What people are saying about

Temple of Dreams

Carolyn Mathews engages us from the start and we're with Seb all the way as he doggedly peels away the layers of intrigue that have shrouded his life to reveal the truth about himself. *Temple of Dreams* is fresh, honest and life-affirming—a feel-good read in the best sense of the term.
Joe Laredo, Writer, Translator of *The Outsider* (Camus) and *The Little Prince* (Saint-Exupéry)

A charming tale of intrigue, self discovery and friendship. The reader follows a short but eventful period in the life of Sebastian, a young man alone in the world, or so it first appears. Carolyn Mathews captures the very essence of two worlds—Now and Then—in her latest novel, *Temple of Dreams*.
Oonagh van Hemuss, Natural Healing Practitioner

A reincarnation from ancient Greece or a mad delusion? Pacy and readable, this imaginative, romantic story of spiritual seeker Sebastian Young carries us along right from the start."
Charles Gates, Archaeologist and Art Historian. Author of *Ancient Cities*

Temple of Dreams

A Novel of Now and Then

Temple of Dreams

A Novel of Now and Then

Carolyn Mathews

Winchester, UK
Washington, USA

JOHN HUNT PUBLISHING

First published by Roundfire Books, 2019
Roundfire Books is an imprint of John Hunt Publishing Ltd., No. 3 East St., Alresford,
Hampshire SO24 9EE, UK
office@jhpbooks.com
www.johnhuntpublishing.com
www.roundfire-books.com

For distributor details and how to order please visit the 'Ordering' section on our website.

ISBN: 978 1 78904 200 9
978 1 78904 201 6 (ebook)
Library of Congress Control Number: 2018951485

A CIP catalogue record for this book is available from the British Library.

Design: Stuart Davies

UK: Printed and bound by CPI Group (UK) Ltd, Croydon, CR0 4YY
US: Printed and bound by Thomson-Shore, 7300 West Joy Road, Dexter, MI 48130

BY THE SAME AUTHOR

Transforming Pandora *Pandora Series – Book One*

ISBN 978-1-78099-745-2

Squaring Circles *Pandora Series – Book Two*

ISBN 978-1-78279-705-0

Pandora's Gift *Pandora Series – Book Three*

ISBN 978-1-78535-175-4

— o —

Allow me to preface your reading with a plea in mitigation of any chronological surprises you might stumble upon as you roam the byways of ancient Greece within these pages. I have to confess I am no historian. In fact, it came as a complete surprise to me that, after three books set firmly in the late 20th and early 21st centuries—chronicling the exploits of the fair Pandora—this novel would require one of its protagonists to reside in ancient Athens, of all places.

The only evidence I could find of any earlier classical Greek influence lay in a dim corner of my bookcase: a slim volume of plays by Sophocles, yellowed with age, innocent of margin notes. (I could never bring myself to write in books.) These plays took me back to Drama lectures at Wall Hall, a late 18th century country house, where US Ambassador Joseph Kennedy and his family spent the second World War. The impressive house and grounds were subsequently transformed into a teacher-training college, but today it's a gated enclave of luxury apartments for a privileged few. *Plus ça change…*

Returning to the subject of a certain character forcing me to embark upon a time trip into the unknown, I apologise in advance to any classicists among you for any inaccuracies you might dig up. I know of only one, which I had to leave in or face having to set the action twelve years later. Which wouldn't have worked. Honest!

Having made that decision, I envisaged the Muses convening a disciplinary meeting to rule on a suspension of my artistic licence. If you're listening, girls, I'll settle for an endorsement. Who in my line of work would refuse one of those?

— o —

The most beautiful thing we can experience is the mysterious.
—Albert Einstein

Chapter 1

'Take him away! I told you I didn't want to see him.'

But the midwife stood her ground, pulling back the swaddling to expose the newborn's golden curls. 'He's beautiful. Won't you hold him for a little while? He's hungry.'

The mother's eyes darkened. 'We agreed I wouldn't have to do that.'

'Just a cuddle...'

The midwife placed the infant in her arms and his tiny lips began wildly sucking in air.

'He'll get wind if he doesn't feed soon,' the midwife fretted. 'I'll fetch him a bottle.'

She was gone before the mother could protest, deliberately taking her time preparing the formula. On her return, she found the baby drinking greedily from his mother's breast, while she sang him a lullaby in an unfamiliar language.

The midwife took a seat by the bed, showing her how to support the child's neck and shoulders so he could swallow more easily, then moving him to the other breast while he was still awake. When the baby had drunk his fill, his lids grew heavy and the mother began to rock him in her arms, still softly crooning the lullaby.

'The adopters aren't due until tomorrow,' the midwife whispered. 'You could change your mind.'

The mother lifted her eyes from her sleeping child.

'I can't keep him. It's impossible.' Her tears splashed the baby's face. 'Anyway, everything's signed and sealed,' she said, tenderly wiping her tears from his cheek. 'I've officially relinquished him.'

The midwife took the mother's hand.

'That can be revoked.'

The two women exchanged a long look, broken when the

mother snatched her hand away.

'You shouldn't be talking to me like this. Please take him now.'

The midwife gathered him up with pursed lips, leaving the mother to pull the sheet over her head and weep her anguish to the pillow.

When an orderly took a cup of mid-morning tea to the room, she found a note on the pillow, secured with a golden brooch in the shape of a snake entwined around a staff.

To whom it may concern: I have decided to discharge myself today. Please give my apologies to Mr and Mrs Young. I wish them well and trust that Sebastian will bring joy to their lives. His father gave me this brooch, which I bequeath to him. A.N.

— o —

Seb pumped the accelerator in frustration. He was stuck behind a broken-down van on a narrow road with a rising gradient, the pelting rain a steady drumroll on the roof. Heaving himself out of the driving seat, he sprinted ten car-lengths to the vehicle and knocked on the driver's window.

'Want a hand, mate?'

The man looked relieved. 'Sure. The breakdown service said they'd be a good half hour. You a mechanic?'

'Nah. I can push you out of the way, though.'

Before the driver's brain could fully grasp the improbability of such a proposal, the van began to rock, prompting him to release the handbrake, upon which his van and its load of plumbing materials shot forward, propelled thirty yards uphill to a muddy lay-by.

As Seb was jogging back to his faithful old hatchback, a young woman in the queue on the other side of the road opened the window of her Mini and shouted as he passed.

'Well done. You're a hero.'

Seb felt his face burn. He'd acted purely out of self-interest: he had an interview at the Asklepios Foundation and was already ten minutes late.

'I've got it on my mobile,' she said, waving her phone at him. 'I'll put it on social media.'

He shook his head but she'd already accelerated away, the back of her raised left hand indicating...what? That she was going to post it, or she'd seen him shake his head? He memorised the pink-lettered web address on her rear window. No way was he going to be plastered all over the Internet.

Once behind the wheel again, he drove at full throttle until, half a mile outside the village of Whitwell, he set eyes on Whitwell Hall for the first time. There it stood, at the end of a long straight drive: a three-storeyed, redbrick Georgian mansion with white window frames, topped off by a handsome clock within a domed cupola.

At the top of the drive he turned left, following the sign which took him behind the mansion to the car park. A long wall bordered one side of the car park, beyond which the crests of distant roofs and treetops hinted at extensive grounds and outbuildings.

Once he'd knocked the worst of the mud off his trainers and rough-dried his hair with a chamois leather, he walked round to the front of the building. Finding the door ajar, he pushed it open, its huge hinges creaking as it gave way.

He'd expected to find a receptionist, but the hall and stairway were deserted save for a dark-haired man in a brown cotton coat, perched on a step stool, dusting the frame of a large mirror.

'Excuse me, I have an interview with Mr Digby. Could you direct me to his office?'

The man turned his head and peered over his glasses.

'What time?'

'Ten o'clock.'

'It's twenty past.'

Seb swallowed hard. He didn't appreciate being taken to task by a cleaner so he disregarded the remark and placed a foot on the stairs.

'Is it on the first floor?'

The man nimbly jumped off the stool and began to walk down the corridor.

'No. It's this way. Follow me.'

They arrived at a door signed 'Director', which the man unlocked. Seb found himself ushered into a spacious, half-panelled room, its upper walls hung with watercolours of wildflowers and herbs.

Motioning Seb to take a seat, the man removed his dusting coat, revealing a grey pinstriped suit and immaculate white shirt. He filled a jug from a water dispenser, sat down behind a polished oval table in front of a large window, curtained and pelmeted in floral chintz, and began to examine a document which Seb assumed to be his application form.

When he'd finished reading, he observed Seb silently for a few seconds.

'Much traffic on the way here?'

Seb nodded, wondering why this old codger hadn't told him who he was from the word go.

'Yeah. Sorry I'm late. You're Mr Digby, aren't you?'

'I am. Who did you think I was?'

'The caretaker, I guess.'

Digby gave a wry smile.

'I have to admire your honesty,' he said, leaning back in his chair. 'On the other hand, your CV poses more questions than answers. You have a handful of General Certificates but no Advanced Level qualifications, yet you're applying for a three-year vocational course equivalent to a degree.'

Seb's eyes had been darting about the room, taking in the furnishings and the artwork. At that moment he was staring at a framed photograph on an ornate side table.

'Mr Young, may I have your attention, please?'

Seb dragged his eyes back to Digby, whose tone had become chilly.

'Why don't you begin by telling me why you want to learn about natural medicine at the Asklepios Foundation?'

Seb hesitated. He could hardly say that his main reason for applying had been a recent recurring dream of a circular, domed building. An Internet search had generated images of ancient Greek ruins, with one exception: a small picture of a similar structure located in the grounds of Whitwell Hall.

Digby was waiting for him to speak. Seb made an effort to remember the more acceptable answers he'd rehearsed, but his brain had jammed. At last, it stuttered into life.

'I...I suppose I've always been good with animals. I used to treat the livestock on our farm. Calling in the vet was always the last resort.'

'Treat in what way?'

'With medicinal plants. One of the stockmen taught me remedies for conditions like bloat, bracken poisoning, milk fever...' An image of Joe in silent communion with a sick animal floated into Seb's mind, reminding him how much he missed his former life.

'This isn't a veterinary college.'

Seb flushed, beginning to wish he'd never applied.

'I know. Joe...the stockman...he treated people, too.'

Digby's tone softened.

'So you're already familiar with natural healing methods?'

Seb nodded.

'Are you working on the farm at present?'

Seb felt an unwelcome stab of grief. But this wasn't the time or place to mourn.

'No, it's in new hands. I work in a pub now.'

Digby's brow wrinkled.

'If you were accepted, you couldn't work full-time. The

course starts on October third, fees for the first year to be paid in advance. Would this be a problem?'

'No. I've got an inheritance coming.'

The flicker of doubt in Digby's eyes persuaded Seb to elaborate.

'My parents died in a car crash six months ago,' he said, rubbing his eyes with the palm of his hand.

'Sorry to hear that,' said Digby, pouring a glass of water and pushing it across the table.

Seb took the glass gratefully and drained it.

'So where are you living?'

'I have a room in a house in Penbury.'

'Do you have any other relatives?'

'Not that I know of. I was adopted at birth.'

At that moment there was a tap on the door and a young woman with long, wavy, red hair swept into the room, her gaze coming to rest on Seb.

'Excuse me, Roger,' she said, in a lilting Welsh accent. 'Sorry to interrupt, but the trustees are waiting for you.'

'That's all right, Sybil. We were late starting the interview. I'll be there in ten minutes.'

She nodded and backed out of the room, leaving a fresh, crisp scent in the air. After that, Digby began speaking more rapidly.

'Let me see. Religion. You've put a dash.'

'My people were agnostics. I haven't got a religion. Does it make a difference?'

'Not at all,' said Digby, smiling. 'The practical component of the course includes an introduction to a healing technique employed by the ancient Greeks. It's conceivable that a student might object to so-called pagan rites. That's why we ask.'

Intrigued, Seb opened his mouth to ask what kind of rites, but Digby had already moved on.

'Education. You've put home-schooled.'

'Yes. By my mother.'

'Any particular reason?'

'I remember starting school but after a while she took me away. She'd been a biology teacher and she said she might as well teach me at home.'

'How did you feel about that?'

'I didn't mind too much. I liked being with my dad and the other workers.'

Digby frowned and Seb added quickly, 'I studied in the mornings and most afternoons I spent outside. School was boring in comparison.' He stopped, fearing he might have said too much. 'I mean, that's not to say I wouldn't be okay with it now...'

Digby's raised hand silenced him. 'Did you mix with other children?'

'Sometimes my mum would invite the farmhands' kids over. But none of the boys could run very fast or wrestle.'

Seb could almost hear his dad's words on those occasions. *Go easy, son. These lads aren't as strong as you.*

'So, you liked sport?'

'Yeah. I joined my dad's rugby club. And we went cycling together.'

Digby finished making notes on the application form and looked up.

'You got good grades for the exams you took. Why did you stop there?'

'When I turned sixteen my dad put me on the payroll as an agricultural trainee.'

Digby shook his head.

'We like our applicants to have a good knowledge of the Natural Sciences.'

'I do.'

'But what proof do you have?'

'None.'

Digby stroked his small, pointed beard, then took a document out of the filing cabinet.

'This is an entrance exam for Contextual Admissions.'

Seb looked puzzled.

'Candidates with low A-level grades due to their difficult home circumstances.'

'Not sure I fit into that category,' said Seb, resenting being shunted into the ranks of the underprivileged.

'Losing your parents and having to move out of your home qualifies you,' Digby said brusquely, placing the exam, file paper and a pen in front of Seb. 'See what you make of it. When you're finished, leave your work on the table and let yourself out. I'll send someone to collect it in an hour and a half. Have you got a smartphone on you?'

Seb took his phone from his pocket and held it out to Digby, who stared at him for a moment, before saying, 'Put it away. I'll trust you not to cheat.'

Exactly fifty-five minutes later, Seb put down the pen, stretched his long limbs and reached for his khaki field jacket. It had seen better days, but he couldn't throw it away because it had once been his dad's. From an inner pocket he took the brooch his biological mother had left him, and traced the golden serpent, coiled around a staff, with the tip of his finger. Then he walked over to the framed photograph which had grabbed his attention earlier and examined it closely.

It was of a tall, tanned man with a broad, open face and a thick head of sandy-coloured hair, swept back from his brow. He was grasping a wooden hiking stick with a serpent carved into its surface. The small brass plaque on the frame was inscribed, 'T. R. Ophis, founder'.

As Seb's gaze swung from the walking stick in the picture to the brooch, an urgent curiosity prompted him to switch on his smartphone to search for T. R. Ophis.

Considering the reputation of the Asklepios Foundation, he'd expected to find numerous references to the founder. But all that appeared was a single paragraph on the Foundation website, describing how the eminent pharmacognosist had purchased Whitwell Hall, a former school, with the aim of establishing a holistic healing and learning centre. He had returned to his native Greece five years later, leaving the organisation in the hands of a charitable trust.

Seb clicked on the picture gallery and scrolled through views of the art studio and lecture rooms along with shots of the grounds: a large herb garden, polytunnels and a housing block for students. There it was, the last image of all, the one which had drawn him here. In a garden dedicated to the founder stood a domed rotunda described simply as: 'Tholos Temple'.

The appearance of Sybil's head round the door put paid to any further investigation.

'Just checking to see you're all right.' Seeing his mobile phone in his hand, she giggled nervously and came fully into the room. 'Oh dear, hope you're not using that to cheat. Roger should have confiscated it.'

Seb blushed and shook his head. 'I'm on my way out.'

'Goodness. Have you finished already? That means you either know a lot or not much at all.'

Seb wasn't sure how to respond. Was she being serious or flippant? He found it hard to judge.

'In that case, I'll lock up.' she said, gathering up his work. 'Off you trot.'

As she did so, something fell to the floor, which she retrieved for him.

'Don't forget your staff of Asklepios.'

Seb took the brooch, muttering his thanks, before darting out of the room. He didn't want her asking where he'd got it, having neither the time nor the inclination to go through the adoption rigmarole.

Once he got back to his car, he set about tracking down the girl who'd recorded him pushing the van. He typed the URL he'd memorised into his smartphone and a website for Belinda's Boutique appeared with the girl's picture on the home page. Her name was Felicity Logan. The address of the boutique was Penbury High Street, so she'd probably been on her way there this morning.

His shift at the pub started at two. He might just have time to make contact with her before then.

Chapter 2

Seb had been loitering outside the boutique for twenty minutes in the hope that Felicity Logan would emerge in search of lunch. Weak sunlight had replaced the rain, but there was an autumnal chill in the air so he took the bull by the horns and went in.

He was surprised at how much bigger the boutique was inside than it looked from the street. He scanned the store. There was one assistant on the till, dealing with a short queue, and another on the shop floor helping a customer. Neither of them looked like the girl in the car.

Feeling awkward among the rows of dresses and blouses, he made for the further reaches of the boutique and was relieved to find a men's clothing section. He was pretending to look at parka jackets when he heard a voice behind him.

'Can I help you?'

He turned to see a figure in a silky grey, mid-length dress with sleek black hair falling to her shoulders and found himself transfixed by eyes the colour of bluebells.

'Would you like to try one on?' She held out her hand to take his jacket and he removed it, ashamed at how shabby it looked in comparison with those on display. As they both surveyed his reflection in the full-length mirror, recognition dawned in her eyes. 'You're the one who moved that van out of the way this morning, aren't you?'

Seb relaxed. 'Yeah. Did you take the video?'

'Guilty.'

'Coincidence, or what?' he said, hoping he sounded convincing.

'Remarkable.' She eyed him up and down. 'I thought you'd be built like a weightlifter.'

He blushed, not sure whether she considered this a good or bad thing.

'I mean, you've got a good physique, not too bulky...' Her voice trailed off as she began searching the rail for the right size.

'Adrenaline helps,' he said, after he'd put on the parka she handed him. 'I was late for an interview.'

'Mmm, that really suits you,' she said, as if she hadn't heard. 'Put the hood up.'

In a practised movement, she tightened the drawstring on the fur-lined hood. 'Just the thing for a day like today.'

He glanced nervously at the price tag, wondering how he could avoid buying a jacket he couldn't afford.

'I don't usually buy fur,' he said finally.

'No problem. It's faux fur.'

'Even so.'

'We've got some without...'

He made a point of looking at his watch.

'I start work at two.'

'Where?'

He straightened his shoulders, getting ready for a change in her manner when she heard the answer.

'A pub in Fairley. The Dog and Duck.'

But her eyes never wavered.

'The interview was for another job then, was it?'

So she *had* heard him.

'No. For a course.'

'Did they offer you a place?'

'Not yet. They said they'd be in touch.'

Her eyes softened as she returned his jacket.

'Shame you have to dash. I'm just going to lunch. You could have kept me company.'

The idea of sitting in a sandwich bar with this girl—more than that, the fact that she'd suggested it—made Seb's heart race. Worse, it rendered him speechless.

'I'm Felicity, by the way,' she said, seemingly unfazed by his silence. Maybe she was used to having this effect on the opposite sex. 'But I prefer Fliss.'

'Sebastian. I prefer Seb.'

She smiled.

'Do you want me to name you on the video, Seb? I haven't got round to…'

'No!' he said, his voice rising at the thought. 'I don't want you to post it.'

Fliss glanced at the cash desk and Seb followed her gaze. Sure enough, the queuing customers were peering in their direction to see what was wrong.

She touched him lightly on the arm and nodded towards a door at the back of the shop. He followed her up some narrow wooden stairs to a room with easy chairs and a small kitchen area.

'Raised voices make the customers twitchy,' she said, as she unlocked a high cupboard, found her bag and took out her mobile. 'Here, take a look.'

She gave him the phone and he watched the vehicle moving towards the lay-by. Then he saw himself appearing from behind it and marching back to his car in the driving rain.

'Do you still want me to delete it?'

Seb didn't understand the question. His face was quite recognisable, despite his hair being drenched.

'Of course. Why would I change my mind?'

Fliss raised her eyebrows.

'Aren't you proud of what you did? I certainly appreciated it. I'd have been late for a meeting otherwise.'

He recalled the countless times the Youngs had warned him against 'showing off'. Like the time the tractor broke down. He'd had to wait till the men had gone home before he rolled the hay bales into the barn. It'd been more of a knack than a feat of strength, just something he'd worked out how to do.

'I don't like drawing attention to myself. It's how I was brought up.'

'Fine.' She took back her mobile. 'There, I've deleted it. Happy now?'

Seb should have felt relieved, but he'd detected an edge to her voice which unsettled him.

'Yeah. Thanks.'

She grabbed a coat and he followed her back down the stairs, through the shop and out into the fresh air.

'See you, then,' he said gruffly, doubtful that this would ever come to pass.

'Bye,' she called, heading off in the opposite direction, leaving him to trudge his way to the multi-storey car park.

— o —

'You're twenty minutes late,' said Chris, pretending to polish the bar top with a drying-up cloth. 'You'll have to make up the time.'

'Yeah, right,' said Seb, grinning. 'Like *you* do when you knock off early.'

'So where've you been?'

'Had that interview today. It overran.'

Chris was staring at him blankly. 'What interview?'

He'd told Chris about it the day before but alcoholic amnesia had probably wiped it from his memory bank.

'For a course at Whitwell Hall.'

'You mean the planting and chanting place? Didn't have you down as a medicine man.'

'Why not?'

'Well, you're pretty normal.'

Seb started to hum to himself as he took glasses out of the washer. He'd waited a long time for someone to describe him as normal. Maybe it hadn't been such a good idea to apply to the Foundation. Maybe life would be easier if he stayed at the pub and became a regular wage slave: a brewery trainee like Chris, going on training courses and getting paid for it.

'I probably won't get in, anyhow,' he said, stacking the glasses on to shelves. 'I'm late applying and I haven't got the right qualifications.'

Chris snorted.

'Qualifications? You mean a man bun and an eyebrow piercing?'

The arrival of a customer sent him to the other end of the bar, leaving Seb to contemplate his next career move.

— o —

That night Seb had an odd experience. He dreamed of a group of people in a courtyard in loose robes, wearing headdresses of green leaves, gathered around an altar. They seemed to be all from the same household, with family members on one side of the altar and servants on the other. There was a strong smell of incense coming from a heap of charcoal burning on the altar. A tall man in a dark purple robe was speaking in a foreign tongue and the others were answering in chorus. An old woman started weeping and it soon became clear that the ceremony was linked to a bereavement.

Her weeping set off some of the other women. One of the servants was nursing a tiny baby, who was soon squalling, too. Another was holding the hand of a small child, whose golden curls made it difficult to tell if it was a boy or a girl. This child was the quietest of them all.

When the tall man stopped speaking, he and an older male family member carried an amphora from the courtyard into the house. Filling small jugs from it, they went from room to room, one upstairs and one down, sprinkling all the floors with what smelled, and looked, like sea water.

Following this, they strewed the floors with soil, then sat in the courtyard with the rest of the family, while the servants tackled the unenviable task of sweeping and cleaning the whole house back to a habitable condition.

When Seb woke up, the dream was still vivid in his memory. He was puzzled about what he'd witnessed, so he kept typing keywords into his laptop until the search engine came up with *Purification Rites in Ancient Greece*.

The one which fitted what he'd seen was a rite performed the third day after a funeral, when the house of death and the occupants (all of whom were considered to be contaminated by the death) were purified. The procedure had to be performed by a free person, which would explain why the servants, who would have been slaves, didn't take part in the sprinkling of the water or the soil.

He knew very little about ancient Greece, apart from some of the better-known myths. Up to now, he'd only had fleeting dreams of a tholos building. How odd, he thought, that he should be dreaming of even stranger things.

But not much had felt normal ever since Pete and Josie's accident. Maybe that's why he'd dreamed of death.

Chapter 3

Later that morning, Seb was doing his usual lap round the park: avoiding dogs, small children and the occasional duck, when his mobile rang. By the time he'd unzipped his tracksuit pocket, the call had gone to voicemail. The message he heard made his pulse race even faster.

'This is Sybil Hughes from the Asklepios Foundation. I've marked your exam paper and I'd like you to contact me.' After a pause she added, 'to discuss your entrance exam.'

Seb's call back was answered immediately.

'Hello, Sebastian. Where are you?'

Seb was puzzled at the question, wondering what difference it made.

'In the park.'

'Oh, good. I didn't want to disturb you at work.'

'I was running.'

'Right. Well, you got eighty-five percent.'

'What did I get wrong?'

She giggled.

'That's a conversation we can have another time. On the strength of your mark, I'm ringing on behalf of the Foundation to offer you a place.'

Seb savoured a pleasing sensation of triumph, until he remembered Chris's taunts about his prospective classmates. Suppose Chris was right and they turned out to be a collection of oddballs and weirdos?

'Can I get back to you?'

'Certainly. But don't leave it too long. The course starts next week.'

At home, he spent a futile few minutes searching for his snake brooch, which he hadn't seen since yesterday. Then he began browsing the online prospectuses of all colleges within a reasonable radius to see if anything 'normal' took his fancy. But all the higher courses demanded A-levels so even an application for next year was out of the question.

Later, at work, he asked Chris about the brewery management trainee scheme.

'Yeah, it's not bad. I should be managing my own pub in a year or so. Go for it. You've got a degree, haven't you? They accept a 2:2.'

Seb turned away so Chris wouldn't see the exasperation in his eyes. He had more brains in his little finger than Chris in his whole skull but little hope of getting anything approaching a decent job without academic evidence.

'I'll think about it.'

At six o'clock Seb was telling himself he'd take his break after serving this customer, when a lone female figure approached the bar and stood in line.

Living up to his reputation as a homing missile for a soft target, Chris glided swiftly along the bar and asked if he could help her.

'Thanks, but I want to speak to Seb.'

Seb glanced at the girl and blushed to the roots of his flaxen hair. Handing the customer his change, he muttered to Chris that he was going for his break.

'You lucky sod,' Chris replied. 'Just don't leave the premises, okay?'

Once Seb was at Fliss's side, he led her to a table at the back of the pub. He offered her coffee and fetched two cups from the machine.

'What can I do for you?' he said, trying to keep his voice cool when all the while his heart was thumping.

'The cleaner found this on the floor. I wondered if it was yours.'

She handed him his mother's brooch, transmitting what felt like a tiny electrical shock when her hand touched his outstretched palm.

'Yeah, it's mine. Thanks.'

It was good to have the snake pin back, but he felt uncomfortable that she knew he'd been carrying a brooch around.

'It must have fallen out of your jacket when I was holding it. Luckily, I remembered where you worked. It's gold, isn't it? Quite an unusual design.'

'It signifies medicine and healing.'

'Oh. I thought that emblem had two snakes…and wings.'

'No, that's the caduceus—the magic wand of Hermes. This is the symbol of Asklepios, god of healing.'

She blinked, and he wondered whether her interest in the brooch was merely polite, but she kept going.

'Is it a family heirloom?'

'Sort of.'

'Was someone in your family a doctor?'

'I don't know. My mother left it for me but I don't know any more than that.'

Fliss's eyebrows almost disappeared into her fringe.

'That statement raises so many questions. Too many for someone on their break to answer. Do you ever get an evening off?'

Seb's dates with girls were up to now infrequent, the most recent a trip with a farm worker's daughter to see a film about a woman who'd lost her memory, with plot holes you could drive a truck through.

'Where would we go?' he said, hoping she wouldn't suggest the cinema.

'My place. My parents are away for the weekend. Are you free on Saturday? I could cook.'

'If I can find someone to change shifts.'

'Okay. Let me know.'

She handed him a card for Belinda's Boutique with her address and mobile number already written on the back.

'Belinda's my mother,' she said, as he contemplated the card. 'But she's never there. I run the shop. She's happy as long as we make a profit.'

He got up, feeling a little lightheaded at the speed at which things were moving.

'By the way,' she said, as he walked her to the door, 'did you get on to that course?'

He'd forgotten he'd mentioned it to her and wished he hadn't.

'Uh, yeah, they offered me a place.'

'Great. Studying what?'

'Natural Medicine.'

'So there *is* a medical connection. Which college?'

'The Asklepios Foundation.'

He studied her face, trying to work out if she now viewed him as a weirdo hippie.

'When do you start?'

Seb still hadn't made up his mind. He was only just coming to terms with life outside the farm: was he really ready to commit to three years in residence at Whitwell Hall? Hadn't he lived a cloistered life for long enough?

'Next week, if I do it. But I'm not sure it's what I want…'

'What other options have you got?'

'None at the moment. Apart from pulling pints in this place.'

'You should go for it,' she said, gently. 'You can always leave if you don't like it. Nothing ventured, nothing gained.'

'I'll see that cliché and raise you "better safe than sorry" and "look before you leap",' he said drily, as he escorted her as far as the door, and she smiled.

She has got a point, though, he admitted to himself, as he rejoined Chris behind the bar.

Seb finished his shift in a bit of a daze, driving back to his bedsit on autopilot. He was beginning to feel excited—about the course and about Fliss. As he entered his room and put on the light, his eye was drawn to a brown envelope on the floor.

Someone must have picked it up from the hall and slipped it under his door. He opened it to find a cheque from the Youngs' solicitor in final settlement of their estate.

At first glance, he read the sum of his inheritance as £200,000 and his heart leapt. That would finance his college fees and still leave a comfortable reserve of capital.

Closer inspection of the balance sheet, however, revealed that in the year before his death, Peter Young had sold all his investments to pay off a bank loan. The final sum, taking into account the proceeds from an auction of the farmhouse contents, amounted to only £2,000 plus a few pence. It was clear that Pete had sunk all his money into the farm so the men could keep their jobs.

Seb placed the cheque in his wallet with a heavy heart. Just as he'd started to get enthusiastic about the offer of a place at the Asklepios Foundation, he'd have to kiss it goodbye. He thought of Fliss: her great looks, her confidence, her family business. What would she see in him now?

He considered his next move. The Foundation would have to be told. He felt a fool now for assuming he'd be able to afford the fees. He wouldn't mention money…just say he was moving on, which could well turn out to be the case. No way did he want to stay in Penbury in a dead-end job.

He poured himself a tot of whisky and toasted Pete and Josie for their generosity to their workforce, misplaced as it turned out to be, as most of the men were laid off anyway in the end.

After his fourth whisky, he fell asleep on the ancient sofabed before he'd even unfolded it. Next morning his mobile rang at eight-thirty, interrupting his fantasy of touring Europe on a Harley-Davidson.

It was Roger Digby.

'Good morning, Mr Young. Sorry to ring you at this hour, but we were wondering whether to place you on the list of students joining us next week. We need a reply today. There is a waiting list, you know.'

Seb's head was muzzy and his neck ached from being rammed against the arm of the sofa.

'Yeah. Uh, thanks for the offer, sir, but...er...unfortunately I don't think I'll be able to take it up.'

Digby harrumphed loudly.

'What's the problem? Have you had an offer from another institution? Is that it?'

'No, sir. But I've been thinking, maybe I should do a bit of travelling to...to broaden my horizons. I've never been outside the UK.' There was silence from the other end which Seb took as a signal to expand on his excuse. 'We didn't go far because my people never wanted to leave the livestock for too...'

Digby cut Seb short, his tone curt.

'Look, I'm ringing to offer you the Teodor Ophis Scholarship. This means all your fees and accommodation will be paid.'

Seb thought of the sum Pete and Josie had left him. That wouldn't cover three years' living expenses. Maybe he could postpone. If he worked on a building site for a year, he could save enough to see him through.

'Could I defer the place for a year?'

Digby must have put his hand over the phone to vent his irritation because Seb could hear a female voice telling him to keep calm. When at last he spoke, his voice was slow and careful, increasing in volume and speed until the final, exasperated sentence.

'Allow me to explain. The founder left enough funds to provide a single scholarship for a deserving case who shows outstanding promise. Up to now, no one's fitted the bill. But after I reported your test results to the trustees and informed them of your circumstances—having to leave your family home, etcetera—they gave the go-ahead. If you don't jump at the offer, young man, there's no guarantee the trustees will extend it!'

Seb dug his hand in his pocket and took out the snake brooch.

'Heads,' he said, under his breath, and flipped the brooch, which landed with the symbol face up. 'So be it,' he breathed.

Meanwhile, Digby's disembodied voice crackled from the phone.

'Mr Young. Are you there?'

Seb picked up the brooch and put it back in his pocket.

'Yes. Sorry, just had to check something. Thanks for offering me the scholarship, sir. I'm happy to accept it.'

Chapter 4

Seb sat in his car, listening to an Indie Hotlist. He'd arrived on the dot of seven, as instructed, but the house was in darkness and nobody answered the doorbell. He rang the number on the back of the card Fliss had given him, but she didn't pick up so he texted her that he'd wait till seven-thirty.

He was thinking about picking up a burger on the way back to his bedsit, and spending the rest of the evening browsing through his new course books, when he was startled by a knocking on the passenger window. It was Fliss, with a small, white dog under her arm, full of apologies for being late.

He followed them into the house, through a spacious hallway with rooms leading off both sides, and into the kitchen.

'I would have phoned you earlier but I didn't have your number,' she said, spooning dog food into a bowl. 'The traffic was bad and Delta's day-carer kept me talking. It's been hectic today. One of the girls phoned in sick...I didn't even stop for lunch.'

When she paused to draw breath, Seb introduced the subject of dinner.

'You must be starving.'

She looked sadly at the glossy white dining table, set for two people.

'I was going to leave early, buy some steak...'

'How about a takeaway?' he said, his stomach growling.

It was only when the food was on the table and they began sharing the dishes, that Fliss started to chill out.

'So what time did *you* finish work today?' she said, propelling the plum sauce his way. She'd set their places at opposite ends of the table so they had to push the foil containers back and forth like curling stones.

'I didn't. Yesterday was my last day.'

'So you decided to do that course?'

'Yeah. I start next week. Went to a specialist book shop in Bloomsbury this morning to get the set books. Set me back a few quid.'

'Are the course fees very high?'

'They gave me a scholarship. No worries about finance,' he lied.

'Great. Let's celebrate!' she cried, hauling a bottle of champagne from the fridge.

In fact, he had no idea how he was going to afford life as a student after his meagre nest egg ran out, but he didn't want to kill the vibe.

By the time she was on her third glass, Fliss had told him she'd been a trainee buyer with a high street store until her mother had opened a beauty salon and made her manager of the boutique. She'd also confided she had an older brother at university and her father was a golf-mad accountant.

There followed a long pause—evidently a cue for him to talk about his own background. But instead, he asked her what music she was into and what books she read.

When the containers were cleared and the bottle empty, Fliss took Seb into a large sitting room, put on some music, and lay on one sofa with Delta while Seb sprawled on the other.

'Do you think you'll miss working at the Dog and Duck?'

Her tone was casual, but Seb knew it was her way of reminding him why he was here.

'I doubt it.'

Fliss lowered her voice, even though there was no one else in the house to hear.

'You started telling me, in the pub, about your mother leaving you the brooch…'

He sighed. He was enjoying the moment and hardly in the mood to talk about a woman who'd abandoned him. But *she* was the reason this knockout girl had invited him round, so he didn't have much choice.

'I was adopted at birth by a childless couple called Pete and Josie Young. They never made any secret of the fact. They told me my biological parents couldn't keep me, and that was it. I never felt the need to find out any more.' Seb swallowed hard and increased the tempo. 'I worked on their farm until they were killed in a motorway pile-up. I had to move out to a bedsit a couple of months ago.' He raised his head to see Fliss sitting bolt upright, a stricken expression on her face. 'That's about it, really.'

'You lost your family and your home all at once!' she exclaimed. 'How tragic.'

She seemed unable to say more. He'd grown familiar with the stunned silence which often followed the telling of his 'story', so he adlibbed to keep the conversation flowing.

'The brooch appeared after the funeral. Josie's cousin offered to dispose of her clothes and stuff, and she sent it to me...said she found it at the bottom of a jewellery box. There was a note pinned to it.'

'What did it say?'

'That she'd decided to make a getaway from the hospital. And she was leaving me the brooch my father had given her.'

'Is that all?'

Seb recalled the line about hoping Sebastian would bring joy to their lives, and decided to keep it to himself, taking a scintilla of comfort from the fact that at least his birth mother had chosen his name.

'More or less.'

'She didn't say who your father was?'

'No.'

Her eyes, dark with sympathy, looked almost purple in the dim light.

Seb was used to the effect this news had on women. In the weeks following the tragedy, there'd been a steady flow of pies and casseroles to his door, baked by the farmhands' wives, delivered by their daughters.

He closed his eyes and concentrated hard on the music to keep the wretchedness of the past few months at bay. Then he became aware of Fliss next to him. When he felt her stroke his cheek, he opened his eyes, took her hand, and kissed it. He didn't usually do that. It was probably the champagne. She snuggled in closer to him, lifted her face to his, and they kissed.

'You'd better stay the night,' she murmured. 'You must be over the limit.'

She got up and led him upstairs.

'I haven't brought anything with me,' he said.

'Don't worry,' she whispered, 'I've got that covered.'

Making love to Fliss wasn't his first sexual experience, but it far outshone his drunken fumblings with the farm daughters. When Seb told her it was the best sex he'd ever had, she giggled.

'I had a good time, too.'

Next morning Fliss made toast which they ate in bed. After that, they took Delta for a walk in a wood, nearby. Once the dog was off the lead, Fliss took Seb's hand.

'Did your birth mother sign that note she left?'

'Only her initials.'

'What are they?'

Seb hesitated. He didn't see what difference it made, but he could hardly deny remembering them.

'A. N.'

'Have you ever thought of trying to trace her?'

'No. She didn't want me then, why should she want me now?'

'Because her circumstances might have changed. And now you're, you know, on your own, you wouldn't be hurting anybody's feelings.'

He let go of her hand to stroke the dog, who was pleading for the ball to be thrown.

'Can't you get in touch with social services?' Fliss persisted.

'There must be some record.'

But Seb had already thrown the ball and taken off in pursuit, racing Delta for it. On the way back to the house, Fliss returned to the subject.

'Your adoptive parents must have been given some information about your mother, Seb.'

'I'd rather not talk about it.'

'But wouldn't you like to meet her? She could tell you who your father is.'

Seb shook his head.

'Pete and Josie brought me up. Fed me, clothed me. It's too late to play happy families with strangers.'

As they approached the front door, he hung back. 'Look, I'd better get going. Got some sorting out to do. I'm moving to Whitwell Hall tomorrow.'

Fliss didn't turn to look at him. Instead, she called, 'Okay, see you,' over her shoulder and crashed the door shut.

Seb was back in his bedsit by twelve-thirty. On the drive back, he'd been trying to work out why Fliss had slammed the door. He remembered being bewildered by Josie's moods at times. On those occasions Pete would raise his eyes to Seb when she left the room and say, 'Women. We'll never understand them, will we?'

The first thing he did was dig out the paperwork for the Foundation scholarship. Sybil Hughes had mailed the forms to him so he could give them to her at the Induction session. As he reached the end, he saw he had to provide a birth certificate. He knew there was one somewhere because he'd needed it to apply for a driving licence. The solicitor had returned Peter Young's papers a few days ago, with the caution that he should read them first before throwing them out. It was probably among them.

He fetched the box of documents from the corner of the room and placed it on the table. The contents had come from a filing cabinet in Pete's office and the majority of the papers turned out to be old financial statements and invoices. By the time he reached the middle of the pile, he'd put everything he'd so far seen into a bin bag.

The next item looked to be just what Seb was seeking: a brown envelope inscribed with the word 'Certificates'. He opened it to find Pete and Josie's birth and marriage documents and his Amended Birth Certificate, naming the Youngs as adoptive parents. He put it to one side, thinking he might as well finish sorting through the rest of Pete's papers. As he reached the bottom of the pile, he found a sealed envelope with his name on it in Pete's handwriting.

Intrigued, he tore it open to discover another birth certificate. With hungry eyes, he read that his mother's name was Anna Norland. She'd been born in Oslo and was a student at the time of his birth.

When he read on, Seb's chest tightened. The original birth certificate declared his father's identity to be Teodor Ophis, born in Athens, founder of the Asklepios Foundation.

Chapter 5

Seb made a dash to the accommodation block, shielding his head from the rain with a slim plastic folder containing his course details and a map of the campus. He climbed the flight of stairs and let himself into the flat that had been his home since yesterday.

The morning's Induction had included a guided tour of the mansion, parts of which resembled a stately home without the barrier ropes. The library and lecture rooms showed signs of their former glory in the decorative plasterwork of their lofty ceilings: even the laboratory benches and tables had an air of antiquity about them, although the equipment looked modern enough.

After lunch, the group met again in one of the larger lecture rooms for an overview of their course delivered by Roger Digby, followed by questions and answers. The second part of his lecture had gone into the philosophy of Asklepian healing and should have led on to a tour of the grounds, except it had to be cancelled due to 'adverse weather conditions'. Disappointing, that. He'd especially wanted to see the founder's garden with its intriguing centrepiece.

No sooner had he pulled off his shoes, than there came a tap at the door. He opened it to find Sybil and a young man in a slouch beanie and long reefer jacket.

'Seb, this is Nick. Your flatmate. He's *finally* arrived.'

Nick surveyed the open-plan living area and kitchen, nodded approvingly and placed his expensively battered leather holdall on the laminate floor.

'Pleased to meet you, man. Where do I put this?'

Seb shook his hand and opened the door of the other bedroom. Both rooms were identical: a bed, bedside cabinet, fitted wardrobe, a shelf, a desk, a chair.

While Nick was inspecting the bathroom, Sybil opened her briefcase and handed Seb an envelope.

'That's your formal offer of a scholarship.' She paused for a beat and added, her eyes full of sympathy, 'Your birth certificate's inside, as well.'

'Thanks,' he said, taking it into his bedroom at once, to avoid any discussion about losing his adoptive parents in tragic circumstances.

Naturally, he'd enclosed his Amended Birth Certificate rather than the original. His discovery that he was the son of Teodor Ophis was something he preferred to keep to himself—especially as he still wasn't sure what sort of person Ophis was. Certainly not one who'd been in it for the long haul, either professionally or paternally.

Nick appeared, minus his outer garments, and went straight to the kitchen cupboards to check out the cookware. Seb couldn't help staring. Despite being recently confined inside a woollen hat, his dark, springy hair was a work of art: fashionably long on top, but short at the back and sides. Dressed in an immaculate crew neck sweater and jeans, he looked as if he'd stepped out of a glossy magazine.

'We're self-catering, right?' Nick said, addressing Sybil.

'Yes.'

'But we're in the middle of nowhere. What happens to people with no transport?'

'The estate shop sells fresh produce, or you can buy a meal in the refectory. It's open weekdays between nine and four, in term time.'

Nick looked at his watch.

'I can just make it, then.'

'Er, afraid not,' said Sybil. 'Today it closed at two. Term doesn't officially start till tomorrow.'

He inspected the fridge, empty but for a carton of milk.

'Any coffee, tea?'

'Help yourself,' said Seb, opening one of the cupboards to expose a solitary box of teabags.

Sybil made for the door.

'I'll leave you two to get acquainted. Maybe Seb can show you where the shops are, Nick.' She flashed a smile at Seb. 'And give you a tour of the mansion, perhaps, as you missed Induction.'

When the door closed, Nick winked at Seb, moving his hands in two eloquent curves.

'Hope I'm in her class. How old do you think she is?'

Sybil's charms had not escaped Seb's notice, but he'd so far regarded her as he might an actress on the screen: fanciable, but inaccessible.

'Late twenties? Maybe a bit older.'

'Even better. I like a woman with a bit of experience.'

Disinclined to take the conversation further, Seb filled the kettle for Nick. When Nick made no move to make his own tea, he made it for him and joined him at the table.

'Any Wi-Fi around here?' said Nick, peering at his smartphone.

'Yeah, but you have to check in at the library first.'

'Right. So did I miss anything important today?'

'Nothing much. Just a tour of the mansion and a pep talk from Digby. The outside tour was rained off.'

Nick seemed satisfied with that, giving Seb a chance to ask if he'd left a job to come to the Foundation. Nick told him he was an actor and had spent three years in Los Angeles playing a long-term role in a TV series. After that, he'd made a couple of movies, but work had dried up so he'd come back to England eighteen months ago to take a course in Screenwriting.

'So you write now?' said Seb, wondering how all this fitted in with natural medicine.

'In theory.' said Nick, grinning. 'Problem is, getting anyone interested in your work.'

'Have you got a place in London?' Seb asked, wondering if he'd have the flat to himself at weekends. He'd grown used to his own company and was apprehensive about sharing with a stranger.

'No. I've been lodging with a friend from drama school. She put me up while I was on the Screenwriting course. My folks live in West Sussex. Not exactly commuting distance.'

Seb forced a grin.

'So how did you hear about the Foundation?'

'Gina, the friend I was staying with, had an appointment with a herbalist here. Her boyfriend was busy so I gave her a lift. I took a look at the prospectus while I was waiting and ended up applying. Not sure I'll see it out, though. Three years is a long time...have to see how it goes. How about you?'

Seb gave him an abridged version of the circumstances that led him to Whitwell Hall, which elicited the customary condolences from Nick.

'It's okay. I'm getting used to it,' Seb answered, automatically.

This wasn't strictly true. He still missed Pete and Josie every day. Especially Pete.

Around seven, Nick suggested heading into Penbury for something to eat. They went in Nick's car and ate Italian, his choice. Seb had warned him against the restaurant. The tables were tightly packed, the service slow, the acoustics bad. But Nick said he was starving and it shouldn't be too full on a Tuesday.

As the restaurant filled up, the combination of high-decibel music with the babble of customers and fortissimo waiters drove Seb to call for the bill as soon as they finished the main course.

Once outside, Nick looked up and down the street. It had stopped raining and the pavements were almost dry. People were out and about. The bars and restaurants were brightly lit and inviting.

'Where to next?' he said. 'Know any good pubs, clubs? The night is young.'

'Are you kidding?' snapped Seb. 'I've had enough racket for one night.'

Nick's face fell.

'Thought you might want to show me the town.'

The last thing Seb felt like was a pub crawl, but he didn't want Nick to take his refusal personally so he offered an alternative.

'Why don't we check out the campus bar?'

It took little more than twenty minutes to get to the mansion car park in Nick's coupé. He sauntered into the common room and up to the bar, with Seb trailing behind. Sybil had explained earlier that it was run by students and open Monday to Friday. But the bar committee couldn't have convened yet because the shutters were firmly down.

'Oh, man,' sighed Nick, surveying the empty room. 'This is definitely not where the action's at.' He started towards the door. 'Think I'll head back into town. Coming?'

Seb's heart sank. His mission was to be normal, he reminded himself, so if he didn't want to come across as a killjoy, he should go with Nick. Then an idea hit him.

'We could take a look at the founder's garden. I'd like to see the tholos.'

Nick regarded his suede chukka boots.

'It'll be muddy.'

'You can borrow my wellies.'

They went straight to the flat, where Seb grabbed a torch while Nick changed his footwear. The campus map showed the founder's garden was some distance from the accommodation block, along a path which led them past rows of polytunnels, stretching across the land like ghostly, elongated igloos. When they reached a high brick wall, they continued until they found the entrance, a tall wrought iron gate, which clicked open at Nick's touch.

The moon was almost full so it was easy to make out the topography. The garden was sizeable: rectangular in shape, criss-crossed by two paths and planted with shrubs, small trees and beds of pink and yellow roses, still in bloom. A cedar of Lebanon with spreading branches dominated the garden. Just beyond, the dome of the tholos temple gleamed in the moonlight.

Seb began to walk in the direction of the tholos but Nick hung back, interested in the building behind them: a single-storey structure with arched windows, extending almost the whole length of one side of the garden. He moved closer to the door and read out the word, 'Abaton', engraved on a blue slate sign.

'Is this where they keep the sacrificial animals?' he said, in a tone of mock horror.

Seb pressed his ear to the door. 'Can't hear anything,' he said, peering through a window.

'Joking,' said Nick, trying the door to see if it was locked.

'Let's have a look at the tholos,' said Seb, feeling foolish.

But Nick had already moved on to a small building situated in front of the abaton. This time the door gave way, revealing a large ornamental urn on a tall, rectangular pillar of white marble in the centre of the room.

They moved closer and saw there was a scalloped basin in the middle of the pillar with a spout above it. On the right side of the pillar was a pump handle.

'Whoa. Reproduction Roman kitsch,' said Nick, laughing. 'That's something I didn't expect to see.'

'The founder was Greek,' said Seb, finding a light switch and flicking it on.

The light revealed a few chairs against the walls and a small sink, above it some cups on a wooden shelf. In the right-hand corner was a marble statue of a woman, holding a snake and offering it a drink from a libation bowl. The name 'Hygeia' was inscribed on the base.

'So it's Greek kitsch,' said Nick. 'Whatever. Let's drink from the fountain. It's only polite, now we're here.'

He pumped the handle vigorously and got enough water to fill two cups.

Nick knocked it back and Seb took one gulp before spitting it out in the sink.

'Tastes like iron filings.'

'I didn't think it was too bad,' said Nick, making for the door. 'But then, my mother's Scottish, so I've been brought up on Iron Brew.'

When they emerged from the pump room they found part of the moon wreathed in grey clouds. It had begun to rain so they crossed the garden at a jogging pace, Seb making sure he didn't outrun Nick.

The base of the tholos consisted of three stone tiers in decreasing diameter, creating three steps up to the outer colonnade all the way round the building. Upon this 'layer cake' rested twenty-four hefty Doric columns, supporting the domed roof and forming a protective circle around the white marble temple.

Seb and Nick climbed the steps and marched around the peristyle in search of an entrance until they came upon a high, bronze door topped by a grille and flanked by two windows. The panels of the door were studded with rosettes and gilded lions' heads. Between the grille and the panels were the words, 'Only pure souls may enter here', in gold lettering.

Finding the door locked, Nick turned to go.

'Come on, man. I'm not sure we qualify for entry, anyway.'

'Wait,' said Seb, sharply. 'I want to know what goes on in here.'

He made his way down to the flower beds and began looking under stones. A little further on, he stumbled upon a wall-eyed gargoyle and couldn't believe his luck when the key that lay beneath him fitted the door.

Once inside, Seb switched on the torch and flashed it round the room. Bordering the interior stood fourteen more columns, set on a wide, black plinth. These columns were Corinthian: smaller than the outer colonnade, their friezes more decorative, with an abundance of acanthus leaves at their heads. Seb's torch picked out some wall paintings and a simple white marble altar at the far side of the room. The floor was laid in a chequerboard pattern of black and white limestone.

'What's that?' they said, almost in unison.

The object which claimed their attention lay in the middle of the floor: a large black circle of stone, enclosing a central white stone with an iron ring fastened to it. Seb was just about to grab hold of the ring when a light went on and a voice rang out.

'What on earth are you doing in here?'

Seb froze for an instant, almost believing the voice belonged to a disembodied being: a temple guardian who'd been alerted by the grotesque gargoyle to the presence of impure trespassers: a three-headed talking hound who'd tear him limb from limb. But when he turned round, the creature who confronted him was Roger Digby, wearing a long raincoat spattered, like his hair and beard, with beads of rain.

'Sorry, sir,' Seb muttered, straightening up. 'We were just taking a look.'

Digby's clenched jaw implied he was struggling to keep his composure. 'Does a locked door mean nothing to you? Hand over the key immediately!'

Seb fished it out of his jacket and gave it to Digby, who snatched it from him and shooed them out of the building, like unwelcome birds who had somehow flown in. He followed behind, switching off the light, securing the door and pocketing the key.

'Is there any particular reason why this place is out of bounds?' said Nick, sounding convincingly nonchalant. 'It's not as if the gate was locked.'

Digby gave Nick a withering glance.

'It was an oversight. The gates are usually locked at six o'clock. Besides, if you'd attended Induction, you'd know that your group will be given a tour of the sanctuary soon enough. Until then, you'll have to curb your impatience.'

'Actually, we wouldn't be here if the common room bar had been open,' said Nick, but Digby was already halfway across the garden. They watched in silence as he disappeared through the wrought iron gate.

'Let's hope he hasn't locked it,' said Seb glumly, as they followed in his footsteps.

Chapter 6

Fliss woke at seven and pulled the cover over her head, willing herself back to sleep. She was just drifting off when she heard her mother's voice in the room.

'Are you getting up soon, Felicity?'

She stuck one arm outside the duvet to wave her mother away and was immediately dive-bombed by Delta who planted several wet kisses on her face.

With a groan, she sat up.

'It's my day off, Mum. Every Thursday. Remember?'

'I know, love. I thought you might be getting up early to do your video thing.'

'I might record something later. If I'm in the mood.'

Fliss sipped her tea and waited for today's assignment: Belinda only ever brought her tea in bed when she wanted something.

'So, have you got any other plans for today?'

She checked the mobile phone beside her bed for messages. Ever since the weekend she'd been hoping to hear from Seb, but he still hadn't been in touch.

'Doesn't look like it. Why?'

Belinda sat on the bed and patted her hand.

'It's Birdie's birthday and I forgot to send a card. I was wondering if you could take it round.'

Fliss immediately felt better. Birdie was someone she could confide in.

'Of course, I will. I'll take Delta.'

'Is everything all right?' Belinda said, glancing at Fliss's phone.

'Yes, Mum,' she pretended, seizing a rare opportunity to give her mother a cuddle before she retreated downstairs.

When Fliss rang Birdie she told her to come at ten, because

her current gentleman friend was taking her out to lunch.

She had to drive past Whitwell Hall on the way to Birdie's house. As she glanced longingly at Seb's new stamping ground, she noticed a sign for the estate shop advertising home-grown organic fruit, vegetables and flowers. On impulse, she turned into the road leading to the mansion. As she neared the house, a sign directed her right, along a winding lane past a row of cottages to a small car park in front of the shop.

There were only two people inside: a young man asking for freshly baked bread and a woman telling him it hadn't arrived yet. The customer looked towards Fliss as she entered, as if expecting her to be the bearer of the bread. As she came closer, he caught her eye and shrugged in comic disappointment, which made her smile.

Passing a freezer packed with expensive handmade ready meals, she found the flowers in a far corner of the shop. She chose a bunch of cheerful gerbera daisies in vivid shades of yellow, orange and red. Birdie was easy to buy for, unlike her mother, who preferred her bouquets to coordinate with the decor of the room.

The shopkeeper took the flowers, continuing her conversation with the young man while she was wrapping them, telling him she could put a loaf by, for him to collect later.

'Okay. I'll take these for now,' he said, indicating his basket of goods, which he rested on the counter. As he did so, his hand brushed Fliss's and he quickly apologised.

'That's okay,' she replied, looking at him properly for the first time and getting the odd feeling she'd seen him somewhere before.

'Your change,' said the shopkeeper, briskly, and Fliss blushed. It probably seemed she was gazing at him because he was so good-looking.

'Excuse me, do I know you?' she said, curiosity getting the better of her. 'Your face is familiar.'

He smiled in a self-effacing way. 'You might have seen me in something. I'm an actor.'

Fliss trawled through her memory banks and retrieved the image of a popular American TV series featuring young people with special powers, banded together to save the future of the world.

'Were you in *Time Guards*?'

'Busted,' he said, with a grin.

'It's coming to me...you're Nick...uh...'

'Porter.'

'Of course. Which one were you?'

'Gideon.'

'The one who used to see visions of the future?'

'No, that was Lukas. I was the time traveller.'

Nick paid his bill and they walked out of the shop together.

'They're not still making them, are they?' said Fliss, recalling the increasingly convoluted plots each new series had produced.

'Not as far as I know. The writers just about sucked the concept dry.'

She smothered a giggle.

'So your time-travelling days are over now?' she said.

'Yup. I'm very much in the present, these days.'

Fliss had reached her car, much to Delta's delight, who was yipping a greeting from the boot.

Nick peered in the rear window.

'Cute dog. So I guess you're not a student here?'

'No. What about you?'

'I started a course this week.'

'Really? How does that work out with your acting?'

'It doesn't. I'm taking some time out. Thought I'd give the good life a go.'

'To build up some superpowers of your own?'

He laughed. 'Listen, I'm new to the area, do you happen to know any decent pubs round here? I'd be glad of the company.'

Fliss was disconcerted at this manoeuvre. And, yes, flattered. Problem was, she was still hankering after Seb. Her hesitation seemed to spur Nick on because his next move was to ask for her number.

Her first instinct was to refuse, but his expression was so beguiling that she decided not to close the door on him completely.

'Why don't you give me yours?'

He complied without a murmur, tapping his number into her phone in a practised movement.

'Have to go, I'm already late for class,' he said, getting into his sports car. 'See you later.'

Fliss selected a playlist of soothing classics for her journey so by the time she arrived at her destination, both she and Delta were relaxed and ready to socialise.

'Happy Birthday, Birdie,' she said when the door opened, thrusting the bouquet at her former nanny.

Birdie trilled her thanks, placing the flowers on the stairs so she could enfold Fliss in a bear hug.

'You get prettier every time I see you. But you could do with a bit of meat on your bones.'

She ushered Fliss into the front room, every surface crowded with cards from people whose children she'd cared for.

'Mum wants you to pop into the salon to see her,' she said, giving Birdie her mother's card, which contained a couple of banknotes.

'Will do. How is she? Still working hard?'

'Always. You know what she's like. Dad wants her to take more time off but she'd rather be at work.'

'That's men for you, pet. He probably wants a few more home-cooked meals.' She pointed to the cocktail shaker on the sideboard. 'Fancy a margarita? I refuse to drink tea on my birthday.'

Fliss was persuaded to have a weak one and a small piece of birthday cake. Inevitably, once the usual fields of conversation had been explored, the subject turned to Birdie's love life.

'I told you Richard was taking me out to lunch, didn't I? He's lovely. Very polite. We met in the supermarket of all places. I like him because he doesn't want to spend every minute together. Once that happens, it gets too boring. That's why I never got married.'

'What happened to the last one?'

'Who, Tony? He was a tightwad. I mean, what man takes you shopping with him and doesn't offer to buy you a little something for yourself? No, I ditched him, and then along came Richard. Nature abhors a vacuum. Anyway, what about you? Any boyfriends? Or are you too busy mucking about on YouTube?'

Fliss spluttered with indignation, risking asphyxia from a cake crumb on its way down the wrong pipe, causing Delta some consternation.

'I'm a fashion vlogger,' she wheezed. 'I've got subscribers…I take it seriously. And I'm planning my next fashion shoot for the website.'

'Sorry, Flissy. What do I know?' said Birdie, patting her on the back. 'I'm old-school, that's all. I'd rather read about fashion in a magazine.' She brought a glass of water. 'Now, where were we? Oh yes. Any nice young men on the horizon?'

Fliss had been confiding in Birdie ever since she could remember, so she launched straight into the saga of Seb, tagging on the morning's encounter with Nick for good measure. When she'd finished, Birdie closed her eyes for a few moments.

'The blond one, I feel, has shut down, due to some emotional trauma. Which wouldn't be surprising, considering what you've told me. The dark one values his freedom…likes collecting hearts. Neither one is up to a committed relationship.' She paused. 'Not at present, anyway.'

Fliss tried to hide her disappointment, which didn't fool Birdie, who plonked a box of tissues on the table in front of her.

'Don't upset yourself, love. Plenty more fish in the sea for a girl like you. Some women go for complicated men, then spend a whole lifetime trying to straighten them out. My preference is for what you see is what you get.'

Fliss pouted like a child.

'I just feel so sorry for him. He hasn't got any family left, but he says he doesn't want to find his mother. I think that's why he hasn't phoned—because I suggested it.'

'Hmm. His instinct's probably right. Sounds like he needs to find *himself* before he goes looking for the woman who gave him up. And he won't thank you for trying to fix the situation because he'll read that as you trying to fix him.'

They talked until a knock on the door heralded the arrival of Richard, a jovial man who'd risen to the occasion by wearing a suit, albeit one which had seen better days.

Fliss took her leave and made for home, stopping to walk Delta on the common. As she walked, she tried to tell herself that Birdie could be wrong about Seb, but Birdie's bursts of intuition had proved pretty accurate in the past. That's probably why her mother wanted her to pop by the salon—for a tarot card session.

At home, she went upstairs and stared at the clothes she intended to feature in her next vlog. Her script was all mapped out in her head but she'd need to glam up first. And after filming she'd have to edit the video or, heaven forbid, do it again from scratch.

In the end, she found a psychological thriller on TV, and stayed with it until the final, implausible twist.

Feeling impatient with herself for wasting the afternoon, Fliss checked her mobile, which she'd purposely left in the kitchen so she wouldn't be tempted to call Seb. There was nothing on it of much interest and she found herself looking for the number Nick had typed in.

Almost of its own volition, her finger pressed the number. Within seconds, a voice answered.

Chapter 7

Sybil Hughes was about to show some slides when the door opened and a voice enquired, 'Is this the Fundamentals of Pharmacognosy class?'

Sybil nodded, looking pointedly at her watch.

'You're half an hour late. I hope you won't be making a habit of it.'

Nick mouthed *sorry* and took a seat beside a woman wearing her grey hair in a long plait, who moved her chair to make room for him, sending a textbook and some handwritten notes flying from the writing board attached to her chair.

Having retrieved the fallen items, Nick raised his eyes to a stony glare from Sybil.

'We introduced ourselves at the beginning of the class, so before I continue, perhaps you'd like to say a few words about yourself and why you're here?'

No stranger to the limelight, Nick promptly obliged.

He explained that he'd discovered the Foundation through a friend who'd come for healing, adding that he'd done some filming in India where he'd been treated by an Ayurvedic doctor for a stomach bug, and how impressed he'd been.

By now he was in full flow, happy to hold the floor. He could have gone on for hours, if Sybil hadn't cut him short.

'Thank you, Nick. You'll be studying Ayurveda with Dr Sharma. This morning, however, I'm outlining the principles of plant description, but before I continue I'd like to check if you're clear on what this module covers.'

Nick shrugged his shoulders.

'I assume it's the part of the course when we study weeds and seeds.'

There was some stifled laughter which Sybil didn't seem to mind. When they'd settled down, she surveyed the twenty students in front of her.

'Would anyone like to summarise why you'll be doing tests on plants and herbs, and putting them under the microscope?'

A hand went up in the second row.

'Seb?'

'To develop new botanical and herbal drugs.'

Her expression was a mixture of surprise and approval.

'That's a good goal to aim for, but we mustn't run before we can walk. The course objective is to familiarise yourselves with the constituents and applications of plants so that when you're a healing practitioner, you'll be equipped to assess and prescribe remedies effectively.'

Nick nodded earnestly and Sybil resumed her presentation. At the end of the session she reminded them they had a practical class in the lab the next day. Then she made an announcement.

'Roger…Mr Digby…has asked me to announce that, as the original visit was rained off, anyone interested in a tour of the sanctuary buildings can meet him in the mansion car park this afternoon at four o'clock.'

As the class filed out, Nick hooked up with Seb and walked with him to the refectory.

'You going on the tour?' said Seb, expecting Nick to share his eagerness to see more of the tholos.

'Um, possibly. What do you think of our classmates?'

Seb swallowed his disappointment at Nick's apparent lack of interest and tried to match his casual tone.

'Okay, I suppose. I don't know them yet.'

'You know more than I do. What did they have to say about themselves?'

'Mostly what they'd been doing before they gave up their jobs to come here.' He racked his brains to remember. He hadn't been paying much attention because he had something else on his mind. 'Oh yeah, and a couple of women who said they had time on their hands now their kids were older. The one you sat next to already has a homeopathic practice but she wants to expand.'

Nick gave a snort of laughter.

'If she expands any more she won't fit in the chair. What about the chicks?'

Seb thought hard.

'The dark-haired girl said she was a PE teacher but they kept giving her random subjects to teach, so she packed it in.'

'And the redhead?'

'Not sure. One of them said she left uni early. Could have been her.'

'Oh well, I'll find out soon enough. She's quite fit.'

Nick wolfed down his sandwich, leaving Seb alone while he table-hopped, schmoozing with his fellow scholars until finally landing on the table where the girl with red hair was sitting.

'The redhead's called Lynette. She's from Rouen,' said Nick, when he finally returned to his seat beside Seb. 'She's not doing the tour, so I offered her a lift back to her digs. She's sharing a place in town with another French girl. If I get on okay with Lynette, maybe you could check out her friend.'

Seb's thoughts circled round the Fliss situation and wondered about confiding in Nick. He was obviously experienced with the opposite sex. Maybe he could help.

'I'm not really looking. There's a girl I've met…'

At once Nick was all attention.

'You dark horse. Tell Uncle Nick all about it.'

'I haven't known her long. Saw her last weekend, but I had to leave early to pack my stuff up. She didn't seem too pleased.'

'Have you slept together?'

Seb felt his face go hot.

'What difference does that make?'

'Not much,' said Nick, laughing. 'I just wanted to ascertain if you were straight. I was beginning to wonder.' Seeing Seb's jaw clench, he added quickly, 'As you weren't showing much interest in the local talent.'

Seb pushed his plate away and got up. They had a free period and hadn't been set any assignments yet so he might just as well stock up on supplies. They'd completely run out of bread.

'See you later. Do you want anything from the supermarket?'

'I can get some stuff in town, don't worry. That reminds me, I've got to pick up some bread from the estate shop. You should go there. Everything's organic.'

'I've heard it's expensive.'

Nick's expression changed to one of sympathy.

'Didn't realise you were on a budget, bro.'

Seb was pulled up short by this remark. He'd saved a bit from his pub job, but he didn't have any regular income at present, so he was being careful. Nevertheless, he didn't want Nick to treat him like a pauper.

'I'm not.'

'Just tight, then?'

Seb chose to ignore Nick's remark and left him to it, none the wiser as to whether or not to contact Fliss.

At four o'clock on the dot, Roger Digby strode towards the spot where Seb and a handful of other students were waiting. He raised an eyebrow when he inspected them.

'Bit of a poor turnout. Do you know if we're expecting any more?'

There were some murmured *don't knows* and some apologies for absence passed on from those who'd had pressing engagements elsewhere.

'Let's go then,' said Digby briskly, and was soon swooped on by an earnest-looking man with a shaved head and loose clothing who kept him engaged in conversation until they reached the garden. Seb walked behind them, interested enough to eavesdrop. It seemed the student had been to Epidaurus and had seen the ruins of the sanctuary of Asklepios.

They came to a wrought iron gate, identical to the one he and Nick had used on Tuesday night, but diagonally opposite, and nearer to the tholos temple. Digby, however, led the group past the tholos and towards the long building against the northern perimeter.

At the entrance to the building, Digby turned to address them.

'There's a description of the sanctuary buildings in your Induction folder but for those of you who may not have read it yet, I'll summarise. The founder, Professor Teodor Ophis, was the architect. He modelled this complex on an ancient Greek healing retreat known as an Asklepion, named after the god of healing, Asklepios. You'll find a statue of him in the rose garden. Asklepios, that is, not the professor. There was an Asklepion on the slopes of the Akropolis, but the most famous one was at Epidaurus. It had a library, baths, an area for sports, accommodation, a hospital and theatre. As you can see, this is very much a scaled-down model. The building behind me is called the abaton.'

He unlocked the door and they filed into a waiting room furnished with comfortable chairs. Its only unusual feature was a bronze head, wings sprouting from its temples, resting on a tall plinth.

'Follow me,' said Digby, walking into a passageway leading off the room. They found themselves in a wide corridor, with windows overlooking the garden to the left and what seemed to be bedrooms, to the right. Digby went into one of the rooms, beckoning the group to follow. The first door on the right was ajar, revealing a toilet and a sink. The main space contained a bed and some basic bedroom furniture.

'As you can see,' he said, 'this part of the building is a dormitory. You might have noticed the head of Hypnos, god of sleep, in the vestibule.'

Someone wondered aloud where the rest of him was, but Digby ignored the laughter and continued. 'Does anyone know what goes on here?'

There were a few sniggers, met by Digby with a look of

scornful resignation.

'Let me rephrase that. What part of the healing process occurs here?'

There was silence until the girl with dark hair spoke.

'Are you saying this is an active healing sanctuary?'

Digby sighed. 'Yes, yes. I covered this in the Induction speech. And it's clearly stated in the course programme that part of the Foundation's remit is to run a healing centre for the general public. In due course, this is where you will do some of your healing practice.'

The girl looked chastened but nevertheless continued. 'I thought the healing centre was in the mansion.'

Digby shook his head irritably. 'The consultation suite and dispensary are only part of it. Treatments vary according to the nature of the condition. Someone who's prescribed the sanctuary experience will spend Saturday and Sunday here...'

He broke off when he saw the shaven-headed man's hand in the air.

'I seem to remember, from my visit to Epidaurus, that in those times the patients slept in the sanctuary and discussed their dreams with the priests the next day.'

'*Enkoimesis*,' said Seb immediately, and everyone except Digby stared at him blankly.

'Come again?' said someone behind him.

'It's Greek for "incubation". Sleep induced by drugs,' said Digby.

'I must have read it...somewhere,' said Seb, avoiding Digby's gaze.

The word had flown from his mouth like a bullet, even though he'd never consciously heard it before. This happened sometimes. He thought of it as the 'latent software' he'd been born with. It was one of the things about him that had seemed to make Pete and Josie uneasy.

'Quite,' said Digby thoughtfully.

'Er, what drugs?' asked the dark-haired girl, directing her question at Seb.

'Opium mixed with other stuff...I think,' said Seb, still at the mercy of his galloping tongue. He looked towards Digby for confirmation, hoping he hadn't been talking complete nonsense.

All eyes now swivelled from him to Digby.

'You seem very sure of your facts, Mr Young, but there's no proof of what exactly was administered, just speculation.'

'What do *you* give the patients to induce sleep?' asked the woman with the long grey plait.

'A natural herbal sedative,' he said, pulling his collar away from his neck. 'You'll learn the formula in your Pharmacognosy class. Let's continue the tour.'

Digby took them farther into the building and showed them a sauna, steam room, cubicles with sunken baths, two treatment rooms for massage and one for colonic irrigation.

'Do you have that before or after they give you the dope?' said plait-woman to Seb. At first he thought she expected an answer, but her toothy smile suggested otherwise, so he grinned back.

Once outside, they walked a few paces to the pump room. Seeing the pump, a student wearing a red bandana round his head started working the handle and seemed surprised when water began spouting into the basin.

'The well water's filtered through a chalk aquifer,' said Digby. 'Quite safe to drink.' He gestured towards the shelf which held the cups. 'Try some.'

Seb watched bandana-man help himself to water and went over to him.

'I wouldn't if I were you. It tastes vile.'

Digby must have heard him because he fixed Seb with a gimlet eye.

'Seems you and your partner in crime gave yourselves an even more extensive tour than I thought.'

To Seb's relief, Digby was interrupted by a student who asked what part the water played in the healing process.

'Good question. The patients are given this water to drink because...' He turned towards Seb. '...Despite what you may think of its taste, it possesses an innate purity. It's also said to play a part in inducing dreams.'

'The well of dreams,' murmured Seb, low enough for no one else to hear.

By now, most of the group had taken a seat and were, in some cases, ogling the statue of Hygeia, identified by someone's smartphone as goddess of health and daughter of Asklepios.

Roger Digby began collecting cups and taking them to the small sink situated in front of a small stained glass window which held the image, familiar to Seb, of a serpent entwined around a staff.

'Well, that's all for today, people,' said Digby, when he'd finished washing the cups. 'I have a meeting at five.'

'What about the tholos?' demanded Seb, more forcefully than he'd intended.

'Sorry, everyone. We'll have to leave that for another day.'

Seb glared at him, convinced that he'd cut short the tour as a punishment for his unauthorised entry to the tholos on Tuesday night. But Digby had already made his way to the door and was announcing that anyone going to the car park should accompany him, but it was quicker for those who lived on campus to use the other exit.

Before he headed off, Digby issued a warning.

'There's something I want all of you to be clear on. The sanctuary buildings must not be accessed by students unless a member of staff is present.' He rearranged his features into a lukewarm smile. 'But you're very welcome to enjoy the gardens themselves during college hours.'

The sole member of the group to leave by the northern gate, Seb tramped back to the flat in the lowering dusk with a creeping sense of loneliness. When he got there, the flat was empty and cold. He thought of going for a run, but it was getting dark. With no job to go to, there didn't seem enough in this new life to fill the gaps in the day.

He turned on the heating and checked his mobile. Nothing. He made a decision and scrolled to Fliss's number, not sure whether to text or call. At that moment, the mobile rang.

'Hi, Seb. How was the tour? Did you find out what lurked beneath the stone?'

'Can you believe it, freaking Digby cut it short. We never got to see inside the tholos.'

Nick laughed.

'Sounds like retribution for our sins. Anyway, mate, two young ladies have expressed a desire for drinky-poos this evening and a light bite. I need you to take one of them off my hands.'

'You mean the French girl and her friend?'

'Yes and no. One of them is, indeed, the French filly. And the other's a girl I met this morning, in the estate shop.'

'Have you decided which one you prefer?'

'No. Not sure yet.'

Seb weighed up the probable prospect of a lonely evening against the possibility of being a gooseberry twice over.

'Seb. You there? Can you be in the pub opposite the library at seven?'

'Okay. I'll put in an appearance, but I'm not guaranteeing I'll stay.'

Chapter 8

Fliss parked her car and stayed put for a few minutes so she wouldn't be early. Nick had seemed surprised when she rang. He probably hadn't expected her to. At least, not so soon. But he'd been eager to meet up. She'd suggested the Bull's Head because they had live music on Thursdays. That way, if the conversation dried up, there'd be something else to focus on.

Just before he rang off, he said a couple of people on his course might be interested in coming, which was a bit of a relief. She didn't want it to feel like a date at this early stage.

She left her car and crossed the road to the pub. Seeing no sign of Nick, she walked farther into the pub until she was stopped in her tracks by a voice in her right ear.

'We're sitting over here.' She turned to find Nick with two drinks in his hands and a wide grin on his face. 'Follow me.'

They walked to a table with a good view of the performance area, occupied by a single female.

'This is Lynette,' he said, nodding towards an attractive girl with red hair, styled in a chic bob. 'She's from *Normandie*.'

His teasing tone produced barely a flicker of a smile from Lynette, who looked Fliss up and down, then cocked her head expectantly at Nick, waiting for the introduction to be completed.

Guessing that Nick had forgotten her name, Fliss gave him the death stare she usually reserved for Saturday girls who turned up late for work.

'I'm Fliss,' she said, taking a seat next to Lynette. 'Nick asked me to recommend a pub, as he's new to the area.'

Yawning as if this was old news, Lynette gave her a brief nod and began studying her phone.

'Can I get you a drink, Fliss?' said Nick blithely, apparently undeterred by her frosty expression.

She asked for a mint spritzer, observing him as he walked

towards the bar. He was just as good looking as she remembered, but a poor prospect if he liked females to be in competition for him. It looked like Birdie was right about him not wanting to be tied down. She just wished Birdie hadn't said the same about Seb.

Lynette put down her phone and Fliss seized the opportunity to ask her what she'd been doing before she came to England.

'I was a beautician. It was a good job but I wanted to extend my knowledge, you know? We have a great interest in France for alternative therapies and remedies.'

'My mother has a beauty salon, actually.'

The girls were deep in conversation when Nick returned with Fliss's drink, bringing some menus with him.

In the queue for food orders, Nick glanced at his watch. It was just past seven-thirty. He was about to text Seb when he caught sight of him, a few yards to the right, sitting at the bar.

'Hey, Seb,' he shouted. 'What's up?'

Seb downed his lager and joined Nick in the queue.

'I knew you'd be in here somewhere, just needed a stiffener first.'

Nick laughed.

'Never needed Dutch courage myself. I drink purely for pleasure. Anyway mate, what are you eating?'

Once they'd ordered, they remained at the bar while Nick filled him in on their dining companions.

'Lynette asked me in for a *tisane*, I think she called it. I had to hold my nose to get it down. We were getting on like a house on fire: she was all over me…then I got a call from the girl I met in the shop. She said this place had live music tonight so I said okay.'

'How did Lynette take that?'

'She was a bit peeved at first but she calmed down when I asked her to come as well.'

'What's the verdict, then?'

Nick shrugged.

'There's not much in it. Lynette's sexy, but way too intense. She was banging on about her *life plan*. The other one's great looking, but kind of distant. I'm thinking she might just have the edge. I like girls who play it cool.' He nodded in the direction of their table. 'Better get going before they come looking for us.'

Nick led Seb to the table and sat down between the two girls.

'Seb, you know Lynette. Fliss, this is Seb, my flatmate.'

Seb was still on his feet when their eyes locked. The level of hurt and dismay in his expression hit Fliss like an arrow to the chest. She fully expected him to get up and leave.

'Park yourself, mate,' drawled Nick, oblivious to the emotional tension in the air. 'You're making the place look untidy.'

Seb sank into the chair next to Lynette and fixed her with unblinking eyes.

'I hear you have a life plan. Tell me about it.'

— o —

Fliss let herself in and tiptoed upstairs in the dark so as not to disturb her parents, who, despite having trouble hearing the TV, developed superhuman hearing at night. When she got into bed, she finally gave herself up to the shock of coming face to face with Seb.

She replayed the evening, agonising at how Seb had almost completely blanked her. If he hadn't started talking to Lynette as soon as he sat down, she might have announced they'd met before. After that, his indifference had made it too awkward to admit.

Nick, in contrast, had been very attentive. He said he'd definitely be paying the boutique a visit. This reminded her of the day Seb had shown up, and made her doubly regret ringing Nick and messing everything up.

It had been an enormous effort keeping up a dialogue with

Nick while straining to hear what Seb and Lynette were saying. Lynette kept touching her hair and leaning into him. Maybe she was trying to make Nick jealous, but it looked real enough.

She'd been relieved when the band started playing; from then on conversation had, of necessity, been kept to a minimum.

Salvation had eventually arrived in the shape of an old school friend, Linzi, who she came across in the ladies. Linzi was dabbing her eyes with cold water, after an argument with her boyfriend, who turned out to be the bass player in the band. Offering her a lift home was the least she could do. In fact, Linzi spent the last half hour of the gig sitting at their table, looking miserable.

Nick's face had fallen when the music stopped and she explained the situation. She also noticed the sharp jerk of Seb's head, as if what he'd heard had grabbed his attention.

When she said goodbye, only Nick and Lynette responded, but Seb did make eye contact. She relived that look over and over, but still wasn't sure if there was any forgiveness in his eyes.

Chapter 9

Seb heard a key in the lock and put an ear to his bedroom door. There was the sound of footsteps and the fridge being opened, but no conversation, so he joined Nick in the main room.

'Okay?' said Nick, when Seb appeared.

'Yeah. Wasn't sure if you'd be alone.'

Nick spread his palms in a gesture of mock despair.

'Must be losing my touch. I start out with two dolls and end up with sweet nothing. Anyway, where'd you rush off to? I thought you and Lynette were getting along.'

'She's okay...not really my type.'

'So you left it to me to take her home. Thanks, buddy.'

'Well, you brought her.'

'Yeah. Must say, it was a bit of a surprise when she didn't ask me in. All I got was an *Au revoir*. Something tells me that you, on the other hand, would have got a *Voulez-vous coucher avec moi ce soir?'*

'Come off it. She's hardly going to sleep with you when you spent all night chatting up another girl.'

'Much good it did me,' Nick said, laughing ruefully. 'Who knew she'd bump into a girlfriend and give her a lift home?'

Seb steeled himself to ask the question he most wanted answering in the world at that moment.

'You planning to see her again?'

'Yeah. I said I'd take a look at her boutique. Might mosey on by tomorrow. About four o'clock. Fancy coming? She's probably got some lovely assistants.'

Seb shook his head.

'Nah, I'll pass.'

Nick gave him a long look.

'I get it. You're still hankering after that girl you told me about. What's your action plan?'

Seb felt himself blush. If Nick knew that same girl was Fliss, he'd take him for a total idiot.

'There isn't one. Don't think I'll bother…I've got enough on my plate at the moment.' He stretched back in his chair and got up. 'I'm for bed.'

Nick yawned.

'Me, too.' He grinned. 'I appreciate you coming tonight, buddy.'

Seb raised his hand in response, fearing he might have screwed up his relationship with two of the coolest people he'd ever met.

— o —

Fliss woke at five-thirty, her head immediately invaded by the dreadful possibility that Seb might have taken Lynette home. And stayed the night.

Unable to get back to sleep, she got up, dragged a drowsy Delta out of her bed and set out for a walk to clear her head. The morning was crisp and bright, the sweet rhapsody of the dawn chorus enough to lift her spirits, temporarily at least.

She left for work early and made a call as soon as she got there.

'What time do you call this, young lady? I'm not even dressed.'

'Sorry, Birdie, but I wanted to ask you something.'

'Hold on a minute.' Fliss heard the tinkle of a teaspoon. 'Go on.'

'Do you know a quick way of finding a mother who gave up a child for adoption? I'm asking for a friend.'

'Who?'

Fliss paused for a second too long, giving Birdie time to work it out.

'Oh, it's that boy you told me about, isn't it? Has he changed his mind?'

'Um, not exactly. But if there's a way of finding his mother, I could give him her address and let him decide.'

'Look, lovey, don't you think you should get his permission before you go digging around? His mother may have had more children. For all you know, she might not want to be found. I wouldn't interfere if I were you.'

'Okay,' said Fliss, hiding her disappointment by deliberately sounding unconcerned. 'It was just a thought. See you soon. Take care.'

Fliss spent the morning checking stock levels, reordering, and arranging a visit to a new supplier. In the afternoon, she went on the shop floor and was taking a turn on the cash desk when in walked Nick, looking every inch the trendy urbanite. He approached the counter, his eyes twinkling.

'Good afternoon. I'm looking for Miss Felicity Logan. Is she free?'

Fliss laughed. 'She will be in five minutes when her colleague comes back from her break. Take a look around while you're waiting.'

Nick gave her a boy scout salute and sauntered off, grinning.

'See anything you like?' she said, creeping up on him a few minutes later as he was inspecting a display of carefully folded jumpers.

'You bet. I thought your stuff might be a bit old-fashioned, being your mum's store. But it's spot on.' He straightened up, looking her up and down approvingly. 'I guess that's why you always look good. You get your pick of the stock.'

'I'm on a break. Do you want to join me?' she said, choosing to ignore a remark she'd heard a million times.

'This is nice,' Nick said, sitting the other side of her desk, sipping tea. 'I tried to ring you earlier, but your phone was off.'

'I turn my personal phone off when I'm working. I've been too busy to check it today. So what brings you here?' When his smile faltered, Fliss immediately regretted putting him on the spot so she answered for him. 'Nothing better to do, I suppose. That's the trouble with students. Too much free time until you have to hand in an essay and then you're up all night.'

'I've yet to experience that pleasure,' he said, visibly relieved at her jokey tone. He paused. 'Actually, I wanted to apologise for last night. Lynette and Seb were a bit off with you.'

'No need,' she said, feeling the blood rush to her face. 'They seemed to be happy with each other's company, at least.'

She steeled herself to ask the question she most wanted answering in the world at that moment.

'So who got the girl?'

The startled expression in Nick's eyes indicated he hadn't expected such a blatant cross-examination.

'Nobody. I dropped her off. That was it.'

Fliss felt her heart swell with relief. Even if Nick got the wrong idea—that she was jealous of him and Lynette getting together—it was worth it to know that Seb hadn't taken her home.

She made no comment, and Nick carried on talking.

'How's your friend? She looked pretty hacked off with her boyfriend.'

'Linzi? Oh, they're always arguing…they've probably kissed and made up already. I asked her to be a model for my fashion shoot. That cheered her up.'

Nick leaned forward. 'Fashion shoot? Tell me about it.'

'It's nothing major. Just some pictures of the new winter lines for the Belinda website. I've got three girls modelling three outfits each. We'll go somewhere like Pendell Woods, weather permitting. My colleague, Milena, is taking the photographs. I'm…'

She hesitated, not sure she wanted to admit she vlogged, in case he marked her down as a shameless self-promoter, which she wasn't. She did it for the sake of the business, not for her own glory.

Opting for full disclosure, she came clean.

'I'll be making a video of the actual shoot, for the boutique vlog.'

'Really?' he said. 'Show me.'

She turned her laptop round so he could see her latest YouTube vlog. He watched it with interest, giving her a thumbs-up at the end.

'It's good. You're very photogenic. And you don't waffle.'

Fliss relaxed, happy to have his approval. 'Thanks.'

'I like the new look you gave the girl. How often do you post?'

'Every two or three weeks.'

She thought guiltily of the garments she had at home still waiting to be filmed. She really should get a move on.

'When's the shoot?'

'As soon as I find some boys. They're harder to persuade...I usually ask my brother's friends but they're away at university.'

'How about me?'

'I can't afford you,' she said, thinking he was joking.

'I'll do it for a sweater. It's getting chilly and my blood's thin from living in LA.'

'Really? That's great. Do you know anyone else who'd be up for it? I need two more. They'll get a £50 Belinda voucher.'

'Okay, I'll ask around.'

She closed the laptop and stood up.

'I'd better get back. Friday afternoon gets busy...people looking for something to wear on Saturday night.'

Nick got to his feet.

'Do you fancy a drink after you finish work?' he said, his voice nonchalant. 'You've only shown me one pub so far.'

Fliss had been expecting something like this ever since he'd come through the door. In truth, if he'd told her that Seb had taken Lynette home, she might well have said yes. But, as Seb hadn't, she lied.

'Sorry. I promised my mum I'd pick the dog up from daycare today.'

'Bring the dog as well,' he said, grinning. 'A few pork scratchings and he'll be fine.'

'She. Anyway, don't be ridiculous.'

'That's a "no" then?'

'Afraid so. But you'll be in touch about the shoot, won't you?'

He nodded.

'And could you send me a full body shot before I interview them?'

'Is that legal?' he said, chuckling.

'Seeing as I'm hiring them for their looks, it's compulsory.'

— o —

When Fliss got home, she told her parents she'd be filming and couldn't be disturbed. She set up a microphone, camera and lights in her bedroom, did her intro in one take, then filmed herself in the clothes she'd chosen. She edited the footage with a fast-motion effect and a honky-tonk piano soundtrack, accomplishing the whole thing in record time.

It's because I'm happier now, she thought, wondering if Seb would ever watch her vlog and, if so, would he like it as much as Nick had.

Once she'd posted the vlog, she typed 'finding birth parent' into a search engine and came up with the Adoption Contact Register for contacting a parent or child. Seb would have to fill in a registration form and his mother would have to be registered as well. At that, some of her happiness evaporated. She'd hit a brick wall, unless she could persuade Seb to register.

Her next search was 'tracing agencies'. She rang the 24-hour contact number and was amazed when a real person answered. She said she was enquiring on behalf of a friend who didn't know where exactly he was born, or the names of his mother and father. He told her that a parent's name and place of birth was required information for a copy of an original birth certificate, so the Adoption Contact Register was his best bet.

If, however, any of those details ever came to light, his agency might be able to help. From then on, it would be a no-find, no-fee transaction.

Chapter 10

Seb hovered over the student notice board in the main hall. He was looking for student societies but most of the notices came from outside organisations. He tried to imagine the person who'd pinned up the one for a Knit and Natter session at a tea shop in Penbury. Plait-woman, perhaps?

'Anything there to tempt you?'

Recognising the tones of Roger Digby, a man he considered more foe than friend, he continued studying the notice board.

'Nothing so far.'

Digby moved nearer the board and began reading aloud.

'Drop-in Mindfulness and Meditation. Sounds like a contradiction in terms.' Getting no reaction from Seb, he read on. 'Swing Dance, Write Club, Comedy Impro, Art in the Park. Any of those up your street?' He pointed to a notice with 'Students' Association' emblazoned at its head. 'They're looking for Bar Committee members. Given your experience, you'd be quite an asset. And it'd keep you out of trouble.'

Seb turned and stared coolly at Digby, resenting the reference to his and Nick's nocturnal visit to the tholos.

'Actually, I'm looking for sports activities. Does this place have anything resembling a rugby team?'

Digby's thin face creased into a scornful smile.

'I doubt we could even cobble together a five-a-side football team. The nearest you'd get to physical activity here is circle dancing. Once a month in the large seminar room. I believe they have live music...a string quartet, no less.'

Seb's shoulders slumped as he brushed past Digby and made for the door. What the heck was he supposed to do at weekends if the place turned into a ghost town?

'Sebastian!'

Seb stopped, surprised that Digby had used his first name.

'I'm on my way home. You're welcome to join me for a cup of tea if you're at a loose end.'

Seb adopted a deadpan expression and turned round.

'Where do you live?'

'In a cottage on the estate.'

'Okay.'

They left the mansion and took the winding lane which led in the direction of the estate shop. As they walked, Digby asked Seb how he was settling in.

'Uh, so far so good. But is it always so deserted at the weekends? I thought the resident students would be around, doing stuff.'

'It's always quiet at the start of term. You'll find, as the assignments pile up, they'll be on campus, hitting the library. Some of the more valuable books can't be taken out on loan. And the students in the two years above you will have their healing practice, as will your year. That's always at the weekends.'

Seb nodded, feeling his morale slowly winching up.

'Where's your friend, by the way? Nick, isn't it?'

'He's gone to see his family. He asked me if I wanted to go with him, but…'

He trailed off, realising that turning down the invitation was at odds with his avowed desire for company, something even he didn't quite understand.

By now, they'd reached a row of handsome brick and flint cottages.

'Here we are,' said Digby, opening the first front door. 'Good boy,' he said, addressing the elderly spaniel who ambled up to them, as he showed Seb into a comfortable sitting room.

Seb took a seat in a wingback chair with a view of a well-tended garden. Beyond this stretched a peaceful scene of green paddocks with a scattering of horses. When Digby finished clinking and clattering in the kitchen, he brought in a tray of tea. The tea poured, he offered Seb a slice of cake.

'My wife's recipe. You should try some.'

Seb took a piece. It tasted of walnuts and honey: it was so delicious, he helped himself to a second slice.

Digby asked if he was interested in the history of Whitwell Hall. Out of politeness, Seb said he was. He was grateful for Digby's invitation to his home, even more so when the dog rested his head on his feet.

As Digby travelled back in time to the Anglo-Saxon burial grounds upon which Whitwell Hall and its antecedents had arisen, Seb zoned out, his thoughts turning to the evening before.

— o —

The student bar was finally open, so he and Nick had ended up in there. They didn't recognise anyone from their year, so they assumed the handful of other drinkers were from years two and three.

He'd been determined not to mention Fliss but after a couple of pints, he put his face into neutral and asked Nick whether he'd managed to catch her at the shop.

'Yeah, I did,' said Nick, winking. 'She even took me upstairs.'

Seb raised an eyebrow in exaggerated disapproval, despite being fully aware that it was Fliss's policy to keep private conversations off the shop floor.

'Only kidding,' said Nick. 'We went to her office. She showed me her fashion vlog. I was impressed. Tried to get her to meet me for a drink afterwards but she said she had to pick up her mother's mutt. Which is why, my young friend,' he said, getting to his feet, 'you have the pleasure of my company this good night. Another pint?'

Seb beamed.

'Won't say no.'

While Nick was getting the drinks, Seb found himself hoping that Fliss had used Delta as an excuse because she didn't fancy

Nick, then immediately felt disloyal to his friend for doing so.

'There you go,' said Nick, putting the drinks on the table. 'I asked the guy behind the bar where all the punters are. He said once the term gets going, Friday night's their busiest night. It's when they hold events.'

'Like what?'

'Quiz nights, stand-up, open mike, that kind of thing.'

Seb rolled his eyes in dismay at a grinning Nick as he had a flashback of a poetry slam he'd been taken to by one of the farm daughters. To his intense embarrassment, she'd read out a love poem he suspected was directed at him.

Later on, Seb was returning from the men's room when Nick jumped up, mobile in hand.

'Hey, mate, wait a second,' he said, taking a picture. 'I've been tasked with scouting out some talent for a porn movie. Specifically, tall blond guys with green eyes.'

'You've what?' said Seb, making a lunge for Nick's phone.

'Steady on. I'm kidding. Fliss is looking for some male models for a fashion shoot, that's all.'

Frowning, Seb sat down.

'Why take a picture? She knows what I look like.'

'She probably wouldn't remember. You spent the whole evening chatting up Lynette, as I recall.'

For a split second, Seb considered telling the truth about his history with Fliss and how the fact he'd ignored her would effectively exclude him from this project. But while this was going through his mind, Nick had pressed send.

'She's got it now. And if you make the cut, a £50 Belinda voucher will be placed in your hot little hand.'

Seb could feel his face burn as he imagined her reaction when she saw his picture.

'Fifty pounds wouldn't go far in that place,' he retorted, the drink making him careless.

'You've been there, then?' said Nick, narrowing his eyes like a detective.

It was too late now to come clean, so Seb told a small lie.

'I went with a girl.'

Nick's eyes gleamed.

'Did you, now? Shopping with a woman suggests a deep, meaningful relationship. Is she still on the scene?'

'Nah. It wasn't like that. After my parents died, I got a lot of attention from the farming community. The mothers thought I was lonely, so they tried to fix me up with a shedload of girls.'

This part was true. Nonetheless, Nick gave a shout of laughter.

'Whoa, boy. You telling me you were fighting them off with a pitchfork?'

'Not exactly. I went out with a few of them, but nothing serious.'

At that moment they were joined by a fellow first-year, who introduced himself as Jim. Seb recognised him as the guy who'd grabbed the pump handle when they were on the tour with Digby. He was wearing the same red bandana, but this time tied round his neck at the back, desperado-style.

When Nick mentioned the photo shoot, Jim instantly put a hand on his hip and adopted a serious expression with one raised eyebrow. It was plain he was joking, but Nick had already snapped him and despatched it to Fliss before he had a chance to object.

The three of them stayed until the bar closed and staggered back to their quarters, Jim disappearing into another block.

— o —

Seb's action replay of the evening before was interrupted by Digby asking him if he wanted another cup of tea.

'Uh, no thanks. I suppose I should be going.'

'Have you any plans for the weekend?' said Digby.

Seb turned his attention to the spaniel, trying to decide as he stroked him, whether to invent some activities or confess that today and tomorrow stretched before him like an arid wasteland.

'Because if not,' Digby went on, getting up and pacing back and forth, 'we could make a visit to the sanctuary.'

For the first time that day, Seb's brain cells began to hum with excitement.

'You mean I could see inside the tholos?'

Digby nodded.

'The sanctuary doesn't open for patients until next weekend. If you're still keen to see it, today would be a good opportunity.'

'Sounds great. What time?'

'We could go now.'

They took a path at the side of the house which led straight to the founder's garden. On the way, Seb asked Digby if the temples of Asklepios had provided the only medical care in ancient Greece.

'When the cult first began, some time in the fifth century BC, yes. For common complaints, the priests offered herbal remedies and crude bone-setting. For more complex conditions, they adopted the Egyptian custom of dream-healing, which we talked about on the tour. As the centuries passed, the sanctuaries evolved into spas, focusing on exercise and diet. They even offered surgery by trained physicians.'

Seb winced.

'Having your appendix out without anaesthetic. That's no joke.'

'They probably used alcohol or opium to numb the pain.'

'So which version of the Asklepion is this model based on?'

Digby smiled.

'We don't offer operations but we can prescribe medicines from natural sources and advise on diet.'

'But surely that can all be done at the healing centre in the mansion.'

'Yes.'

'In that case, who uses the abaton?'

'Anyone who needs healing of the *psyche*, the Greek word for the soul.'

Seb was digesting this answer when Digby added, 'You came up with the term "enkoimesis" for induced sleep on the tour, as I remember. Where did you hear that expression? I don't think it's in the handout.'

Seb shook his head, blushing, still unable to offer any explanation other than it popped into his head.

'Well, how or why it came to you, that's the reason I've brought you here today. Any more questions?'

'What was the tholos used for?'

'Nobody's quite sure. Maybe it'll "pop into your head" and the mystery of ages will be solved.'

They approached the garden from the opposite direction to the way he and Nick had come on Tuesday night, arriving at the same gate after a mere five-minute walk. Once inside, they headed for the tholos, climbed the steps, and walked a few paces along the peristyle to arrive at the high, panelled door.

As Digby unlocked the door, Seb felt his pulse racing. He had no idea why this building held such an attraction for him but he couldn't wait to explore what lay beneath the circular stone.

He followed Digby inside, the natural light from the windows allowing him to see the interior more clearly than he had on his last visit. His target was the central white stone, but he didn't want to seem over-eager, so he asked Digby about the painted panels. There were seven of them, positioned at regular intervals around the room, easily visible between the columns.

Digby started with the panel nearest him, of two young women, each with a snake entwined about her arm.

'Hygeia and Panacea, daughters of Asklepios.' Next, he pointed to a picture of a handsome youth, wearing nothing but a flimsy loin cloth and a laurel wreath, holding a golden bow. 'That's Apollo, father of Asklepios and god of medicine, among other things.'

He nodded towards the picture next to it. 'And here's the man himself, of course. Asklepios. Strange that his father's always depicted as a beardless youth, and he as a rather stout patriarch with an abundance of facial hair.'

Seb giggled. The painting, positioned on the wall behind the altar, showed a seated Asklepios with an unruly head of hair beneath a sort of cap, his droopy moustache merging with a curly beard. The top half of his body was bare, resembling that of a wrestler, his lower half covered by a loose, white garment which must have slipped from his shoulder. In his left hand he held a staff, around which a serpent coiled. At his right foot, lay a dog.

The sight of the staff made Seb automatically reach into his pocket and touch the serpent brooch.

'Any snakes here?' said Seb, half serious.

'The Asklepion sanctuaries had a pit of snakes to accept offerings of food on behalf of the gods,' said Digby. 'I'm afraid we don't keep any here.'

'Too bad,' said Seb, and Digby smiled.

'Sometimes the snakes were put in the abaton, where they moved around the sleeping patients.'

'The dogs, too,' said Seb, plucking that information out of thin air.

Digby gave him one of his searching looks.

'Indeed. They would have licked the supplicants' wounds, if they had any.'

As they moved on, it occurred to Seb that maybe this would be a good time to ask Digby if he'd known Professor Ophis. On the other hand, he wasn't sure whether he really cared what kind of man his biological father was. To distract himself, he studied the painting nearest him. In the foreground, the artist had drawn a seated goddess surrounded by sheaves of wheat and poppies, with what looked like a snake curled around her arm. Behind her, danced several male and female figures, each carrying a flaming torch in one hand and a drinking cup in the other.

'*They* look as if they're having a good time,' said Seb.

'We'll never know how good a time,' replied Digby drily. 'The Eleusinian cult imbibed a rather interesting potion at their festivals. Unfortunately, as there are no reliable records of any of the secret rites of the mystery cults, we can only speculate.'

Digby moved towards the panel which depicted a Titian-haired matron with a somewhat serious expression.

'Rather more to my taste is Mnemosyne, goddess of memory. In terms of the incubation therapy, she's the most important deity. Supplicants always said a prayer to her before going to sleep, in the hope they'd remember any visions they had.'

'Who are these guys?' said Seb, examining the last panel, an image of two naked, winged males carrying a body.

'Hypnos and Thanatos: twin gods of sleep and death, carrying a dead warrior. Ancient Greece was all about war...against Persia...between the Delian League and Sparta...so death was a great preoccupation.'

'The Delian League? Who were they?'

'An alliance of Greek states under the leadership of Athens. The Athenian empire, in other words. Sparta had a similar coalition.'

He walked to the centre of the room and beckoned Seb forward.

'Would you like to do the honours?'

Seb strode forward, seized the iron ring and gave it a tug. Expecting the stone to be much heavier than it was, he was surprised when it easily released from its resting place, to reveal a shadowy basement area below.

Seb peered through the aperture, trying to figure out how to access the lower chamber. He looked across at Digby, who simply continued to observe him as if this was some sort of test.

Puzzled, he went down on his hands and knees and felt inside the circular hole but he could find no fittings of any kind, just the lip on which it rested.

'Is this when you produce a magic rope ladder?' said Seb, willing himself to stay calm and polite when what he really wanted to do was tell him to get on with it or he'd throw his skinny carcass down the hole.

In reply, Digby advanced towards the altar, which stood some feet in front of the columns, and disappeared behind it. Seb reached the spot in time to see Digby lift up a wooden trap door, exposing a flight of wooden stairs.

Digby flicked on a light switch and motioned Seb to follow him down to a subterranean chamber, furnished only with a large wooden chest and two chairs.

His first response was disappointment at its lack of any obvious purpose. But as he got closer, the wall lights revealed a pale gold floor-labyrinth on a jet black background, laid out in polished granite tiles.

'Wow,' he said, spellbound by the way the gold sparkled in the light. 'This is beautiful. Do you actually use this? I mean, the people who come here for treatment, do you put them in here?'

'Of course.'

'And what does it do for them exactly?'

'Do you want the esoteric explanation or a more universally accepted version?'

Seb shrugged. 'Both. I'm here to learn.'

'We usually tell the patients it's a contemplative practice, like meditation. But the Greeks believed it was more than that. For them, it was a technique for revitalising body and soul. They believed the seven-path spiral of the labyrinth corresponded to the seven spinal energy centres in the body, and that walking the labyrinth could awaken the life force, which lies like a coiled serpent at the base of the spine.'

Seb allowed himself a moment to mull this over. While he did so, his hand was once again drawn to the brooch in his pocket.

'Is that what the staff of Asklepios is all about? The snake coiled around the staff signifying the energy rising up the spine?'

'It could be,' said Digby, giving him a long, thoughtful stare. 'Ancient cultures held the snake to be a symbol of healing, regeneration and transformation, so in Greece it came to be associated with Asklepios. There's also a more mundane explanation, as there often is with things esoteric—it signifies his ability to heal a poisonous snakebite.'

Seb glanced upwards to the circular hole in the ceiling where the white stone had been.

'What's the point of that, exactly?'

'It's so we can check the patients are all right without disturbing their contemplation.'

Seb began to walk the labyrinth, circling back and forth, reaching the centre and returning on a similar spiral trail.

'We tell them to take it slowly and pause for reflection when they get to the centre,' said Digby, when Seb arrived back at the beginning.

'Sure. I was just getting the feel of it.'

Digby looked at his watch.

'I'm afraid I have to get going. Some domestic chores await. My wife's away this weekend.'

'Any chance I could come back some time and do it properly?'

It was hard to see Digby's expression in the faint light but he seemed to be deliberating. After a long pause, he replied.

'Very well. How about this evening? Come prepared to spend the night in the abaton. You might as well have the whole experience while you're at it.'

Chapter 11

Later that day, having followed Digby's instructions as far as he could, Seb presented himself at the door of his cottage. He'd managed to fast, and to drink only the pungent spring water that Digby had given him. But white clothing had been harder, as he didn't possess any, apart from a T-shirt that had seen brighter days.

A trip into town had yielded some white boxers and a cheap white sweatshirt. Digby had said to bring what he could, so he assumed there was a plan B. Would Digby supply white track pants, perhaps, to substitute for his jeans?

Digby answered his knock promptly, only pausing to check Seb had left his phone at home before picking up a holdall and striding down the front path. He was clearly eager to get on with the activity, whatever that would turn out to be.

Inside the tholos, he asked Seb to remove his shoes and jacket, then took some white cotton slippers and a long, white robe from his holdall. It had wide sleeves and no fastenings, apart from a cord at the waist, and was loose enough to wear over clothing. He explained that it signified the purity of the patients' prayers and intentions, and also kept them warm, as there was no heating in the tholos. While Seb was putting it on, he placed some items on the altar.

Returning to his holdall, he produced two small pieces of the honey cake Seb had tasted earlier in the day, wrapped in a paper napkin.

'It's a little ritual we like to perform. An oblation to Asklepios and Hygeia. Would you mind placing this on the platen?'

Seb took the cake and padded towards the altar, which was set with two lighted pillar candles flanking a silver altar plate. He performed the task, waiting for the moment Digby would produce a mechanical snake, whose jaws would open to receive the offering.

Digby had not moved from his spot so Seb looked back at him for further instructions.

'Would you like to pray for a healing in return for your offering, as the Greeks would have?'

Seb was stumped. Rituals and prayers were uncharted territory for him. He felt the lines were blurring now, between familiarising himself with the sanctuary sleepover and being treated as a patient himself.

'But I haven't got a medical condition. I'm as strong as an ox.'

'Not all illnesses are physical.'

'Right,' said Seb, wondering whether Digby thought he needed psychological help. 'So you want me to pretend I'm a real patient?'

'Look,' said Digby, his expression indicating that he didn't take kindly to time-wasters. 'You can stop the process at any time if you're uncomfortable with it. I assumed, because you were so eager to come back here, that you'd be prepared to completely immerse yourself in the experience.'

'Yeah, of course,' said Seb, fearful that Digby would call a halt to proceedings. 'Um, how do I phrase this prayer, exactly?'

'Walking the labyrinth creates an opportunity for healing on *all* levels. So why not ask for that?'

'Do I have to say it out loud?'

'If you want to be like the Greeks, yes. They spoke out loud when they communicated with their gods.'

Seb bowed his head, because he'd seen pictures of people doing this in church.

'I ask for healing on all levels,' he parroted, glancing at Digby for further instructions.

'Who are you addressing your request to?' said Digby, as if talking to a child.

'God?'

'Which one?'

Seb looked vacant for a few moments, then bowed his head for a second time. 'I ask the god *Asklepios* for healing on all levels.'

'Fine,' said Digby, switching on the labyrinth lights. 'We can go downstairs now.'

When they reached the lower chamber, Digby took some nightlights in glass containers from the large wooden chest, placed them around the circumference of the labyrinth and lit them with a pocket lighter.

'You'll find a bottle of spring water in there and a blanket if you get cold,' he said, nodding towards the chest. 'I'm afraid there's no water supply in the building, therefore no WC. So if you need to "go", the nearest place is the abaton. That's where I'll be. I'll come back and check on you in an hour.'

'What happens if nothing happens?' said Seb. A whole hour spent walking round in circles didn't hold much appeal.

'Don't overthink the process. Just walk the labyrinth until you reach the middle, pause for contemplation, and retrace your steps. You can do it as few or as many times as you want. The spiralling motion puts the walker into a state of mind that's conducive to meditation. Revelation, even.'

'Revelation?'

'In the sense of an epiphany: a realisation of something not seen or recognised before. It can be felt during your walk or even some time later. Don't expect anything and then you won't be disappointed.'

Digby switched off the wall lights and disappeared up the stairs, leaving Seb feeling like a tourist abandoned in a foreign city without a guidebook.

— o —

A light from above seeped through Seb's closed lids. Opening them, he made out a shadowy figure peering down at him through the viewing aperture directly above the centre of the labyrinth, where he was sitting cross-legged, wrapped in a blanket.

'Sebastian. Are you cooked yet?'

Seb raised a hand in acknowledgement and was joined in seconds by Digby, who helped him to his feet.

'How do you feel?'

'A bit spaced out. I wasn't asleep, but I seemed to be in a different place. What time is it?'

'Nine-thirty. I came at nine and you seemed to be in contemplation, so I left you to it.'

'I wasn't aware of you.'

'No matter. Let's get you to the abaton.'

Once outside, Digby led him to the big old cedar of Lebanon in the centre of the garden and told him to take off his slippers and place his hands on the trunk.

'This tree's been here over three hundred years. Think about its roots…how abundant they are, how far into the earth they go. Imagine you're this tree. Your branches grow up into the sky and your roots down into mother earth.'

'Why did I have to do that?' said Seb, on their way to the abaton.

'It's a quick and easy means of grounding yourself after an extended period of contemplation. That's one of the reasons every Asklepion had a grove of trees.'

Seb imagined ancient Greeks in short tunics hugging trees, and tried to keep a straight face.

Digby opened the door of the abaton and led Seb through the vestibule to a bedroom towards the end of the corridor.

'This is your room for the night. It's customary to have a bath before the incubation. You could say it's an outward sign of the imminent cleansing within.'

Still in a somewhat dazed state, Seb took the towel Digby gave him, and followed him to the spa area.

'Do your usual clientele use those?' said Seb, as they passed by the sauna and steam room on their way to a bathroom.

'If they want to. Depends when they arrive.' Digby opened the door of a large cubicle and indicated the sunken bath. 'You'll have to settle for this, given the time of night. There's bath oil on the side and a nightshirt on the hook, there. Come back to the room when you're ready. You can leave your clothes here.'

Seb undressed and stepped down into the bath, his attention caught by a mural of the stern-looking woman he'd seen earlier in the tholos, whose name escaped him. The artist had painted an inscription at the bottom of the picture: *Memory is the mother of all wisdom.*

As water gushed into the bath, the aroma of lavender filled the cubicle, making him wish he hadn't been quite so liberal with the bath oil. Nevertheless, he sank down into the water, his eyes closed, trying to remember what he'd been thinking about when he'd stopped circling the labyrinth and come to rest in the centre.

After a while, the water cooled and he was no nearer retrieving the memory, so he dried himself, pulled on the white nightshirt and returned to his room, where he found Digby waiting for him, wearing a robe identical to the one he himself had worn in the labyrinth.

Digby motioned him to get into bed. As he did so, Seb noticed a glass of pale green liquid on the bedside locker.

'What's next?' he said, a little alarmed at the possibility of a drug-induced experience.

'A prayer to Mnemosyne to help you remember your dreams.'

Seb recognised the name and was able to put a face to it.

'That was her in the bathroom, wasn't it?'

'Yes. One of our students painted the mural. It serves as an aide-mémoire for the patients.'

'Okay. I ask the goddess Mnemosyne to help me remember my trip.'

Digby retained a neutral expression, leaving Seb wondering why he hadn't challenged his turn of phrase.

'The glass beside you contains water with some drops of tincture added. Sip it slowly. It'll send you off to sleep quite soon.'

Seb reached for the glass of liquid, sniffed it and looked at Digby.

'Will it have any after effects? Like, do I have to stop driving for twenty-four hours?'

'It's completely safe, Sebastian.To quote Paracelsus, *It is the dose that makes the poison*. I'll be in the next room, checking on you every so often. We never leave patients unattended in the abaton.'

Seb took a sip. It was quite bitter, but at least it didn't strike him as an illegal substance, not that he was an expert.

Digby took a slim book from his pocket and opened it. 'In the meantime, I'll be doing some chanting.'

Seb couldn't suppress a giggle. Was he hallucinating or was Digby impersonating a medieval monk?

'I'm serious,' said Digby, frowning. 'The *therapeutai* believed that these chants, and the following dream, would unlock an inner capacity to heal oneself, which everyone possesses but few know how to access.'

Before Seb could probe any further, Digby had begun chanting in a language he didn't recognise. When he'd swallowed the last drop, he lay back and surrendered to sleep.

Chapter 12

I open my eyes and stare at the ceiling, my head thumping as if fifty hammer-wielding bees are attacking the inside of my skull. I hear cheering in the distance and try to call out, but can only manage a groan. My hands fumble for a sheet, but all they find are patches of mud clinging to a film of oil and sand which covers my body.

My eyes scan the room as best they can: it is small and bare, except for a water basin. Beyond it is a larger room with benches scattered with garments. Then I hear footsteps, followed by a cry.

'Apollos! You are awake. Praise Athena.'

A man kneels beside me and looks into my eyes, his own eyes dark and sorrowful. He fills a cup from the water tap, gently lifts my head and puts it to my swollen lips.

'Drink slowly.'

I sip it to the last drop and let my throbbing head slump back.

'Where am I?' I croak, my voice so weak he has to place his head close to mine to hear me.

'The stadium. You competed against Tellias in the pankration.'

My battered body indicates to me that victory was not mine.

'Who are you?'

His face pales and he answers in a whisper. 'I am Philemon, your friend. Don't you recognise me?'

The name means nothing to me. He proceeds to ask whether I remember this thing or that, but I can only shake my head, and eventually he leaves the room. I try to sit up but the pain in my upper body is too great, and I sink back on to the pallet, the straw stalks like arrows to my aching flesh.

I can feel myself drifting off to sleep. At one point I am briefly aware of a cover being laid on my naked body, but not roused enough to open my eyes. I am, from time to time, conscious of the coming and going of men in the adjoining dressing room. Some sound like trainers, giving advice and discussing the events with the competitors.

I hear two of them discussing me, as if I'm not there.

'He fought well, but Tellias is built like a bull. They say he's the strongest man in Attica.'

'Do you think he'll survive?'

'Depends whether a blow damaged his heart.'

'Or his head. His trainer, Brygos, says he remembers nothing.'

When I next awake, it's to the sound of two voices close by, one of them Philemon's.

'When do you think he can be moved, Brygos?'

'At dusk, when the crowd has dispersed. I'll arrange for two slaves to carry him to the precinct. The physician will give him something for the pain and bind his ribs.'

My next impression is being carried on a litter over rough ground and Philemon grabbing the pole as a cursing bearer stumbles. I feel the journey will never end, each false step a dagger in my chest.

When at last we reach the temple precinct, an official takes us to an examination room where he instructs the bearers to lift me on to a high bed. I hear Philemon explaining I've been injured in the pankration and have lost my memory. The official tells Philemon he will fetch a physician and leaves the room in the wake of the litter bearers.

I want to sit up but the effort is too great and brings on a coughing fit which culminates in my vomiting into a bowl, fetched by Philemon in the nick of time.

'Is the pain bad?' he asks, his brow wrinkling with concern.

I can only nod. Every breath is agony now. I could happily elect to die at that moment, without hesitation. Not knowing who I am gives me that freedom, for with no knowledge of any loved ones, I have no qualms about leaving them.

Philemon must have seen something of these thoughts in

my eyes because he tells me that earlier in the day he'd sent a messenger to my uncle with word of where I'd be.

'His name?' I whisper, my breath rasping as I speak.

'Aristokles.'

The name means nothing, but I nod my head, hoping he'll elaborate.

'He'll tell your sister, Xanthe.'

I try to picture them, hoping their images will appear, but draw a blank. My mental efforts are interrupted by a man who introduces himself as a temple doctor and expertly examines me, establishing the location and intensity of the pain as his hands skim the surface of my body. At the end of the examination he asks me my name. I've heard it enough times that day to repeat it.

'Apollos. I know nothing else.'

He speaks to Philemon out of my hearing, instructs his attendant to prepare a draught and leaves the room. I take this opportunity to close my eyes, until the attendant brings me the foul-smelling concoction. I almost choke when the liquid hits the back of my throat but manage to keep it down. Once I've recovered, he helps me from the bed, telling me to grasp his hand as he pulls me to my feet. Taking my weight, he guides me to a bath set in the floor and lowers me into it. Nearby, stands a water cauldron mounted on a three-legged stand with a small fire beneath it.

By this time I am shivering so much my teeth are chattering and Philemon asks the attendant to hurry with the water. The man makes a show of testing the temperature, then fills two jugs and starts pouring warm water on my head, chest and arms, while Philemon removes the oily sand from my body, first with a sponge and then with a curved metal scraper. More than once, the scraper hits a bruise, or a wound, and I flinch.

'Doctor's orders,' says Philemon, gently. 'He can't treat you until you're clean.'

Finally, my ordeal over, the attendant dresses me in a thin white robe and with Philemon's help, steers me along a colonnaded portico to a smaller room where the doctor is waiting.

'Well, now, young man,' he says as they help me on to the bed. 'Has the bath revived your memory? Can you tell me any more about yourself?'

I still have no recollection of home or family, nor any idea of my occupation or social status. The only compass I have to navigate with is Philemon. I search my mind for any vestige of what he's told me but it has already dropped away.

The doctor waits for me to come up with something but when I remain silent he gestures to Philemon to speak for me.

'He is the son of Theas. But both his parents are now deceased. He lives in the house of his uncle, Aristokles...'

Philemon's voice falters, his face expressing regret, no doubt because with these words he has broken the news to me that I am an orphan. But I shed no tears. How can I mourn those of whom I have no recollection?

The doctor seems satisfied with this information and asks an attendant to unpin my tunic while he fetches two bronze cups. He applies some liniment to my upper body and I realise my flesh no longer feels on fire: thanks, I'm sure, to the brew I took earlier. He massages my chest and arms using the cups. At times he lingers over a certain spot and my breath catches from the smarting provoked by the suction of the cup. When he attends to my back he uses long, gliding strokes on either side of my spine. Once he's satisfied with his work, he applies a different ointment to the damage on my face.

'These bruises will be gone within a week or two. The gash on your cheek will leave a scar, though.'

He hands me a mirror of polished bronze. Two half-closed, bloodshot eyes squint back at me from a swollen face covered in scabs and bruises, and I wonder if I'm going to stay this ugly or if my reflection will improve in time.

'Thank you,' I say. 'And when will my memory return?'

His expression becomes as fixed as a mask.

'I've only known two cases of amnesia. A hoplite witnessed his comrade sacrificing his life to save him and he went into a state of shock. He was fortunate. His condition was transient and he regained his memory after ten days. The second, like you, suffered a blow to the head. There was some improvement, but he remained forgetful.'

I hear a sharp intake of breath from Philemon and our eyes meet. In his gaze is a sadness which is deeper than mine.

'What happens now? Do I go home?'

The doctor's face softens into a smile.

'Not yet. This will be your room for the next few days. Rest is the best cure for body and mind. I'll come and apply the cups again tomorrow.'

'And his ribs?' asks Philemon. 'Do they need binding?'

The doctor closes his eyes, as if consulting a higher authority.

'No. The bandages could lead to constriction of the lungs. The ribs will mend but he must refrain from strenuous activity for at least forty days. This means no wrestling practice, so the palaestra is completely out of bounds. He's lucky to have escaped without any worse injuries. I've heard that Tellias once killed an opponent at the Isthmian games.'

I'm listening to this with horror and, on seeing my expression, Philemon thanks the doctor and escorts him to the door. When he returns, he brings with him a cup of water.

'The attendant will fetch you some bread and soup soon. Do you think you'll be able to keep it down?'

Feeling drowsy and wanting just to sleep, I whisper, 'Perhaps.'

I feel his hand on my arm and I open my eyes.

'I have to go now. I'll come back tomorrow, after the equestrian contests. Is there anything you want me to bring?'

'Do I have my tunic here?'

'Yes, but it's dirty. They used it to cover you. I'll ask Xanthe to send a slave with a clean one. But you must promise not to leave the sanctuary.'

'Who is Xanthe?'

Philemon looks at me sorrowfully.

'Your sister.'

With a muttered farewell he hurries from the room and I sink into a dreamless sleep.

Chapter 13

Sebastian opened his eyes at the sound of a window blind being raised. He lay motionless for a few moments, looking at the ceiling, trying to work out where he was, when a white-clad figure bent over him.

'Sebastian, are you awake?'

He hauled himself into a sitting position and stared at the nun, whose voice sounded vaguely familiar. He remembered falling asleep in this room, but her presence made him wonder if he was still dreaming.

'How are you feeling?' she said, handing him a glass of water.

As he drank, it dawned on him that this was Sybil, dressed in one of the long white robes, a wide white headband compressing her pre-Raphaelite hair into an unruly bun.

'Okay, I think. I could murder a coffee. Where's Mr Digby?'

'He had to go home to see to Bentley.'

'Who?' said Seb, his mind still hazy.

'His dog. You slept longer than expected. Roger didn't want you to be left alone, so he asked me to keep an eye on you.'

'Is he coming back?'

'No,' she said, her eyes twinkling. 'I told him I'd escort you off the premises.'

Seb felt a wave of disappointment.

'Does this mean I miss out on the last part of the process?'

'Not at all. I'll have a look in the kitchen and see if there's anything to drink while you get dressed. Your clothes are in the bathroom. When I get back, you can tell me what you remember of your dream. I take it you had one?'

Seb nodded and Sybil left the room, returning about fifteen minutes later with what looked like two mugs of coffee and some powdered milk. Now dressed and seated by the window, Seb stirred in some of the powder, took a sip and gave a yelp of disgust.

'I'm afraid chicory coffee is all I could find,' she said, giggling behind her hand. 'We usually offer herbal teas but we haven't stocked up for this term yet.'

Seb placed the mug on the windowsill and waited for Sybil to begin.

'If you're wondering why I'm wearing white,' she said, 'it signifies my position as your guide. One of what the Greeks would call, the *therapeutai.*'

'Attendant to the gods,' said Seb, thoughtfully, remembering that Digby had used that term.

'It's nice to think so,' said Sybil, looking impressed. She picked up a pen and one of two bound notebooks on the table beside her. 'So, what have you got to tell me?'

'Well, it was a really vivid dream. I think it was a continuation of what must have started in the labyrinth, because when I saw this really beaten-up guy, I felt I already knew him.'

'Go on,' said Sybil, leaning forward.

'He was being treated in a sort of hospital…' He paused, trying hard to remember the episodes in sequence. 'He was somewhere else before then, though.'

'Think about the sounds you heard,' she urged. 'That sometimes jogs the memory.'

Seb remembered the crowd cheering in the distance and the opening scene came back to him.

'It started off with him lying on a sort of primitive mattress, groaning. He was naked, covered in oil and mud and sand. There were some men in the adjoining room, stripping off. They were competing in athletic events, so it must have been a dressing room in a stadium. I could hear the spectators shouting and cheering.'

'Did you get an impression of what era this was?'

'The clothes made me think of ancient Rome or Greece. Somebody mentioned Attica.'

Sybil nodded encouragingly.

'Did you notice what the weather was like?'

'Hot. The room stank of blood and sweat.'

'Hmm. There was a summer festival in Athens called the Panathenaea in honour of the goddess Athena. They held a range of contests: poetry, music, athletics…it could have been that. Anything else?'

'Yes. He must have had concussion because he couldn't remember anything. His friend told him he'd lost the contest. I'd never heard of the sport before. From the state of him it could have been wrestling or boxing.'

Sybil took picked up her smartphone and checked something.

'Probably pankration, a combination of wrestling, boxing and judo. Athenian males of fighting age had to be battle ready. The farmers among them would have kept fit by labouring. The soil was poor so they had their work cut out. The moneyed classes spent a lot of time in gymnasiums and wrestling schools. But there was quite a contrast between training and competing. Only eye gouging and biting were banned in the competitive pankration.'

Seb shuddered. 'Sounds brutal.'

'It was. Did you get the name of the injured party?'

'Apollos.'

'And his friend?'

'Um, it sounded like an old-fashioned girl's name. Philomena.'

'Philemon?'

'That's it.'

Seb tried to picture Philemon and remembered the tears in his dark eyes.

'He was upset. He escorted Apollos when he was carried to a sort of hospital in the grounds of a temple. They had to walk on rocky ground…it was quite hard going.'

Sybil paused in her note-taking and looked up.

'Did you see a citadel higher up?'

Seb searched his memory, recalling a shadowy silhouette of a large building.

'I think so, but we didn't climb that high.'

'That would have been the Parthenon, on top of the Akropolis. The hospital has to be the Asklepion, on the lower slopes. So we must be in the Classical period.'

'When was that?'

'Some time in the fifth or fourth century BC. Tell me more about his treatment.'

When Seb finished, she asked him to describe Apollos.

'Tall, muscular. His hair looked as if it'd been bleached by the sun. His face was swollen, so I can't be sure of his age. In his twenties, probably.'

'Was he clean shaven?'

'He had a bit of a beard, more like heavy stubble.'

'What about his friend?'

'He was slim, dark-haired.'

'Was he older or younger?'

Seb wondered what difference that made. Philemon had a softer look but his manner had suggested he was past his teenage years.

'Did *he* have any facial hair?' Sybil prompted.

'Possibly. Why?'

'I don't know how much you know about those times, but if he was younger, it's likely they were lovers.'

'What? That's rather a sweeping statement, isn't it?' he said, flushing. This was a sore subject for him, having been suspected by Nick of being gay.

'I'm not exaggerating, Seb. It's an historical fact. The Greeks had a custom of an older male acting as a mentor for a young male. The close relationship was accepted as part of the youth's overall education: sometimes it was sexual, sometimes not. When the youth matured into a young adult the association was supposed to end.'

Seb screwed up his face in disgust.

'Are you telling me the Greeks were a bunch of paedophiles?'

'Not from their point of view. As long as the sexual element in the relationship wasn't primary, the bond between mentor and protégé was tolerated by society and thought by some to be the highest form of love. It's believed to have extended to females as well, to a lesser extent, although it was more common in Sparta. Married women had liaisons with unmarried girls for the same reason…it was considered an educative experience.'

Seb laughed out loud.

'That's their story and they're sticking to it.'

Sybil grinned.

'Of course, you have to take into account the fact that women spent most of their time at home. In the bigger houses, they even had separate quarters. With most women so segregated, it's not surprising that male and female bisexuality was accepted.'

Seb grunted his disapproval.

'Still sounds decadent to me.'

'Different days, different ways,' she said casually. 'Were there any women in your dream, by the way?'

'No, although Philemon spoke about sending a message to Apollos's sister.'

'Not to his parents?'

'Philemon told the doctor they were dead.'

'Hmm,' said Sybil, 'I wonder where he lived.'

'With his uncle.'

Seb waited until Sybil had stopped writing and asked a question of his own.

'So if the women were so segregated, how did the Greeks ever meet their wives in the first place?'

'Marriages were usually arranged between families of the same class. The man was expected to be married by the time he reached thirty. The bride would be fourteen or fifteen. If the husband wanted to keep a mistress, use prostitutes or continue a same-sex relationship, he did.'

'A bit tough on the young wives,' said Seb. 'Didn't they object?'

She shrugged.

'They were trained by their mothers to do their husband's bidding. They knew their function as a wife was to keep house and produce heirs. Being in love, or their husband being monogamous, wasn't necessarily part of the bargain.'

'Seems harsh,' said Seb, feeling sorry for the women and imagining how boring their lives must have been. 'And more than a touch misogynistic.'

'No more misogynistic than a society which believes that Eve was to blame for the Fall of Man by eating the fruit of the tree of knowledge.'

Seb looked thoughtful.

'We had a book of Greek myths at home. There was a story about Pandora, the first woman, who unleashed evil on the world when she opened a forbidden box. Must have been their counterpart to Eve.'

Sybil nodded.

'The poet Hesiod described Pandora as the first of "the deadly race and tribe of women who live amongst mortal men to their great trouble." So it's not surprising that most Greek men believed that Zeus put women on earth to punish them.'

'How so? By waiting on them hand and foot?' said Seb, feeling aggrieved on behalf of all ancient Greek females.

'In those times, the Greeks took the view that intense passion was a kind of madness. Erotic love was regarded as a disruptive force, leading to conflict and death. It features a lot in their tragedies.'

'Fascinating,' said Seb, in a tone indicating that it was anything but. Sybil's dream appraisal was coming across more like a history lesson. He hadn't eaten for twenty-four hours, and all he could think of was a fry-up.

Sibyl coughed delicately.

'Sorry, I've digressed. Is there anything else you'd like to say about your dream?'

'I'm just wondering how come I understood everything they said, even though they'd have been talking Greek.'

She smiled, as if indulging a small child.

'Dreams don't work like that, do they?'

'If you say so. But I had a dream set in ancient Greece a couple of weeks ago, just before I came to the Foundation, and it sounded like a foreign language to me.'

Sybil asked him to explain and he told her about the family group gathered round a courtyard altar.

'That's interesting. Almost like a trailer of the big picture to come.' She reflected for a moment. 'Your ability to understand could be because this incubation therapy carries with it a bit more *power*. We'll have you speaking in tongues, next,' she said, giggling. 'Getting back to last night's dream, was there anything that stood out?'

Seb closed his eyes and waited for inspiration, but none came.

'So the god Asklepios didn't visit you in the night and present you with a miracle cure?'

Seb uttered an involuntary snort, not sure if she was serious or joking.

'It would've been a wasted journey for him. There's nothing physically wrong with me.'

Sybil seemed about to speak but checked herself.

After a few moments, Seb added, 'As far as I know.'

Sybil gazed at him, crossing one arm and holding her chin with the other.

'Good. Okay, I'm going to ask you a few questions. It won't take long. You must be hungry.'

On cue, Seb's stomach growled.

'I'd like you to think of how you experienced this dream,' said Sybil, picking up pace. 'Were you an observer or a participant?'

Seb leaned back and closed his eyes, trying to evoke the way the dream had unfolded.

'Some of it *was* similar to watching a film. Like the journey from the stadium to the temple. I seemed to be looking down on the slaves carrying the litter and stumbling over the rocks.'

'Did you have a bird's-eye view of all the events?'

Seb half-remembered a sensation of sipping the water that Philemon had given to Apollos in the dressing room, and of lying on the treatment bed while the temple doctor attended to him.

'No, not all of the time.'

'Then who were you when you weren't an invisible observer?'

Seb hesitated, unwilling to place himself centre stage.

'Dreams with different points of view are quite common, Seb,' said Sybil, her voice low and encouraging.

'Okay,' he said, as if pleading guilty. 'Sometimes I felt I was experiencing what Apollos was going through. Other times it was more like watching a play.'

'So when you were "in his body", so to speak, did you feel the pain of his wounds?'

'I suppose I did, in a way. But it wasn't physical suffering, more like the torment in his mind.'

'How did that feel?'

'Well, there was a lot of anger at his opponent at first. Then he was overcome with shame and disappointment at losing.'

Sybil nodded.

'So you were feeling his emotional reaction. If you'd been feeling the physical pain itself, naturally I would terminate the process. As it is, we'll be able to continue.'

Her words puzzled Seb. Surely he'd completed his part: spent a night in the abaton, delivered a dream. All she had to do was analyse it, maybe offer him a herbal remedy for something or other—probably stress, given the week he'd had—and they could each go on their merry way.

He watched her close her notebook with a satisfied flourish. Taking the other notebook from the table, she held it out to him. Its green cover was embossed in gold with the staff of Asklepios.

'This is your dream journal, Seb. You should write down your account of last night's dream as soon as you can, and any further memories that might come to the surface. It's possible you'll have more, so keep it by your bed and record them as soon as you wake up.'

She stood up and removed her white robe, packing it into a floral backpack. 'I'd like to see you again after your next dream. My phone number's on the back page.'

Seb took the journal and remained seated.

'Is that it?' he said, unable to conceal his disappointment. 'I thought you were going to interpret the dream and make an assessment.'

'That's not how it works here, I'm afraid. It's your *experience* of the dream, not the interpretation, that triggers the healing. The psyche is a self-regulating system and dreaming is its way of healing itself. I think there's more to come.'

Seb felt a mixture of emotions. As far as he was concerned, the aim of the exercise had been to mirror the experience of a patient spending a night at the sanctuary. When Digby had said the process unlocked an inner capacity to heal oneself, he hadn't warned him that it could be ongoing. What he'd thought of as a one-off drama was being commissioned by Sybil as a series. And he was expected to continue whether he liked it or not.

'Look, Miss Hughes,' he said, struggling to sound calm, 'I'm very grateful to Mr Digby for letting me see how temple sleep works. But if you could just give me an idea of how long the treatment usually takes—maybe some examples of past case histories—I'd like to leave it there.'

'You'll get all that later in the course,' said Sybil, more sharply than he expected. 'I'm afraid I must insist on seeing you again. Whether you like it or not, Seb, you're now one of my cases.'

'But I didn't come here to be healed,' said Seb, his voice rising. 'I'm as strong as an ox.'

'I agree you haven't come with a physical ailment. But remember, the ethos of the Foundation is to treat the whole person. Dream incubation can bring to light hidden psychological disorders. All we've got so far is the theme of memory loss, which might or might not be significant. As I said, it's the dream itself that sets off the healing process. The healer lies within you. I'm not your healer, I'm your facilitator. And my advice is more sleep, "perchance to dream" —hopefully.'

Seb decided then and there to refuse to continue but Sybil countered that move before he even opened his mouth.

'We expect nothing less of the Foundation's scholarship student.' She paused. 'How can I put it? There's no such thing as a free lunch.'

Groaning inwardly, Seb stood up and followed her along the corridor, through the vestibule and out into the morning light. She was wearing a dress which hugged her figure, emphasising the contrast between the trimness of her waist and the curve of her breasts and hips. He compared her to the sylphlike Fliss, and found he admired both body types in almost equal measure.

'Do I need to sleep in the abaton again?' he said, when they got outside.

'No, no. That's neither necessary nor convenient.'

Seb felt a vague sense of disappointment.

'Will I need to take the same stuff I did last night?' he asked, as they reached the gate.

'Only if your dream doesn't continue naturally. Actually, I'd better give you some, just in case. We don't keep it in the abaton.'

It turned out that Sybil lived in the same row of cottages as Digby. She invited him in but he declined, eager to get back to his place and cook himself some bacon and eggs.

She went inside and returned with a small paper carrier bag containing a dropper bottle of the tincture which he could either mix with water or place directly on his tongue. He turned to go but she put her hand on his arm.

'This is a piece of lapis lazuli,' she said, shaking a midnight blue stone from a small organza bag onto her palm. 'If you put it by your bed, or under your pillow, it will help you recall your dreams. And you can have it beside you when you write them up, as well.'

Seb thanked her and put it in the bag. *Worth trying anything to speed up the process,* he thought, as he retraced his steps past the sanctuary and the polytunnels until he reached his accommodation block.

As he put his key in the lock, he heard music coming from inside the flat.

Chapter 14

Seb walked into the kitchen and found Lynette sitting at the table, eating toast and reading a magazine.

'What are you doing here?' he demanded. 'Is Nick back already?'

'Very nice to see you, too,' she replied, her voice laden with sarcasm. 'Actually, my washing machine broke down and Nick said I could use this one. Is that all right with you?'

'How did you get in?' he insisted, too irritated at her occupation of his territory to muster any semblance of politeness.

'Nick left it with the lady in the estate shop. Any more questions?'

'When will you be finished?'

'When the laundry's done.'

Sighing with resentment, Seb went to his room. He wanted to cook his breakfast but he couldn't with her sitting in his kitchen.

Cursing Nick for inflicting an unwelcome visitor on him, he retrieved his mobile from the yew chest Joe had made him for his seventh birthday, to store his model kits, and switched it on. He felt better when he found a text from Nick warning him that Lynette might appear with her smalls in tow. This allayed his suspicions that Nick might have been trying to push them together to get Lynette off his own back. That still might be the case, but the tone of the text was apologetic, so he'd give him the benefit of the doubt for now.

There was also a missed call from Fliss which made him want to shout, 'Yes!' but he had to mime it instead. He wanted to ring her then and there, but how could he, with the French girl a few feet away, separated only by a thin wall?

Trapped in his room, he placed the piece of lapis lazuli on the desk and opened the journal. At first, his pen hovered over the blank page but as soon as he described Apollos lying on the straw mattress, one memory led on to another with scraps of detail emerging above and beyond what he'd already told Sybil. Every so often he glanced at the lapis stone, its flecks of golden pyrite glinting in the light, and the pictures in his mind became clearer.

His flow was interrupted by a brisk *rat-a-tat* which made him jump. Before he could answer, Lynette opened the door.

'I'm finished now. Would you like a drink before I go?'

'I wouldn't mind a coffee,' he said, in a better mood now he'd begun to log his dream.

Minutes later, Lynette placed a mug of coffee on his desk, hovering rather too long before sitting on his bed.

'Is that college work?' she asked.

He turned to face her, wishing he'd closed the journal before she'd come in.

'No. I was just jotting down some ideas,' he said, struggling to come up with an answer that would satisfy her.

'What sort of ideas?'

An image of his encounter in the hall with Digby came to his rescue.

'I saw a flyer for a Creative Writing group on the notice board.'

'That sounds interesting,' she said, her eyes widening. 'When is it? I might join you.'

Lynette's enthusiasm sounded genuine enough but Seb was beginning to doubt her motives.

'Er, on reflection, I'm not sure I'd be much good at it.'

'Really? You seem to have written down quite a lot of ideas.'

Seb closed the journal and put it in the desk drawer.

'I was actually looking to play rugby but I couldn't find anything on the board.'

'My God!' she said, pouting theatrically. 'You're one of those jocks who likes sliding around in mud every weekend. I misjudged you.'

He stared at her blankly, trying to work out how playing a sport could be considered a bad thing.

'How did you get here?' he said finally, deciding it was time to address the subject of her departure.

'My flatmate lent me her car in exchange for doing her washing. Is that a hint that I've outstayed my welcome, by any chance?'

'No,' he said, lying through his teeth. 'This place is hard to get to on a Sunday if you don't have your own transport. I just wondered...'

Lynette gave a languid stretch, arching her body. It reminded him of a cat getting ready to pounce.

'Will you answer something that's been puzzling me, Seb?'

'If I can,' he muttered, his heart sinking.

'Have I done something to offend you? We had such a good conversation in the pub on Thursday night. And yet today you seem so distant.'

A wave of embarrassment engulfed him, closely followed by a tsunami of irritation.

'I was just a bit surprised to see you here, that's all,' he said, through gritted teeth. 'I'm sorry if I came across as rude.'

She bared her teeth in a smile.

'No problem. I know how grumpy men can get. Especially when they haven't got a girlfriend.'

Her insinuation that he was bad-tempered because he was sexually frustrated made him nervous. He had to get her out of his bedroom. Fast.

'How do you know I haven't got a girlfriend?'

'Is that where you spent the night?' she said, like a wronged woman.

Seb got to his feet, choosing to ignore the question.

'Do you need any help carrying anything to the car, Lynette?'

She shrugged. 'No thanks. It's a bit late to play the gentleman.'

'Okay,' he said, biting back a stronger reply. 'Well, see you around.'

Seb picked up his empty mug and took it to the kitchen sink, washing it slowly and carefully to ensure he wouldn't have to talk to her before she left.

As soon as the door closed, he screwed up his courage and called Fliss's number.

'Hello, Seb. How are you?'

At the sound of her voice, friendly and relaxed, all his apprehension vanished.

'Fine, thanks. You called me?'

'Yes. Nick put your name forward as a model for the fashion shoot. I just wanted to check that he'd cleared it with you first.'

He should have told a white lie and said he had, but the alpha male in him chose not to cover for Nick.

'Not really, to be honest.'

There was a short silence at the end of the line.

'Oh. I'm sorry to hear that. We're planning to do the shoot next Sunday. You'd have to come to see me before then to try on some outfits. Nick and Jim are doing it. I hope you can make it too.'

Encouraged by the warmth of her tone, Seb reflected on whether now would be a good time to clear the air about what happened on Thursday night.

'So can I add you to the list?' she said. It was the slight tremor in her voice that made up his mind.

'If you like. I mean, I'm surprised you're asking me, after the way I ignored you in the Bull's Head...' The memory of how devastated he'd been to see her there stopped him short for a few seconds. 'It was a bit of a bombshell, though, you turning out to be the girl Nick met in the estate shop.' He was struggling now to control his anger. 'He said *you* rang *him*, so you didn't exactly play hard to get.'

There was a sharp gasp from Fliss followed by what sounded like a heated defence, which he couldn't hear clearly due to the din of the door buzzer being repeatedly pressed.

'Can you hold on a sec. There's someone at the door.'

He swung the door open, eager to get rid of whoever it was, and found Lynette on the threshold.

'I forgot my magazine,' she announced loudly, marching towards the table.

Seb backed away from her, making it obvious that he didn't want the person on the other end of the phone to hear her voice.

'Bye, chéri, see you soon,' she boomed, exiting with a knowing smirk.

Silently cursing Lynette, he attempted to resume his conversation with Fliss. But the line was dead. And there was no answer when he rang her back.

His blood racing, he threw on his running gear and pounded his way around the grounds. When he got back, he realised he still hadn't had anything to eat so he drove into town for something more substantial than bacon and eggs. The Bull's Head was the first pub he came to, so he ordered a Sunday roast. This turned out to be a good move, as the waiter directed him to a wall banquette with a view of one of the large TV screens. By a stroke of luck, a premier league football match was just starting.

The two men seated on the other side of the table nodded amiably to him when he sat down. Comfortably cocooned, he dined to the accompaniment of their commentaries on players, managers, referee and linesmen. He had no objection to this. On the contrary, it gave him the benefit of company without the burden of contributing any more than an occasional compliant comment to the discussion.

At full time, the older of the pair said he'd better get back to see the grandkids before they went home, he and his friend nodding goodbye to Seb before shouldering their way through the crowd. Having long since finished his lunch and stopped drinking after his second lager, Seb, too, made for the door.

Outside, the chill of the autumn afternoon brought him

swiftly back to his earlier preoccupation: how to make things right with Fliss. He returned to his car and tried to decide what to do. He couldn't bring himself to phone her in case she still refused to answer. But he had to explain to her why Lynette was in his flat.

Twenty minutes later found him driving past her house, checking if she was home. The presence of her Mini in the drive suggested she was, but the VW Golf and BMW beside it indicated that her family was also in residence. His brain went into overdrive, imagining her father opening the door, blasting him for upsetting his daughter, and telling him to go forth and multiply and never come back.

The road was a cul-de-sac which widened to an arc. Having slowed down, he decided to pick up speed and circle the arc. He was now approaching her house on the other side of the road. The question was, should he keep going or stop and knock on the door?

Chapter 15

As Seb walked up the drive to Fliss's house, the front door opened and a man in a suit and tie emerged, followed by a petite woman in a silky blue dress, cropped jacket and very high heels.

He assumed they were Fliss's parents and cursed his luck at running into them. His instinct was to turn tail and wait until they'd gone but it was too late for that. The woman was making straight for him.

'Hello, have you come for a fitting?'

Seb's brain froze for a moment. Then he made a decision. If this was the only way he could get into the house, so be it.

'Hi. Yes, I have.'

'I'll tell Felicity you're here. Who shall I say?'

Fearing that Fliss might refuse to see him, he was about to give Nick's name, until it struck him that she might know Nick was away for the weekend, so he took a chance that their red bandana friend hadn't already been fitted out.

'Jim.'

She went back into the house and shouted something up the stairs while the man got into the BMW and started the engine.

'She's not expecting you,' said the woman, as she teetered past him. 'But she said go up anyway.'

When Seb got to the top of the stairs, he heard Fliss call out, 'In here', and followed the sound to a large room with two rails of clothing. Fliss and another girl stood in front of a fitted wardrobe with mirrored doors, discussing the outfit the girl was wearing.

'Hi,' he said, his legs like rubber. 'Sorry if I'm interrupting…'

Fliss's eyes blazed when she saw it was him. Then her gaze moved to a spot behind him and he realised she was looking for Jim.

'Jim's not here. I thought you might not see me if I said who I was,' he said, throwing all caution to the wind.

She coloured, making a small movement of her eyes in the direction of her wide-eyed companion.

'You're not on my list for today,' she said, as if talking to a troublesome customer. 'Would you mind waiting downstairs? We'll be finished soon.'

He slunk away, feeling every inch the interloper, and found Delta waiting at the bottom of the stairs, a plaited rope in her mouth. She greeted him and ran into the kitchen so he followed her in for a tug of war. He was helping himself to a glass of water when he heard voices in the hall and the sound of the front door closing. He turned and saw Fliss standing in the doorway, her mouth set in a straight line.

'What can I do for you?' she said, maintaining her glacial tone.

'I've come to apologise for what I said. I was out of order.'

'Okay,' she said, taking a carton of juice from the fridge and pouring herself a glass. 'Anything else?'

Seb shifted from foot to foot, not sure what he was supposed to say now.

'Someone interrupted our call,' she said silkily, bending down to pet Delta.

'That was Lynette. Her washing machine broke down and Nick said she could use ours. She forgot her magazine...came back for it at just the wrong moment.'

Fliss raised her eyes and trained them on his.

'Did you sleep with her?'

He yelped like a dog who'd been kicked.

'Hell, no. She's on my course.'

'Is that the only reason?'

'I don't like her.'

Fliss finished her drink.

'Look, as you're here, I might as well organise your clothes for the shoot. That's if you've decided to do it.'

This wasn't quite the reaction he'd hoped for, but it was better than being ordered off the premises so he followed her upstairs and obediently tried on several garments, behind a panelled screen. She finally settled on three outfits, her manner during the fitting betraying no hint of their previous intimacy.

Once the trying-on was complete, she sat on the floor and began typing notes on the clothes into a pink laptop. Seeking to prolong their time together, Seb asked when she was seeing Nick and Jim.

'Tomorrow evening. You were all supposed to come here together. That's what I was ringing to tell you.'

Seb thought about this and envisaged an awkward conversation looming on the horizon.

'Nick's going to wonder how I got here first. Unless he gave you my number?'

'No.'

'In that case, one of us will have to tell him we were already acquainted when he introduced us in the Bull's Head.'

'I'll leave that to you,' she said, her eyes steely. 'You're the only one who can explain why you behaved as if we were strangers.'

'I'm sorry. I was shocked to see you there.'

'That's no excuse.'

He racked his brain for something to get her onside.

'Look, it was awkward. Just before we joined you, Nick was comparing you and Lynette.' He took a deep breath. 'He told me he fancied "the girl in the shop" more than her. So when I saw the girl in the shop was you, what could I do?'

'How about saying "hi"?' she snapped. 'But you obviously value Nick's friendship more than ours.'

He closed his eyes and massaged his forehead, scrabbling around for a more convincing defence.

'Believe me, I wish I could go back and change how I reacted.' He started pacing the room. 'Trouble is, everything's moving so fast. One day I'm planning to go travelling, the next I've let myself in for a three-year course I'm not even sure's right for me, and I'm sharing a flat with a stranger. Who wouldn't feel freaked out?'

Fliss made no comment, returning her attention to her notes. Seb stopped pacing and played his last card.

'And on top of that, I've found out more about my mother.'

She snapped her laptop shut.

'Help me up,' she said, and he obediently took her arm. As she rose, her body drew close to his. He wanted to embrace her but released her hand, leaving her to make the next move.

'Why didn't you ring me on Monday?' she said, her mouth inches away from his ear.

'I was busy moving in.'

'Tuesday?'

'That was Induction day. Then Nick arrived.' He thought about their evening exploring the sanctuary and the confrontation with Digby. 'It was full on.'

'What about Wednesday, Thursday?'

'I was always going to ring you…when I'd adjusted to life on campus.'

The truth, though, was more ambiguous than that. Her coolness when they parted last weekend had made him doubt she wanted to see him again. And made him wonder if he could be at ease around someone whose moods he couldn't fathom.

Fliss hadn't moved away from him so he took a chance and softly kissed her lips. She responded by leaning in closer and returning his kiss, this time longer and deeper.

'When are your parents due back?' he whispered.

'Why?' she said, with a deadpan face. 'Do you want to be introduced?'

'Not if I can help it.'

'Don't worry. They've gone to a golf club dinner. They won't be back till after twelve.'

She took him by the hand and led him to her room. After

they'd made love, he made a move to get out of bed.

'Wait,' she said. 'Tell me what you found out about your mother.'

He sighed, remembering how she'd wanted him to trace his mother and wishing now he'd never mentioned the subject.

'It's not something I enjoy talking about.'

'Come on,' she said, with more than a hint of reproach in her voice. 'At least tell me how you found out.'

'I found my original birth certificate. My mother's name is Anna Norland. She was born in Oslo. Looks like I'm half Norwegian.'

'Really?' she said, her voice breathy with excitement. 'That probably accounts for the colour of your hair.'

'Maybe,' he said, thinking instead of his resemblance to the photograph of Teodor Ophis in Digby's office.

'Did it say on the certificate who your father was?'

'No.'

'That's a shame. Never mind. If you ever contact your mother, you can ask her.'

'I still don't have any plans to do that.'

He couldn't see the expression on her face but he sensed her disappointment.

'The odds are she's kept me a secret, and I wouldn't want to barge into her life and disrupt everything.'

Fliss sighed. 'There's a national Adoption Contact Register where you can post your details, in case she wants to contact you. Where's the harm in that?'

He didn't answer. Instead, he got up and showered. Fliss wasn't in the bedroom when he came out of the en suite. He met her on the landing. She was in pyjamas, her hair damp.

'I used my parents' bathroom,' she said. 'You'd better go now.'

As he descended the stairs, she called out, 'Were you born in Norway, then?'

He wanted to say yes, to put her off the trail, but he'd already lied to her about his father and didn't want to compound the felony.

'No. This country.'

'Where?'

This question required another white lie.

'It wasn't a place I recognised.'

Once she heard the front door close, she dialled the tracing agent's 24-hour number. This time the answer machine kicked in.

'Hello, this is Felicity Logan. Things have moved on. I have further information about my friend's mother.'

— o —

When Seb got back to the flat he found Nick lounging on the sofa, playing a game on his laptop. The floor was strewn with cardboard and polystyrene packing. A widescreen television stood in the corner of the room, showing *Sunday Match of the Day* in high definition.

'Hey, man,' said Nick, barely raising his eyes from the laptop screen. 'How you doing?'

'Good,' said Seb. 'What's with the TV?'

'Thought I'd treat us.'

'Thanks, mate,' said Seb, sitting down beside him and reliving some of the soccer action he'd already viewed in the pub.

'Been anywhere interesting this weekend?' said Nick, his eyes still focused on the computer game.

'If you call spending the night in the sanctuary interesting, then yeah.'

'You're kidding,' said Nick, giving Seb his full attention. 'You mean you broke in?'

'Hardly. Old man Digby would have rusticated me on the spot if he'd caught me.'

'Sounds painful,' said Nick, sniggering. 'Come on. Spill.'

Seb launched into an account of his chance meeting with Digby, the introduction to the labyrinth, and his night in the abaton. When he got to the part where he woke to find Sybil in his room, Nick whistled his approval.

'You lucky dog. I wouldn't mind waking up to the delicious Miss Hughes. Wish I'd stayed here now.'

Seb matched Nick's tone.

'No such luck. She was only interested in the dream. Digby was supposed to be there but he had to feed his dog or something, so he sent her instead.'

Nick groaned.

'This place is full of ice maidens. How could she resist a strapping specimen like you?'

'Yeah, right,' said Seb, embarrassed.

'Was it a good dream?'

'Very good. Believe it or not, it was set in ancient Greece. This guy had been injured in some kind of extreme martial arts contest, part of some big festival in Athens. They took him to a temple for treatment. It was an Asklepion, but not a scaled-down version like the one here. This was the real McCoy.'

'That's bizarre,' said Nick. 'You were in a temple sanctuary dreaming about an ancient Greek in a temple sanctuary. So what did the lovely Sybil make of that?'

'She was interested...kept asking questions. But she said she didn't have enough to go on. Apparently, I'm now one of her cases and she wants to see if the dream continues.'

'Hmm,' said Nick. 'Are you *sure* she doesn't fancy you?'

Seb made a face and swiftly changed the subject.

'Anyway, when I got back I could have done without Lynette being here, making herself at home as if she owned the place.'

Nick looked contrite.

'Sorry, mate, but how could I refuse? You know what women are like, you have to keep them sweet. Otherwise they can bear a grudge. Was she friendly?'

'A bit too friendly.'

Nick nodded knowingly.

'Classic. When you first met she thought you were interested in her, but you didn't follow up so now you've become a challenge.'

A chirp from Nick's phone announced a message.

'It's a summons from the lovely Felicity,' he said with a slightly bemused air. 'She wants me and Jim to go to her house for a fitting tomorrow evening. She must have forgotten about you. Do you want me to remind her?'

At the sound of Fliss's name, Seb's heart had started to pound. He hadn't planned to tell Nick about them tonight, but it looked as if he had no choice.

'No, it's okay,' he said, trying to sound composed. 'She rang me earlier.'

Nick looked surprised.

'Really? How did she get your number?'

Seb's mouth suddenly felt like the Gobi Desert.

'Truth is, I've known Fliss for a couple of weeks.' He could feel his face burning. 'We spent last weekend together.'

'Wait. So this was before I met her?'

'Yeah.'

'Why didn't you say so?'

Seb shrugged.

'Ah,' said Nick, a gleam of comprehension in his eyes. 'I get it. You thought she'd been coming on to me so you blanked her.'

'Uh, more or less,' he said reluctantly. 'But, looking back, it was a stupid thing to do.'

Seb momentarily closed his eyes, waiting for the axe to fall. When he looked up, Nick was taking something out of the fridge.

'Quite understandable, mate,' he said, offering Seb a can of lager. 'When I said I fancied her, I had no idea…'

Seb took a gulp of the cool amber liquid, savouring his relief at the way his friend had taken the news.

'So, what made her ring you?' said Nick, his curiosity clearly piqued.

'I guess when you sent her my picture, she assumed I was happy to resume contact. She was telling me about the shoot but she heard Lynette in the background and hung up.'

'Crikey! This is better than a soap opera.'

'More a comedy of errors. I went round to her place this evening and bumped into her parents. I told her mother my name was Jim.'

'Did she ask for proof of identity?' said Nick, grinning.

'No probs. I showed her a red bandana and she let me in.'

Nick allowed himself a chuckle before he resumed the interrogation.

'What did Fliss say when *you* appeared?'

'She was not amused. But she finally accepted my apology. While I was there, we got the fitting out of the way. Hence, only you and Jim have the summons for tomorrow.'

'You've had a busy weekend, old china. An exclusive abaton experience *and* a romantic reunion. And there's me worrying you might be lonely.' He turned off the TV. 'Anyway, tell me more about this dream.'

When Seb finally turned in for the night, he put a few drops of the tincture on his tongue, placed the piece of lapis lazuli under his pillow and closed his eyes.

Chapter 16

My uncle is holding a party tonight. The house is fragrant with garlands and wreaths; extra couches have been borrowed from our neighbour; all the oil lamps have been filled; and the large wine krater manhandled into the centre of the men's dining hall.

Downstairs the kitchen is bustling, and judging by the pervading aroma of frying fish, charcoal has already been lit in the courtyard brazier.

I am resting in my room, on doctor's orders, somewhere between sleep and waking, my thoughts wandering back and forth between past, present and future. It is twelve days since my defeat in the stadium and my body is still a long way from full recovery. Alas, the same is also true of my mind.

My sister Xanthe has spent many hours since my accident speaking to me of times past: of the years we lived in the house of our father, and of the last two years spent in the house of my mother's brother, Aristokles.

While many memories, with Xanthe's help, have returned, every so often come shadowy hints of scenes I cannot retrieve. But who can say if they're true memories or mere daydreams?

The memory of my mother's death is, however, quite clear, though I was only five years old when she died giving birth to Xanthe. Many men in my father's place would have abandoned the newborn on Mount Lycabettos, to die of hunger—or worse, to be devoured by wolves. But my grandmother begged him to allow her to live, arguing it would be a sacrilege for a child of noble blood to be 'rescued', as some were, to be raised as a slave. My father, being at heart a kindly man, mercifully allotted Xanthe a nursemaid, to my grandmother's eternal gratitude.

When the women of the family came to lay out my mother's body, I was playing outside the room and heard them disputing which was a better fate for my little sister: death by exposure or being raised by a nursemaid, and growing up with her spirit stunted from the lack of a mother's love.

They stopped when my grandmother joined them, leaving me puzzled by their words, because I loved my nurse Dorcas more than any other, having rarely felt my mother's embrace.

I told my sister this, during one of our recent forays into the past, and she said she'd overheard two kitchen maids discussing our mother. They said she'd become low-spirited after my birth, and thereafter had avoided the duties of motherhood. This revelation saddened me and has made me think more sympathetically of her than before.

As for my dear father, may his memory never die, he was mortally stricken by apoplexy just before I was due to become an ephebe and start my military training. Although the land and properties passed to me, my uncle considered the upkeep of the city house too great a responsibility for an eighteen-year-old, not to mention the expense. His solution was to lease the house and for my sister and I to move into his residence.

'May I come and sit with you, Apollos?'

Xanthe is standing in the doorway. She is usually in the women's room at this time of day, with Aunt Eupheme.

I motion her to come in and she sits on a stool beside my couch.

'Has Arachne released you from the loom?' I say, taking her hand.

The ribbon on her ponytail dances as she laughs: like the weaver in the legend, our aunt takes a great pride in her craft. We have a secret nickname for our uncle as well. His is 'Homer', because he thinks himself something of a poet and would hold a party just so he could sing one of his compositions.

'You're looking much better now,' she says, her doe eyes scrutinising my face. 'Do you think you'll go to the party?'

'I think I must. Uncle Aristokles has invited Philemon. I can't let him enter the fray alone.'

My sister's eyes shine when I speak my friend's name.

'Will you bring him into the courtyard when he comes? I'd like to show him Echo, while she's still such a pretty little pup.'

'And what if Echo is nowhere to be found? Should I take Philemon straight into the dining hall?'

'No, of course not,' she says, with a look of dismay. 'She'd probably be in the stables.'

'Last time we found her there, she stank of manure. You were an hour scrubbing her clean,' I remind her.

Xanthe pulls a face.

'Apollos, stop trying to foil my plans. Why do you always want to keep Philemon to yourself?'

My sister is fifteen. Many girls of her age are already married. In the eyes of the world, she is ready: our aunt has schooled her in all aspects of household management and even taught her to read and write. Most importantly, the dowry my father left her is inducement enough for any suitor.

When I reached eighteen and attained citizenship, I became her official guardian, so it is my responsibility to find her a suitable match. Being reluctant to see her go, however, I have neglected to announce that the family is open to offers of marriage. Uncle Aristokles, on the other hand, deems the time for her to fly the nest is overdue. Impatient with what he sees as my indolence, he has latterly taken the duty upon himself.

To his irritation, Xanthe rejected the first candidate on the grounds of his shortness of stature. In the last two weeks, while I was recovering from my wounds, our uncle produced a second suitor: a man recently widowed, seeking a mother for his small children. Needless to say, she refused him as well. As would I have, in her place.

'—Apollos! Will you promise to bring Philemon to see Echo?'

'All right, I promise. But is it really Echo you want him to see?'

She blushes and I immediately regret baiting her.

'He's such a dear friend. He gave me a nightingale for my twelfth birthday, do you remember?'

I did remember. And also how heartbroken she'd been at the sight of its lifeless body at the bottom of the cage a few weeks later. The harbinger of spring who never lived to see summer. It must have been a hen bird because it never sang.

'Do you think he likes me enough to pledge?' she whispers, tears spilling down her cheeks. 'Will you ask him? If he does, he must tell Uncle before he makes me marry someone I don't want to.'

My heart sinks to my feet. Philemon has never spoken to me of Xanthe as a future wife. In fact, he has never spoken to me of any young woman. Truth is, he's still mourning the loss of his mentor, Diogenes, who died at the Battle of Sybota, felled by a Corinthian arrow.

'I don't know the answer to that, Xana. He's never made mention of any feelings for you, above friendship. But it makes no difference because, like me, he's too young to be married...' I feel myself growing more irritated and my voice rises. 'Ye gods, we only finished military training a few weeks before the Panathenaea. We've hardly begun to find our way in the world.'

Xanthe begins to sob so hard she can barely catch her breath. I try to soothe her but she won't be consoled.

'I don't want to m-marry someone more than t-twice my age. I don't want to go to a s-strange house and leave you.'

I am lost for words to make her feel better. I will sorely miss her when she goes, but our uncle's word carries a weight that mine does not and I fear that soon he will run out of patience.

I feel my own eyes grow damp and find myself gruffly asking her to leave me so I can rest. Of course I cannot rest, so I go downstairs to ask Tromes to draw water from the well and bring it to my room. I prefer the baths at the gymnasium but, since my injury, have become used to bathing at home.

Once he has filled the copper tub and assisted me by pouring water on my back, he applies the ointment to my cuts and bruises. Since I have known Tromes for many years—he came with us from our father's house—I am comfortable with this familiarity. He brings me a fresh robe and I leave the house to make my way to the gymnasium, in search of Philemon.

On arrival, I ask around for him. Nikias, one of our friends, greets me warmly and tells me he was there until an hour ago. Unused as I've recently become to walking any great distance, I nevertheless determine to continue my search and take the road to his house, where I am admitted by a houseboy who removes my sandals and shows me to an inner room.

While I am waiting for Philemon, his mother appears and welcomes me with a kiss on the cheek.

'How are you, Apollos? Sit down, you look worn out. Philemon was devastated when you were so badly beaten. How is your aunt? Is Xanthe any nearer finding a husband? Your uncle's patience is not a bottomless well. I hear he's having a party tonight. I expect there are great preparations afoot. Word has it that the sophist Protagoras is going.'

On and on she goes, never pausing for breath. It's as if she is so used to her questions being ignored that she never expects an answer to any of them.

'Mother,' says a voice behind me. 'I think Melitta wants something from the storeroom.'

'That girl,' grumbles Philemon's mother. 'If it's more olive oil she wants, then I'll know she's been using it as a skin balm.'

As she takes her leave, Philemon gives me an apologetic smile and sits down. The houseboy comes into the room, places two drinking vessels on a small table and half-fills them with water. He returns with a customary jug of wine to top them up, but we both decline.

'What brings you here, Apollos?' says Philemon, once the boy has gone. 'Has the party been cancelled?'

'No, Philemon, it's not that.' I take a long draught of water and wonder how I can say what I've come to say without compromising my sister's dignity. 'I felt like some company. I went to the gymnasium and they said you'd left, so I took a chance you'd be at home.'

He smiles and nods expectantly, as a tutor does when encouraging a pupil.

'Xanthe wants you to see her beloved pup this evening, before the feast. So perhaps you could come a little early?'

'Of course. Have you just bought it for her?'

'No, I captured it more than a month ago.'

'Captured?'

'Yes. It was running wild in the Agora, being chased by some street urchins. I managed to get to it first. No doubt somebody's wife or daughter is still mourning the loss of her lapdog. I took the pup home and Xanthe fell in love with her.'

'You never mentioned it,' he says, looking hurt.

'I didn't think it important.' Observing that Philemon is still frowning, I add, 'You were away, overseeing some work on your farm.'

'Ah yes,' he says, his face clearing. 'The gathering of the barley. It was a good crop this year.'

I feel it's time to stop prevaricating so I get to the crux of the matter.

'I'm afraid I've been neglectful of Xanthe in an important respect. I should have been looking to make her a good match, but I left it to my uncle. She's already refused two, and I fear the next match might be signed and sealed without consulting her.'

Philemon's gaze wavers and he jumps up to refill his cup.

I refuse his offer of more water and, without enthusiasm, continue.

'Xanthe was raised by a nursemaid until we moved to our uncle's house. Aunt Eupheme, having no girls of her own, seems to have neglected to advise her of the conventions of a betrothal. Xanthe's got it into her head that she has the final say. Today she told me where her heart lies.'

I've been staring at the floor and when I raise my eyes I see the blood has drained from Philemon's face.

'My friend, it pains me to put you on the spot like this. I don't enjoy this role of go-between, but she has developed a fondness for you and wonders if, perhaps, you reciprocate...'

I can hardly bring myself to go on, so palpable is Philemon's discomfort. When he interrupts, I feel a surge of relief.

'No, no, no, Apollos. The affection I feel for her is akin to that of a brother. And, besides, I am in no position to marry.'

'Of course,' I say, wiping the sweat from my brow with my fingers. 'I told her you were far too young to think of marriage.'

'Good,' he says, relaxing back in his chair. 'Your sister is charming. I hope her husband is kind to her. Now let us speak of other matters. The envoys have been sent out to proclaim the Greater Mysteries. Do you think you'll be well enough to attend?'

Soon we slip into an easy dialogue. I am eager to hear the gossip of the gymnasium and the Agora, and time passes quickly. When I get up to go, Philemon escorts me to the street door. I walk a few steps and remember I have something else to ask. I turn to find him still standing by the door, watching me.

'Will you still come and see Xanthe this evening before we join the feast?'

'Whatever you wish, Apollos,' he replies, bowing low in mock imitation of a Persian. 'I am at your command.'

Chapter 17

It is dusk and the guests have begun arriving. My uncle has given me the task of greeting them, as he is still getting ready. In his absence, the houseboy is neglectful of his duties and there's a buildup of guests waiting in the anteroom to be relieved of their sandals and shown to a dining couch.

I catch sight of Philemon at the back of the line. He nods in greeting and points towards the courtyard which tells me he's going to speak to Xanthe. I had expected to be present at their meeting but she'll probably be glad I'm not there.

My uncle appears at last in a blue robe of fine-combed wool, his beard curled, old-fashioned style. As he moves among the company, I take this opportunity to slip away into the courtyard to rescue Philemon. Here I find Xanthe sitting by the well, watching Philemon orbiting the altar to Zeus, clutching a ball fashioned from remnants of wool, the pup on his tail. He stops in his tracks when he sees me and throws Echo the ball.

'So, what do you think, Philemon? Is Echo good enough to take hunting?'

Even to my own ear, my words sound excessively hearty. And when Xanthe tuts her disapproval at my suggestion, I feel keenly that she resents my interruption.

'I'm afraid I have to drag Philemon away, Xanthe. The feast is about to start and it's time you went upstairs.'

She sighs and gathers the panting Echo in her arms.

'Very well, but will you ask Uncle if he'll let the flute-girls play for us later?'

Philemon and I exchange a glance. Depending on who's attending the party, the flute-girls may be otherwise engaged once the wine starts to flow.

'If he gives his permission, I'll let you know. Don't come down.'

When Xanthe has gone, I ask Philemon if their meeting went well.

'I think so. I was careful not to be too familiar.'

'What did you speak of?'

'She told me how much she loved dancing and singing in the virgins' chorus during the night-vigil in honour of Athena. And of how they all loved their training classes with the composer. I suspect life seems a little dull now the festival is over.'

My heart aches for her, but there is nothing I can do to enliven her daily life. Particularly as, inevitably, she will be leaving us soon.

'I hope she didn't broach the subject of betrothal,' is all I can find to say.

'No. It was I who introduced the subject. I told her my father had entered into an agreement with the guardian of a distant relative, on her father's death. In a few years, when she's of age, we are to be married.'

'Is this true?' I exclaim, astonished. 'Are you really betrothed?'

He laughs.

'By Zeus, no! I said it to save Xanthe opening her heart to me.'

'Thank you, my friend,' I say, feeling a warm rush of gratitude for his consideration of her feelings. 'I expect there'll be a few tears on her pillow tonight but at least she won't be harbouring false hopes.'

He puts a hand on my shoulder, and drops it as we enter the dining hall. We are the last to go in and have missed our chance of sharing a couch. A house slave conducts me to the side of a reclining stranger who looks old enough to be my grandfather, while Philemon is paired with my cousin Autolykos, whom he barely knows. All in all, I feel we are paying a high price for dawdling outside.

The feast master, a crony of my uncle's, is waiting patiently for the guests to finish admiring a freshly painted mural of Erato, muse of lyric and erotic poetry, before he decides on the mix of water to wine. Erato is in the foreground, tuning her lyre, while in the background, her eight sisters are holding emblems of their expertise. When he's satisfied the last word of praise for the artist—and, more importantly, for my uncle's good taste—has been uttered, he formally declares one part wine to three parts water and no more than two refills of the krater. This is greeted by polite nods, the guests being sober at present and on their best behaviour.

I smile when I see the image on the interior of my drinking bowl: a maenad defending herself against a priapic satyr with a thyrsus pole. I deduce a set of bowls has been borrowed from our neighbour, as my high-minded uncle's taste in decoration usually runs to Dionysus crossing the sea, bordered by grapes and dolphins.

Once everyone's drinking bowl is full, the flute-girls enter. Before they start to play, they bestow each diner with a crown of myrtle, paying particular attention to a guest they might have met before or would like to get to know better. When it is my turn, the girl leans in close, whispering that she is free to see me later if I desire it, but I smile and say nothing. If I feel the need of female company I go to Nikoleta's place where the girls are known to be clean, a tip my father gave me when I was seventeen.

My uncle is keen to get the feast started and bids the slaves hurry. He is a generous host and no doubt wants to demonstrate the extent of his larder. Once we have eaten our fill, and the dogs have cleaned every last morsel from the floor, the slaves clear away, push the tables under the couches and replenish our drinking bowls.

So far I have had little communication with my dining companion, apart from the usual pleasantries and a shared appreciation of the cook's roast pheasant, served in a particularly good wine and juniper berry sauce. He has been engaged in conversation with a guest on the couch flanking ours: Bacchylides, the lyric poet who composed the virgins' song for the procession. He is also my uncle's tutor in the art of writing and intoning lyric poetry. 'A job for life,' I've heard my Aunt Eupheme complain.

Clearly eager to unveil his latest ode, Uncle Aristokles whispers in the ear of the feast master, who immediately calls for us to stand to make libations to the gods. When this is done, we sing the Hymn to Apollo after which some of the company return to their couches, while others stand chatting, hindering the boys who are trying to mop up libation wine from the floor.

During this interval, I seek out Philemon and Autolykos, who greets me by lamenting how much his father has spent on this party just so he can rub shoulders with the 'eggheads', as he calls them. He bemoans the falling sales of shields in recent years at the manufacturing workshop he administers for Aristokles, blaming the fall in profits on the peace treaty with Sparta.

'Chian wine, indeed,' he grumbles. 'It's wasted on most of them. What's more, the mural is by Parrhasios, and must have cost a small fortune.'

The conversation takes a more positive turn when he asks how my wounds are healing, which prompts him and Philemon into a thorough appraisal of the Panathenaic athletics. This is a topic I am eager to hear of, having missed most of the games due to my enforced recuperation in the Asklepion.

We are interrupted by the entry of the lyre player, our signal to return to our seats, unless we have arranged to sit elsewhere. I had intended asking Autolykos to trade places with me but, on consideration, feel it might cause offence so I hold my tongue.

The lyre player presents a branch of myrtle to the guest nearest the door, as he offers him the lyre. The guest declines, indicating that he wishes the lyre player to accompany him.

His choice is a well-known drinking song in praise of Dionysus and those familiar with it join in the chorus with inebriate gusto.

When the myrtle branch reaches my uncle, he takes the lyre and launches into his composition: a paean addressed to

Athena. The work is competent but uninspired. To his credit, he maintains the correct metre throughout, but a few surreptitious winks and nudges from the audience suggest their whistles and cheers may be ironic. I catch the eye of my couch partner and we exchange a furtive smile before straightening our faces in support of our host.

The singing begins again, this time more ribald. It's not till the final chord is played that I remember Xanthe's wish to hear the flute players. I wait until the guests have struck up conversations and approach my uncle, who grasps my arm when he sees me. It's clear the wine is beginning to have a benign effect.

'Apollos, my boy. I'm glad you felt well enough to attend. I hope you appreciate your placing.'

'How could I not come to hear your verses, Uncle?' I say, matching his good humour. 'As for my placing, I'm afraid my companion and I have not yet exchanged names.'

My uncle's gaze has shifted to a point behind my shoulder.

'Protagoras,' he says, raising his voice to be heard above the chattering and laughter. 'You have dined with my nephew, Apollos, but I understand you have not been formally introduced. He was a finalist in the pankration and is still nursing his wounds.'

I turn to face the gentleman who shared my dining couch, who proffers his hand.

'I noticed you had some difficulty getting up. I hope the condition is temporary.'

His tone is solicitous and I assure him that the temple doctor is confident my strength will be restored in due course.

I can see my uncle is eager to have the philosopher's attention so I swiftly make my request for the women of the house to be entertained by the flute-girls during the drinking games. Perceiving a cloud of disquiet cross his face, I offer to oversee the performance.

'Very well. But make it clear to their master that all must be conducted with propriety. Oh, and tell him I'll give him a few extra obols when we settle up.'

My uncle immediately turns to Protagoras to enquire if he has many pupils at present. I leave them to their discussion and go in search of the flute-master, finding him and his girls in the kitchen, demolishing the remains of the banquet.

Once the man has agreed—my request was a formality, as he would have been very foolish to refuse—I climb the stairs to the women's room and ask the maid to fetch my aunt. I can hear Xanthe and the maids chattering within but do not step over the threshold.

'My dear Aunt Eupheme,' I say, when she appears, smiling in my most appealing way. She can be a martinet to her family and the slaves but I know she has a soft spot for me, which I play on, for Xanthe's sake. 'Uncle Aristokles sends a message. He says the flute-girls are at your disposal if you'd like a recital.'

'It depends if they're well-behaved and decently dressed,' she answers, with knitted brow. 'Though I suppose your uncle wouldn't have suggested it if they weren't properly turned out. How was his poem received, by the way?'

'Warmly. Did you hear the cheers?'

'Was that for him?' she says, the relief on her face belying the indifference of her tone.

I nod and she looks back into the room, which has become very quiet. They must be straining their ears for her answer.

'Go on, then, Apollos, you can bring the girls up. Will you wait outside until they've finished playing?'

'Of course.'

Once the flautists are delivered to the women's quarters, I am quite happy to spend a peaceful interlude away from the party. The strains of the flute mingle with the clangour of the kottabos game going on below, the guests striving to pitch their wine dregs into a bronze bowl in the centre of the floor, so they'll be lucky in love.

It's the custom to name the object of one's affections on the throw. But the person who holds my heart cannot be revealed, so I'm glad to be spared the humiliation of plucking a name out of the air and suffering taunts from the crasser members of the company as to which brothel she inhabits, how much she charges, and worse.

The exit of the flute-girls from the women's room coincides with the last of the entertainment, which turns out to be the flute-master doubling as a juggler. He has already started when I get back to the dining hall so I watch from the doorway until, with a dramatic flourish, he throws his final hoop.

I catch Philemon's eye and he leaves his group and joins me.

'Where have you been? Did you feel unwell?'

Unaccustomed to being cast in the role of weakling, I bridle at his tone and answer brusquely.

'On the contrary, I've been on guard duty upstairs.'

Philemon frowns, then light dawns in his eyes.

'Oh, I see. Old Democrates and his cronies were calling for the flute-girls to cheer them on. That's why they were nowhere to be found. You'd escorted them to the women's chamber.'

'Yes. It meant I was mercifully spared the kottabos. Did you play?'

Philemon shakes his head.

'I went outside to see if you were in the courtyard and managed to avoid it.'

'A lucky escape?' I ask, wondering if Philemon also has a secret love. He's too old for another mentor, so perhaps he's formed an attachment to a girl.

'You did well, Apollos,' he declares, swiftly changing the subject. 'Xanthe's wish for some musical entertainment was granted. What a good brother you are.'

I hear myself grunt and wonder if I was as curmudgeonly as this before the blow to my head.

At this moment, the feast master calls for order.

'If you have not already done so, please welcome our honoured guest, Protagoras, who is gracing us with his presence this evening.'

As members of the company approach Protagoras to make themselves known to him, I steer Philemon to the now vacant place beside me. At first we amuse ourselves by commenting on the other guests but grow silent as the philosopher enters a debate with Bacchylides on whether a poet writes from inspiration, or from an innate talent for choosing words that exactly strike the right note.

'I can appreciate your interest in the mastery of accurate expression,' says Bacchylides, smoothly. 'It is, after all, why the fathers of your pupils pay you a fortune to instruct their sons in the *art* of rhetoric.' His emphasis on the word 'art' dripped with sarcasm which drew some guffaws from the room. 'The skills of argument and reasoning are all very practical for the law courts and the citizens' Assembly, but poetry is another matter. My poetry, I believe, is divinely inspired. And I thank the gods every day for smiling on me.'

Protagoras shakes his head in a way that indicates he has heard this argument a hundred times before.

'Concerning the gods, my friend, I have no means of knowing whether they exist or not, nor of what form they may take. Therefore, I cannot be certain whether your verse is divinely inspired or the result of your own natural ability, honed by years of practice.'

His words provoke some bibulous jeering. A flying chestnut, discharged from the back of the room, narrowly misses his right ear. The feast master strides forward to shout 'Order!' and the room settles down.

'Do you doubt the existence of the gods, sir?' asks Philemon, who, like me, is not familiar with this man's doctrine.

'Only because we cannot *prove* their existence,' says Protagoras, changing his speech to a gentler tone. 'The way to wisdom is to take control of one's own life…to learn to live to one's full potential, aspiring to excellence in all undertakings.' He glances at Bacchylides. 'Whether it be poetry or politics.'

'So this is your advice for the younger generation, is it?' says Bacchylides, in a sneering tone. 'Ignore the gods and be charged with impiety?'

A hush falls on the room. The penalty for the crime of impiety is death.

Protagoras assumes an expression of innocence and holds out his hands.

'I simply commend all young men to cultivate the virtues of grace, eloquence and self-control. Who, in this room, could denounce me for that?'

For a moment, it feels as if the tide of feeling might flow against him, but the atmosphere is leavened by a red-faced man, the worse for drink.

'Don't waste your time trying to reel the boy in, sophist!' he shouts. 'His father can't afford your fees!'

Philemon joins in the general laughter but I sense his shame. Riled at this insult, I counter, 'And your father, if you knew him, taught you no manners.'

My uncle throws me a look of daggers and nods to two of his friends to pacify the man, who is drunk enough to start a fight. My guess is that the krater has been refilled more frequently than decreed when the feast master's back was turned.

At that moment, a well-known politician, drawn to the gathering, no doubt, by the lure of Protagoras's presence, focuses attention back to the debate.

'I've heard, sir, that you teach a certain doctrine: "Man is the measure of all things". Can you explain in what sense you see this to be so?'

Protagoras strokes his beard, as if deciding how much this audience can take.

'An *explanation* is never as good as two arguments which can be debated, so I'll state two propositions for you to consider,' he says finally, opening his arms to include everyone in the room. 'The first proposition is to understand the word "measure" in the sense of "touchstone". We all have a personal viewpoint. The way things appear to me, in that way they exist for me. And the way things appears to you, in that way they exist for you. What is true for one man may not be true for another.'

'You mean death is bad for the man that dies, but good for the undertaker?' says the politician.

'In its simplest sense, yes,' answers Protagoras, causing the politician to scowl at the suggestion he might be less than brilliant.

There follows mixed murmurs of assent and dissent, silenced by those who want to hear the second proposition.

'The second proposition is to understand the term "measure" in the sense of mathematical ratios. To accept this view, we must believe the human body possesses a symmetry, corresponding to a certain ratio revealed by Pythagoras.'

He gestures towards a man I recognise as an architect commissioned by Perikles to work on the reconstruction of the Akropolis.

'As some of you here will already know, the Parthenon is one of many temples designed according to an aesthetic canon, the precise dimensions being governed by this same Pythagorean formula.'

The architect nods and smiles, clearly gratified at the guest of honour's recognition of the ancient geometry at play in the creation of the new Parthenon.

'Furthermore,' the sophist continues, 'Pythagoras calculated that the same mathematical ratios apply to the very movements of the planets, which means we can compare the symmetry of the ideal human to the order and harmony of the Cosmos itself.'

He pauses to let his words sink in, and then continues.

'Man is therefore a microcosm of the macrocosm.'

This statement produces mostly frowns and blank looks. A few guests, including the politician, are nodding their heads sagely as if they knew this all along. Protagoras surveys his audience, inviting a response. After a few moments, a voice rises above the murmurs.

'So this means,' says Autolykos, in a tone full of awe, 'that Man, Temple and Cosmos are identical in design.'

The room falls quiet, some faces reflecting hesitation, some doubt, and some alcoholic stupor. In the eyes of a few, however, I detect the radiance of an epiphany. Then a voice breaks the silence. It is mine.

'I'd say the first proposition shows men as being creatures of limitation and the second as being divine.'

'And therefore,' adds Bacchylides the poet, quick as a flash, 'we must all of us be capable of divine inspiration.'

At that point, the red-faced drunkard projects a stream of vomit on to the embroidered hem of the philosopher's tunic and the party descends into chaos.

Chapter 18

Sybil asked Seb to wait in the main hall while she got a key to the consultation suite. He was relieved she'd managed to see him so soon after the dream, so he could talk about it while it was still fresh in his mind. He'd written it down as soon as he'd woken up, ringing her at eight o'clock and delivering his journal to the admin office first thing, so she could read it before they met after morning lectures.

Having unlocked the door to the suite, Sybil hesitated between a room with a medical examination couch and one without.

'Do you prefer to sit or lie down for the debrief?' she said.

'Sounds like an MI5 interrogation,' he said, feigning a worried expression.

'What would you like me to call it, then?'

'How about a grilling?' he said, smiling to show he wasn't serious.

'Shall we settle for report?'

He walked into the room with the examination couch.

'Lying down feels a bit Freudian,' he said, nonetheless thudding his long frame down onto it, announcing, 'Oh well, in for a penny...'

Sybil took his journal out of her bag and placed it on the desk.

'I enjoyed reading this, Seb. I can tell from the way your handwriting flows that your memories are coming quickly. That's a good sign. We're getting a much clearer picture of Apollos in the second dream, aren't we? I notice you've added a few more details to the first dream, as well.'

Seb settled back on the couch and basked in her praise.

'Yeah. Sometimes it almost writes itself.'

'Really? Did Roger mention the spinal energy centres to you, before your labyrinth walk?'

'Yes. He said there were seven of them, matching the seven

spirals of the labyrinth.'

'Well,' she said, lowering her voice as if she were about to impart a secret. 'There are known to be other, emergent energy centres and one of them, at the base of the skull, enables advanced dream recall and interdimensional communication. One of the names it's known by is "the well of dreams" and I'm wondering if perhaps this centre began to open after your time in the labyrinth.'

'I'm cool with that,' he said, grinning. 'As long as I don't get abducted by aliens.'

Sybil refused to be amused.

'I've got some questions ready,' she said briskly, putting on her glasses in a businesslike fashion. 'So shall we get started?'

He nodded, though he'd have liked longer to get his head together. He'd just come from a lecture on the Fundamental Principles of Ayurveda and his brain cells were bulging with vata, pitta and kapha.

'Shouldn't you be in white, Miss Hughes?' he said, playing for a bit more time. 'I thought that's what *therapeutai* wore.'

'No, no. That was correct for the abaton but our meetings from now on will be elsewhere.' She paused for a moment. 'You can call me Sybil during these sessions.'

Seb felt himself colour, wondering if she'd detected the hint of sarcasm in his voice. He nodded and she went on.

'Okay, so first question. How much of the dream did you experience as an outside observer and how much, if any, as a participant?'

Seb didn't have to think twice. It was what had made the dream different from the first.

'I felt as if I was in his body all the time. I don't remember having a bird's-eye view at all.'

'That's interesting,' she said, making notes in her own journal. 'And did you experience his emotions in the same way you did before?'

'I think so. I remember feeling his dismay...and sadness... when his sister said she wanted to marry Philemon.'

'That's understandable. What about his mental state? Did his mind seem a bit fuzzy?'

'Not fuzzy. It was more like an occasional feeling of detachment.'

'That could be because his attachment to people and places will only resurface when his memory fully returns. Or it could be because his thoughts are being filtered through *your* mind.'

Seb digested this while Sybil continued.

'His memory, or part of it, *is* returning, isn't it? Did you get a sense of that?'

'Uh, a bit. Fragments of the past seemed to float into his head sometimes.'

Sybil nodded.

'You wrote that he'd been about to start military training at the time his father died. Did any memories of the training materialise?'

'I had a vague impression of being in a garrison...being taught how to fight in heavy armour...how to use a bow and a javelin.'

'And he's finished his two-year military training, so he must be about your age. Twenty, twenty-one?'

'Guess so.'

'Which means he's younger than we first thought.' Seb noticed her cheeks had turned pink. 'He revealed something about his friend, Philemon, too, didn't he?'

Seb felt a little uneasy discussing this, as if he were breaking the confidence of a friend.

'Are you talking about the mentor business?'

'Yes. And that would have been common knowledge, by the way,' she said, as if reading his mind. 'Because, as I told you before, it was considered the norm.'

'If you say so,' he said, still feeling uncomfortable.

'So the question is,' she went on, her voice quickening, 'did

Apollos ever have a loving relationship with a mentor?'

'I don't know,' he said flatly.

'Are you sure? Think back to when his mind dwelt on Diogenes, Philemon's lover. Did an image of someone *he* was fond of appear?'

Seb answered without hesitation.

'No. The only amorous feeling I remember him having was for his "secret love". I got the impression this person was female.'

'Did you pick up anything else about her?'

'No.'

'Perhaps he'd learned to close her image down, since it was a covert relationship.'

'Would that be possible?'

Sybil shrugged.

'I'm not sure. What we don't know, of course, is how much of his memory might have been lost forever. He did suspect some of it might be missing, didn't he?'

'Missing, presumed dead,' murmured Seb, half to himself.

During the silence which fell while they pondered this, it occurred to Seb that Sybil seemed to be a heck of a lot more interested in Apollos's mental health than she was in his own.

Sybil looked at her watch and sighed.

'I've got a seminar group at two o'clock, so we'd better press on. Let's talk about the symposium.'

'You mean the party?'

'Yes. The word "symposium" originally meant drinking party.'

'Okay. I heard it as "party". My dream Greek must be straying into the vernacular.'

Sybil made no comment. She obviously didn't find the linguistic angle as interesting as he did, so he forced himself back on track.

'Well, I was impressed with the krater mixing bowl. It was enormous, and beautiful, in its way. Like an upturned bell with two handles.'

'Was it decorated?'

'Yeah. It was painted with red figures on a black background. They were engaged in combat, wearing nothing but their helmets. I remember a figure with a sword hanging from a waist belt and he was attacking the guy next to him with a spear.'

Sybil began to giggle.

'How the ancient Greeks loved the human form. Any excuse to paint or sculpt a muscular naked male! Of course, in reality, a warrior would have worn a short tunic with a breastplate and greaves to protect him. And a large shield.'

'Come to think of it, he *was* holding a shield. And, funnily enough, it had a snake symbol on it.'

Sybil pulled out her smartphone and began to type.

'Ah, here it is…I wasn't sure. The snake is one of the symbols of Athena, so that warrior would have been fighting for Athens, as you'd expect, given its pride of place in an Athenian household. In fact, Apollos and Philemon would have received a shield and a spear from the state halfway through their training as hoplites.'

'That's foot soldiers, right?'

'Yes. Although, from the sound of it, Apollos could apply to the cavalry now he's done his two years. Didn't Xanthe say something about her dog disappearing to the stables? This could put Apollos and his family in the elite cavalry class. Only the richer Athenians could afford to own and maintain a good mount they could ride into battle.'

The ancient Greek preoccupation with war was not an interest he shared, so he deliberately steered the conversation in a different direction.

'What about the philosopher at the symposium? Was he a real person?'

'Protagoras? Of course. He was a contemporary of Socrates. He taught the doctrine of relativism: that knowledge, truth, and morality are not absolute. They exist in relation to culture, society, or historical context.'

Seb felt himself blush. Sybil was making him feel like a schoolboy who hadn't done his history homework.

'After I'd written up the dream, I hardly had time to make it to class, let alone check every detail,' he muttered, in defence.

'My first degree's in Classics, so I have the advantage,' she said, almost apologetically. 'Anyway, what did you think of the discussion at the end, about man being the measure of all things?'

Seb wasn't sure whether he bought either of the philosopher's proposals. But he'd enjoyed listening to him.

'For me, the discussion was the most interesting part. An improvement on watching a bunch of guys telling jokes and riddles, singing the equivalent of rugby songs, and getting hammered. Shame it ended with that idiot spewing all over him.'

She smiled.

'Getting drunk was par for the course. And Protagoras was an itinerant teacher. He would have been used to a bit of heckling.'

'At the time, I wasn't sure which argument he supported. But, from what you say, it'd be the first one.'

'Actually, no one's *really* sure, as none of his writings have survived. The authorities burned his books because he doubted the existence of the Greek gods. We only know about him from other philosophers. He was renowned for teaching that there were at least two opposing arguments on any matter, and for demonstrating how to make the weaker argument stronger. This was so his students, the young men of Athens, could persuade others to their argument, either in the citizen's Assembly or a court of law.'

'I still say it was doubtful he *did* agree that Man, Temple and the Cosmos were identical in design,' said Seb, thoughtfully. 'Anyone who states he doesn't have proof of the existence of the gods is an agnostic, and hardly likely to believe in divine design.'

Sybil consulted her smartphone and read aloud from the link.

'*Ancient Greek myths showed the gods to be amoral and capricious. For that reason, Protagoras disapproved of the custom of constantly appeasing them with ceremonies and sacrifice*. Looks like you could be right. Although challenging the existence of the mythological gods isn't the same as denying there's any kind of higher divinity.'

'Whichever way you look at it, he was a man before his time,' said Seb, admiringly. 'I'm surprised there weren't more like him.'

'There must have been doubters, but they wouldn't have admitted it, because anyone refusing to recognise the established gods would be labelled an atheist, even though they simply wanted to liberate society from the yoke of believing in myths. In fact, it says here that Protagoras was eventually expelled from Athens for impiety.'

'Tough. But better than a cup of hemlock,' he said, feeling a tingling at the back of his head.

Sybil took off her glasses and stared at him.

'That's how Socrates died, for the same crime. How did you know that?'

'I didn't. The phrase just came into my head. It happens sometimes.'

Sybil directed a rueful glance at her watch.

'I'd better get back to my list of questions. Let's see, um, Apollos seemed pretty convinced by the second proposition, didn't he? So it seems he's attracted to the mystical.'

'Yes. That was genuine. I felt it.'

She nodded in approval, prompting Seb to ask her what *she* thought of man being the microcosm of the macrocosm.

'It's a pretty common belief, if you think about it. It's in Genesis: *God created Mankind in His own image and likeness*.'

'What does that mean?'

'I've always thought it meant that God is the Infinite Spirit and we've got a small part of the same spirit within us, the bit that lives on when we die. How about you?'

'No good asking *me*. I was brought up an agnostic.'

Sybil looked sad for a moment.

'A lot of people think that's the only rational position to take.'

From the way she said it, Seb perceived it was not a view she shared.

'Leonardo da Vinci believed in divine proportion, you know,' she continued. 'Think of his drawing of Vitruvian man, set within a circle and a square. Sunny told me that Professor Ophis designed the sanctuary buildings according to the golden ratio of Pythagoras.'

Seb had difficulty swallowing this chunk of information, particularly as her mention of his father had made him want to shout *Eureka!*

'Who's Sunny?'

'Sunil Sharma. He teaches Ayurveda.'

'Dr Sharma? I've just come from his class. Did he know Professor Ophis?'

'Yes. He's the only member of staff who's been here from the beginning. Roger was appointed by the trustees after the professor left.'

Up to now, Seb had told himself he had no interest in a man who would get a young woman pregnant, stand by while she gave the baby up for adoption, and then leave the country. He'd done the calculation as soon as he'd seen Teodor Ophis's name on his birth certificate. The foundation was inaugurated twenty-five or so years ago which meant that Ophis had only stayed for five years. The sum added up to a father who had no interest in being one. Teodor must have left around the time he was born. Yet the possibility of finding out more about this shadowy figure was exerting an urgent magnetic pull on him.

'There's not much in the prospectus about him. Where is he now?'

'I have no idea. You'll have to ask Sunny next time you see

him.'

Sybil consulted her notes.

'So, to summarise, Apollos is still recovering physically…and mentally, with regard to his memory, but we don't know if it'll completely return. One of his current concerns is the reluctance of his younger sister to enter into an arranged marriage. He and Philemon have recently finished military training and are no longer ephebes. They're fully-fledged citizens with a responsibility to fight in defence of their city-state whenever they're called upon. Philemon had a mentor whom he's mourning, and Apollos has a secret love, still to be revealed.'

Seb swung his legs to the floor and sat sideways on the couch.

'Just an everyday slice of ancient Greek life,' he said dismissively, not quite sure where this dream had got them in terms of, well, anything at all, really.

'I look forward to the next chapter,' said Sybil, getting up and handing him his journal.

Seb remained seated, feeling there was more to say.

'Sorry, Sybil, this probably sounds stupid, but how precisely has this session thrown any more light on my so-called condition?'

'We haven't established that you have a condition yet,' she said, breezily.

'Exactly. So why are we continuing?'

'Case studies are a good learning and teaching tool. I'd like to have a more complete picture of the subject you're dreaming about before we stop.'

Seb bridled at this.

'When you said last time that another dream may throw more light on any underlying psychological disorders, I took that to mean *my* psychological disorders, not the ancient Greek's. You seem more interested in him than me.'

'And with good reason,' she said, in her schoolmarm voice. 'I'm assuming that you dreamed about him because his life is in some way a reflection of yours, so I'm trying to see if there are any similarities. Do you see any?'

'Not really, apart from being about the same age. I don't have a younger sister, as far as I know. And I won't be training to go into battle any time soon.'

'Well, for example, you're both orphans. Can you think of anything else?'

Seb racked his brains for something less obvious.

'Our physical strength, perhaps?'

Sybil looked surprised, prompting him to elaborate.

'I was stronger than most boys my age. That was the reason my mother kept me away from school. She was frightened I might accidentally hurt someone.'

At that moment Sybil's phone rang. At the end of the call, she said she had to go but would be in touch. And if he thought of any more similarities, to make a note of them.

They walked together to the outer door and she locked up. Seb was eager to find Dr Sharma but as he increased his pace she called out to him.

'Remember what I told you before, Seb, it's the dream itself that sets off the healing process. As long as you're dreaming, you can't lose.'

Chapter 19

Seb took the stairs two at a time and sped to the admin office, hoping that the Course Administrator would be around.

He'd become acquainted with Brenda when he'd collected the key to his flat. She was worried he wouldn't find it, so had offered to go with him in his car, saying the walk back would do her good. He'd been glad to have someone else there to show him the ropes when he first set eyes on his new quarters. He'd been almost sorry to see her go.

'Hello, Sebastian. How are you?'

'Fine, thanks, Brenda.'

'What can I do for you? Actually, I've just put the kettle on. It's white coffee, no sugar, isn't it?'

He sat at one of the spare desks that lecturers sometimes occupied when they used the office equipment. In fact, he'd been half-hoping to see Sharma collating photocopies at one of them.

'I'm looking for Dr Sharma,' he said, gratefully accepting a chocolate digestive. 'Is he still around?'

'Let's see,' she said, peering at a timetable on the wall. 'He's with the third-years this afternoon. If you'd come ten minutes earlier, you'd probably have found him in the staff room. Is it anything I can help you with? If you've got an essay to hand in, you can leave it with me.'

Seb tried to assess Brenda's age. In her fifties, he guessed. Sybil had said Sharma was the only member of staff who'd met Ophis, but she might have been referring to the teaching staff.

'I want to find out more about the founder, actually. Miss Hughes said Dr Sharma knew him.'

'Are you writing an article for the student magazine?'

Seb relaxed. She'd just provided him with the perfect motive.

'I'm thinking about it. You haven't met him, by any chance, have you?'

'Me? Good heavens, no!' she exclaimed, as if he'd asked if she'd ever danced with the Prince of Wales. 'He left over twenty years ago.'

'No worries,' he said, as casually as he could. 'What time does Dr Sharma's class finish?'

'Four-fifteen. But he'll want to get on his way then. He doesn't hang around.' She stopped, as if remembering she was talking to a student. 'He likes to avoid the traffic.'

'I might try anyway,' said Seb, concealing his disappointment with what he hoped was a bright smile.

'Otherwise, you could try to catch him at the three o'clock break. He's in room 107.'

'Thanks for the hospitality, Brenda. I'd better shoot.'

'That's all right, dear. Not a word to the other students, though. I don't do this for everybody,' she said, smiling at him the same way the farm wives had, with a mixture of kindness and what he guessed was sympathy.

Seb raced back to the flat to fix himself a sandwich. There was no sign of Nick, so he didn't have to explain where he was going when he left twenty minutes later.

Just before three o'clock he stood at the door of the refectory and surveyed the room. There were a few people in the queue but he didn't know any third-years, so he couldn't be sure if they were here yet. After five minutes there was no sign of Dr Sharma so he made his way to room 107. He put his ear to the door but could hear nothing. At that moment, the door opened and he almost fell inside.

Dr Sharma regarded him with a quizzical expression.

'You're one of my first-year students, aren't you?

'Yes. Sebastian Young.'

'What are you doing here?'

'There's something I'd like to ask you.'

Sharma's expression had changed to one of annoyance.

'I'm on my way to the staff room. Can't it wait till the next class?'

'But that's next week.'

'What can be so pressing that you can't wait till then? I gave you reading homework this morning, didn't I? I don't have time for tutorials until after your first essay.'

'It's not actually an academic question. I want to write an article on the founder for the student magazine...there's not much about him in the prospectus. I mentioned it to Miss Hughes this morning and she said you were the only member of staff who knew him. Is that right?'

'I believe so, yes.'

Sharma was walking at a fast pace towards the staircase which led up to the staff room. He probably thought his unwelcome pursuer would retreat when they reached the stairs but Seb ascended with him.

'Then I wonder, sir, if you'd be good enough to tell me about him...when you're not so busy,' he added, too late to appease his quarry.

They came to a large, impressive door and Sharma put his hand on the doorknob.

'I doubt any of the students would be in any way interested in his biography,' he said peevishly, his eyes bulging slightly behind round, metal-rimmed glasses. 'I strongly suggest you choose something else to write about. Now please go away and leave me in peace.'

Feeling as if he'd been kicked in the gut, Seb dug his hands deep into his jacket pockets to quell a sudden desire to punch Sharma in the face. As he did so, the fingers of his left hand came into contact with his mother's brooch, which instinct told him to release from its hiding place.

'Will this change your mind?' he barked, thrusting the brooch close to Sharma's face, a shaft of light from a skylight above illuminating the golden staff and serpent.

Sharma recoiled from the object, as if Seb had produced a

flick-knife from his pocket. But when he saw that Seb was standing perfectly still, he leaned forward for a closer look.

'Where did you get this?'

Seb was in no mood to recount the circumstances of his birth, so he decided to tell the truth, but not the whole truth.

'It was found in my mother's things after she died. I believe it belongs to Professor Ophis.'

Sharma looked at his watch, sighed, and produced his mobile.

'Give me your phone number.'

Seb entered his number into Sharma's phone.

'Where do you live?'

'On campus. I'm the scholarship student.'

Sharma didn't reply. Instead, he disappeared inside, leaving Seb staring at the closed door.

— o —

Seb waited all week for Sharma to ring, with no result, leaving him to wonder if he'd taken his number just to get rid of him. If so, it wasn't surprising. Sharma must have seen through his pretence of writing an article as soon as he produced the brooch.

The worse thing was having no one to confide in. He'd become used to keeping his own counsel, but he found himself wanting to tell Nick and Fliss what was going on. He kept quiet because that would have meant admitting to having Teodor Ophis's name on his birth certificate. He imagined their reactions. Nick would rib him about it endlessly, whereas Fliss would probably take off on a flight of fancy about his biological parents getting back in touch with each other and the three of them living happily ever after, the thought of which made him shudder.

By the time Sunday dawned, he'd resigned himself to having to wait until the following morning to speak to Dr Sharma, after his Ayurveda lecture. And what if Sharma snubbed him? This nagging fear made him glad of the distraction of the photo shoot.

Fliss had the whole thing planned down to the finest detail. He, Nick and Jim were to drive to the shop and change into the first of their outfits. It had to be his car because Nick's was a two-seater and Jim's ride was a Yamaha. If the weather was good, they'd go to Pendell Woods. The female models would be travelling in a people carrier along with Fliss and Milena, who was taking the photographs.

The weather forecast had promised a mild, bright day and was true to its word. On the way to the shop, they joked about how high on the scale of ridiculous the poses they'd be ordered to strike would be, and what the changing facilities would consist of.

'I hope you've got a pop-up changing pod for the great outdoors,' said Nick, after Fliss told them to leave their own clothes in the boutique changing room. 'Jim is very modest.'

She laughed.

'Just go behind a tree. You'll be okay if you're quick.'

'I'm not talking about the toilet arrangements.'

'Neither am I.'

'You are joking.'

She gave a mock sigh. 'Of course I'm joking. We've got throws you can hold around the person who's changing. Don't worry, your modesty will be preserved at all costs.'

Seb was the last to leave the changing room. As he began to draw back the curtain, he heard female voices coming from upstairs. They were getting closer, so he stayed inside.

'I just love what I'm wearing, Fliss. Thank you *so* much for inviting me.'

He hung back a little longer before joining his mates who were waiting at his car. As they set off, tailing the people carrier, he broke the bad news.

'Bloody Lynette's one of the models. What the flaming hell is Fliss playing at!'

'You mean that French bird on our course?' said Jim, from the back seat. 'She's quite fit. Am I missing something?'

Nick turned round and winked at Jim.

'Lynette's got her eye on him. Which is awkward, as he's going out with Fliss. Looks like this photo shoot could be *vairry* interesting.'

Seb shot Nick a dirty look, which only made him chuckle.

Jim joined in. 'I quite fancy the little blonde. Is she taken?'

'I have no idea, Jimbo. Do you, Seb?'

Seb grunted. 'Her name's Amy. She works in the shop. That's all I know,'

When they got to the car park at Pendell Woods they stayed in the car and watched the group in the people carrier disembark. The driver, a man of about sixty, took two suitcases from the boot, giving one to a sturdily built woman of about the same age, and the other to Amy.

'Are they her grandparents?' said Nick.

'No idea,' said Seb, becoming aware of how little he really knew about Fliss. They'd last seen each other on Friday, when she'd come to a DJ night in the common room bar, but no mention had been made of Lynette.

They got out and joined the group, Seb standing as far away from Lynette as possible.

'Thank you all for coming,' shouted Fliss. 'Just a quick introduction: Linzi, an old school friend of mine; Amy, who works in the boutique; and Lynette, who's doing the same course as Jim, Nick and Seb. Our driver, Richard, has offered to be our sentry so nobody crashes the shoot. And Milena's on camera duty today. She's very experienced, so if you do exactly as she tells you, we'll sail through it in no time.'

All eyes then switched to the older woman, but before Fliss had a chance to present her, she introduced herself.

'I'm Birdie. It's Bridie really but Felicity calls me Birdie because she couldn't pronounce my name when *I used to look after her*.' She emphasised the last words as if to establish her position as a figure of authority. 'I'm in charge of the male models.'

Fliss coloured as Nick started sniggering.

'Birdie's got your outfits,' said Fliss, a touch apologetically. 'And Amy's sorting out the girls' clothes because I'll be shooting a video.'

There were polite nods of interest at this.

'It's a five-minute walk,' continued Fliss, 'so we'd better get going before anyone else gets there.'

The chosen spot was a clearing with natural props: a massive log and any number of living trees to hug, still in leaf even though the end of October was approaching. Seb was itching to ask Fliss what Lynette was doing there, but Birdie was standing guard so he kept his distance.

Under Birdie and Amy's supervision, the models all appeared in the right costumes at the right times, allowing Milena to work with military precision. Even when a large, lolloping red setter invaded the set, he ended up in the last clutch of photographs before his owner arrived and hauled him away.

The only fly in the ointment for Seb was when Milena took some couples shots and she told him to stand next to Lynette.

'Hello, Seb,' she whispered, barely moving her lips. 'I think you're surprised to see me, no?'

He had to make a snap decision. Should he agree with her or not?

Seb glanced across at Fliss who was videoing them.

'Not at all. Fliss told me you'd be here,' he fibbed.

Milena barked out an instruction for them to angle their bodies and look into each other's eyes. Seb reluctantly obeyed, keeping his gaze on the bridge of her nose.

'She rang me last night,' she breathed. 'Her other model let her down.'

'I know.'

Mercifully, Milena lowered the camera, allowing Seb to escape.

'Can I have Nick and Linzi, please, and then we're done.'

Back at the shop, and changed into their own clothes, the three young men went up to the staff room where they found Birdie and Richard setting out soft drinks and buffet food.

'Let's fill our boots, lads,' said Nick, piling his plate high and making a beeline for Linzi.

Seb downed a bottle of lemon and lime and looked around. Jim was deep in conversation with Amy. The other girls were still downstairs. He'd just decided to text Fliss when Birdie hove into view with a plate of food.

'Here, eat something.'

Surprised, he took the plate and put his phone away.

'Thanks.'

'Come and sit down with me a minute,' she said, heading for some wooden chairs set against the wall. 'We haven't had a chance to chat.'

Seb's heart sank but he went along with it for politeness' sake.

Birdie allowed him some time to eat before speaking.

'Flissy tells me you're adopted.'

He nodded, dreading what might be coming.

'I suppose you know she's got a bee in her bonnet about you tracing your mother.'

He sighed.

'I wish she'd leave it alone.'

'Why is it you don't you want to find your mum?'

He shrugged.

'I wouldn't want to remind her of, I don't know, a part of her life she wants to keep secret. And suppose we didn't hit it off? She could take a dislike to me, or vice versa.'

Birdie patted his hand.

'I understand what you're saying. I told her it's not a straightforward situation. She might have got married and had more children. So don't think *I'm* encouraging her.'

He had no idea that Fliss had discussed his situation with

anyone else, so he assured Birdie the thought hadn't entered his head.

'On the other hand,' she said, gently. 'Very few mothers give up their babies without suffering years of regret afterwards. Imagine her wondering how you were and what you were doing, especially on your birthday.'

Seb looked down at his plate, hoping she wouldn't see the inconvenient tears which had welled up at her words.

'Just remember, though, if you close too many doors your life will become small. Sometimes it's worth taking a risk for what you gain in the long run.'

When Seb looked up, he saw she had a small card in her hand, which she pressed into his.

'Get in touch if you ever want to talk. You might not think so, but I'm quite a good listener.'

Moments later, Fliss appeared.

'Is Birdie giving you a reading?' she said, taking a seat beside him.

'Seb and I were just chatting,' said Birdie, sharply.

'Why was Lynette on the shoot, Fliss?' said Seb, feeling suddenly tired.

She took his hand and squeezed it.

'Because I asked her.'

'When?'

'That night in the Bull's Head, when you ignored me. I needed a redhead because Milena's friend had pulled out.'

'She told me someone let you down at the last minute and you rang her last night.'

Fliss exhaled a scornful snort.

'And you believed her?'

Seb shrugged.

'Yeah. I even said I knew. Why didn't you tell me she'd be here?'

'Because she's not important.'

'But I look like a fool now.'

'And whose fault's that?' she said, jumping up and joining Linzi and Milena, who were chatting on the landing.

Seb watched her go, too annoyed to follow her.

Lynette was the first to leave, appearing briefly to pick up her voucher. Seb, still sulking, said a cursory goodbye to Fliss and left with Nick and Jim shortly after.

'Okay, gentlemen,' said Nick, as Seb drove away from the shop. 'In view of the fact I drew a blank with the fair Linzi—her excuse being she's got a boyfriend she's true to—I suggest we make tracks for a local hostelry and see if they accept Belinda vouchers.'

'You and me both, man,' said Jim, ruefully. 'I really fancied Amy. I was feeling the vibe but she didn't reciprocate.'

'She's probably not into the ageing hippie look,' said Nick. 'I could restyle you, if you like. I know a good hairdresser: a short back and sides would take years off you.'

Listening to his two friends kidding around, Seb envied their ability to sail through life on an even keel. While he was still adrift, awaiting the arrival of fair winds and following seas to carry him to his true destination.

Chapter 20

Dr Sharma had avoided all eye contact with Seb during his class. Their brief had been to give a summary of a section of their coursebook to the rest of their group. Fortunately, Lynette was in a different set; he didn't know if he could have been civil to her if they'd been forced to work together.

After break, they reconvened for Sharma's lecture, 'Tracing the Path of Disease'. As the others made their way out at the end of class, Seb remained seated.

'You coming, mate?' said Nick.

'Go ahead, I'll see you in the refectory,' he said, pretending to look for something in his rucksack.

Nick darted him an enquiring look but Seb made a quick movement with his head towards the door, hoping he'd get the message.

Once everyone had left the room, he approached Sharma, who was packing his stuff away in his briefcase.

'Dr Sharma, do you remember what we talked about last Monday?'

Seb's heart was pounding. Sharma was still avoiding his gaze and Seb was regretting ever raising the issue in the first place. Getting the wrong side of a tutor this early in the course was foolhardy, to say the least.

Finally, Sharma raised his head. His eyes were wary.

'I have spoken to Professor Ophis. He's agreed to video call you. Are you usually free at 7:00 p.m.?'

'Yes,' said Seb, unable to believe his ears. 'Thank you, sir. Do you know when...?'

'No,' said Sharma, tersely, giving him a piece of paper. 'Write down your email address. I'll send it to him so he can add you to his Skype contacts.'

'Is he in Greece?'

'I'm not sure. I suggest you confine your questions to your conversation with him.'

Sharma gestured towards the door and Seb took the hint. On his way to join Nick, having cooked up a reason for wanting to speak to Sharma privately, he tried to imagine Teodor's reaction when Sharma had told him about the brooch. He hoped he'd been able to remember who he'd given it to. Unless, of course, he had a stash of brooches he awarded to all the women he slept with.

— o —

Seb sat in front of his desk, staring at his laptop. He'd set up a Skype account, which was asking him to add contacts, but there was only one person he was interested in talking to and he didn't know his email address.

At seven-fifteen, his laptop played a strange futuristic sound, making him jump. He chose the option 'answer with video' and a slightly blurred image of a handsome man, with greying temples, came into view. Teodor's features hadn't changed much from the photograph in Digby's office so his image was no great surprise to Seb.

'Hello, Sebastian. I hear you're my scholarship student. I was beginning to think the committee had forgotten all about awarding it. Congratulations.'

'Thank you, sir.'

Seb had expected him to speak with a Greek accent, but it was barely discernible. He spoke in a version of the hard to locate, 'international' accent of an intellectual cosmopolitan.

'No need to call me "sir", Sebastian, Teo is fine. My friend, Sunny, tells me you want to write an article about me. I was quite surprised. This is the first request I've ever had.' He smiled engagingly. 'What do you want to know, exactly?'

Seb glanced at his two 'show and tell' exhibits: his birth

certificate and the brooch, which he'd placed out of sight of the webcam.

They'll have to wait, he thought. If Teodor wants to pursue the fiction of an interview, then I'll go along with it.

He picked up the pen he'd placed on his desk for just such an eventuality and held it poised over a jotter. 'If you could give me a potted biography, that'd be great.'

'Certainly. At least, I'll try. Well, I was born in Athens sixty years ago. I studied Pharmacy at the University of Athens. Then an MSc in Medicinal Chemistry at the Université Paris Descartes, followed by a PhD in Pharmacognosy. After that I taught Pharmacognosy at the University of Athens, where I became a professor.'

Teo paused, looking pensive.

'Up to then, I was happy in my work. But when my wife died, I couldn't bear to live in the same house, or even the same city. I sold up, left my job and decided to visit some of the friends I'd met during the course of my work. One of those friends was Sunil Sharma. He mentioned that Whitwell Hall was on the market and I bought it with the money my wife left me. So I founded the college in her honour, though not in her name. Asklepios took the laurels for that.'

'Your wife must have been quite young when she died,' said Seb, feeling an unexpected sympathy for the man. Though he couldn't help adding, 'Did you have any children?'

'She was thirty-two. No, we didn't have any children.'

'What did you do after you left the Foundation?'

'I went back to Greece for a few months. My parents were getting old and I felt they needed me. Later on, I did a stint at King's College and produced a few research papers. One of my interests was the phytochemical analysis of Mediterranean medicinal and aromatic plants, to isolate and identify bioactive metabolites. On the strength of that, I got a job with Paris Descartes.'

Seb struggled to subdue a feeling of pride in his father's achievements, which felt uncomfortably like disloyalty to a mother he'd never known.

'Are you in Paris now?'

'Yes.'

Seb's curiosity had been satisfied to a degree, but he still had little idea of Teo's personal life.

'What about you?' said Teo, out of the blue. 'What prompted you to consider a career in holistic healing?'

Seb decided there and then, before their relationship became too chummy, that it was time to come clean about his motive for speaking to Teo face to face.

'It started when my adoptive parents died. They were farm tenants, which meant I was out of a home and a job. So I looked around and found this course. When the director offered me a scholarship, I had to produce my birth certificate. I'd never seen the original before…' He reached for Exhibit A, the certificate, and held it close to the webcam. 'Can you see the names of my biological parents?'

Teo put on his glasses and leaned forward.

'It's not very clear. Why don't you tell me?'

'Anna Norland, student, and Teodor Ophis, founder of the Asklepios Foundation.'

His expectations of Teo's reaction to the document had ranged from outright denial to acute embarrassment, but all Teo did was sit back and nod his head sadly.

'It must have come as a shock to you. I'm surprised your adoptive parents didn't tell you who your real parents were at some point.'

'Is that all you have to say?'

'My dear boy, what do you want me to say? You must have known that Sunny would tell me about the brooch. I want you to know that I have no objection at all to being found.'

Seb could feel his anger rising and dug his nails in his palms to control it.

'Did you know she was pregnant?'

'Of course. That's why my name's on the birth certificate. We registered the birth together, at the hospital.'

'Can you tell me why my mother didn't keep me?'

Teo's face crumpled.

'We were in love, but she was already married. She told me she was going to leave him. If she'd divorced him, I would have married her. But in the end, she decided to return to Norway.'

'Already married? I thought she was a student.'

'A mature student. In those days we ran a postgraduate course. Her husband was in Norway.'

'How do you know I wasn't *his* child?'

'The dates didn't match. He was in the navy, so when she went home between terms he wasn't always there.'

'I'd have thought a married woman would have heard of birth control,' said Seb, hearing, and regretting, a spiteful tone in his voice.

'She thought the birth control pill was dangerous, so she used another method, called the diaphragm. We both believed it was a safe option. It turned out to be less than effective.'

Seb's presumption of Teodor as a lustful older man recklessly pursuing a naive young woman fell to earth and burst into flames.

'Have you kept in touch with her?'

'No. She didn't keep you, so what would be the point?'

'But do you have an address for her?'

Seb wasn't even sure himself why he was pursuing this line of enquiry.

'No. I only know she lived in Oslo.'

'Do you think she ever told her husband about you?'

'I doubt it. His name was Erik, like the famous Viking, Erik the Red—the one with the filthy temper. From what she said, he was aptly named.'

'What was she like?'

Teo produced a large handkerchief and blew his nose.

'She was a lovely young woman. Tallish, slim, with long dark hair and beautiful green eyes. And a very good herbalist.'

'Have you got a picture of her?'

'No. I destroyed the few I had of her. I was quite distraught at the time.'

'Didn't people notice she was pregnant?'

'Of course, but she was married so they wouldn't have thought anything of it.'

'So what happens next?' said Seb, feeling drained.

'I suggest you give yourself time to digest what I've told you. I'll email you, and we can keep talking.'

'Okay,' said Seb. He'd just heard a key in the lock, so expected Nick to knock on his bedroom door at any moment. 'By the way, did Dr Sharma know about all this, at the time?'

'Not at all. Your mother and I were very discreet. If he suspects anything now, it's because of your recent altercation.'

Seb felt a pang of guilt about his loss of control when he'd thrust the brooch into Sharma's face.

'I'm sorry that happened. Put it down to a rush of blood to the head. I wasn't interested in my biological parents until recently. I suppose it was the coincidence of coming to study at a place founded by a man whose name turned out to be on my birth certificate…'

'Quite understandable. Quite understandable.'

Seb felt as if his father was figuratively patting him on the back to calm him down. The unexpected thing was, he liked the feeling.

'I guess I should apologise to him?'

'If you like. But I'll tell him anyway that I'm going to touch base with you regularly, as you're my scholarship student. If anyone asks about the article, you can say I prefer to remain a man of mystery. Can you answer one question for me, please, before you go?'

'Sure.'

'How did you get the brooch?'

'When my adoptive mother died, it was found in her effects.'

'So did Anna give it to Mrs Young so she could give it to you?'

'I suppose she did, yes. She used it to pin a note on the hospital pillow when she discharged herself.'

'What did the note say?'

'Something like, she wished Mr and Mrs Young well and hoped I'd bring joy to their lives. And that my father had given her the brooch, which she bequeathed to me.'

'But you didn't get it till after Mrs Young died?'

'No.'

Teodor looked sad.

'I'm going to end the call now, Sebastian. I'll be in touch.'

As his father disappeared from the screen, accompanied by another weird sound effect, there was a knock on his door.

'Come in,' Seb shouted, shoving his birth certificate in the desk drawer.

'Am I interrupting something?' said Nick, his eyes wandering to the laptop, causing Seb to wonder if he'd heard Teodor's last few comments.

'No, mate,' he answered, shutting the lid of his laptop. 'I was watching a YouTube video about Skype. Have you ever used it?'

'Not lately, but all the time when I was in LA. Why, who do you want to video call?'

Seb shrugged and walked into the kitchen area.

'It's free. I'm exploring ways to save money.'

Nick looked concerned.

'Are you really short of money? I'll buy your Belinda voucher, if you like. I've got my eye on a pair of snazzy strides.'

Seb laughed.

'I won't say no. Two thousand quid isn't going to last me three years.'

'You'd better start doing the lottery, old son. In the meantime, we've been invited to a poker night by a mate of Jimbo's. So I'll give you fifty quid for the voucher and that'll be your stake money.'

Before they left, Seb retrieved Exhibit B—his mother's brooch—lying unexhibited behind his laptop, and slipped it into his pocket.

Much later that evening, the last thing Seb did before he got into bed was feast his eyes on the ten twenty-pound notes he had won.

All in all, it hasn't been a bad day, he thought, closing his eyes and drifting away.

Chapter 21

I hand the attendant the squealing suckling pig and he holds it down on the altar while the priest sprinkles water between its eyes. The animal tosses its head in response, the priest taking this as a sign of consent to being sacrificed.

In a flash, he slits the creature's throat, its blood cascading into a libation jar held by the attendant who is bare to the waist, his torso spattered with blood. Once the pig has ceased moving, the priest plunges his long knife into its belly and examines the entrails to see if the sacrifice is acceptable to the goddesses Demeter and Persephone.

Philemon is standing next to me and covers his mouth and nose when the stench is released. His family estate keeps a handful of sheep and goats, mainly for wool and cheese, so he is unaccustomed to the reek of slaughter. The priest indicates, with a wave of his blade, that my pig is satisfactory and dismisses me.

Once Philemon's offering is in turn dispatched and approved, we go in search of a group of comrades we served with on military training. We find them on the lower slopes of the Akropolis, resting after our trek back to Athens from the Bay of Phaleron. We swam in the ocean to purify ourselves before the sacrifice of the pigs, to avoid the stain of bloodguilt for the deliberate slaying of a living creature.

We throw down our cloaks and join the group. The conversation turns to our first initiation five months ago in the spring, when we travelled together to Demeter's shrine at Agrai, by the River Ilissos, to be inducted into the Lesser Mysteries. There, we took part in rites of atonement, for no one with unatoned bloodguilt can be initiated into the Greater Mysteries. Our instructors said they would see us here, at the Greater festival. We'll probably meet them at tonight's feast.

Today is only the second day of the celebration. The Grand

Procession from Athens to Eleusis, where the Greater initiation ceremony takes place, does not leave until the fifth day, and we are all impatient to get there. Such secrecy surrounds The Mysteries that we have only a sketchy idea of what we're in for, and we joke about what we might witness in the telesterion, the huge initiation hall. Our guesses become wilder and more raucous until some Thracian passers-by, distinguished by their cloaks of many hues, rebuke us for irreverence.

The city of Athens is swarming with visitors, more arriving every day. The envoys have travelled all over Hellas to announce a sacred truce of any hostilities to ensure safe passage for the celebrants. The festival is open to any adult: male, female, free or slave, as long as they speak Greek and are free of bloodguilt. Those already instructed in both Mysteries come to celebrate Demeter, goddess of grain and a fruitful harvest. Others, like us, are here to complete their initiation.

Yesterday evening, after invoking the blessings of the gods, the hierophant informed all initiates that we must fast each day from dawn till dusk, and directed the crowd to swear an oath, in unison, never to reveal the secret rites of the Greater Mysteries.

By the light of the full moon, the priests and priestesses led the procession from the Agora to Demeter's sacred temple, the Eleusinion, at the base of the Akropolis. We walked behind the honour guard of ephebes, who had earlier escorted the goddess's sacred objects from her temple in Eleusis to Athens, borne in baskets by her priestesses. Upon arrival at the temple, they carried them inside, accompanied by singing and dancing from the female neophytes.

I have no idea what is in the baskets. I once asked my father, who scolded me for daring to suppose he would break his vow of silence, and told me I was lucky he hadn't ordered my guardian slave to beat me.

I am not the only one whose curiosity is growing by the day. My comrades are discussing that very subject at this moment.

Finding that none of us has any idea what form the sacred objects take, we fall to complaining how hungry we are, reminiscing about our garrison life on meagre rations, even further reduced some days on the whim of our sergeant.

One of my comrades makes our mouths water with a story of how he and I went hunting early one morning, bagged a brace of hare, cooked them over an open fire and devoured the lot. I go along with the tale, but for the life of me I cannot recall the occasion and feel a sharp pang of fear that my weakness of memory, since the blows to my head from the fists of Tellias, is beyond repair.

Sunset is approaching and soon we will feast on sacrificial pork and the gift-offerings of fruit and grain from other city-states. The feasting, dancing and singing will go on far into the night, illumined by the harvest moon. After that, we'll take some bedding from our knapsacks, wrap ourselves in our cloaks and sleep on the ground.

— o —

It is day three and this morning we witnessed the members of the cult of Asklepios and Hygeia arrive from Epidaurus. They entered through the Sacred Gates and made their way up to the Parthenon to pray to Athena, before descending to the precinct of Demeter.

At sunset, the priests made sacrifices to Zeus, Athena, Demeter and Persephone, but I did not stay for the great feast. Instead, I am back at the Asklepion sanctuary, where the scent of frankincense and eucalyptus reawakens memories of the days I spent here, when my mind and body ached with the shame of defeat. This time, however, I am in the hallowed confines of the abaton, the only one of my group fortunate enough to be spending the night here.

At least Philemon and the others are enjoying the feasting.

Later, as tradition demands, they will come here to keep a vigil outside, under the stars, while we empty-bellied incubants sleep on pallets covered by the hides of sacrificial animals. I am one of scores of pilgrims. So many, that some have to sleep under the porticos.

To pass the time until the sleeping draught arrives, I reflect on the circumstances of my good fortune. Soon after sunrise this morning, Philemon and I, along with others of our group, gathered at the entrance to the Asklepion sanctuary to request a night in the abaton. There were so many petitioners that the temple high priest announced he would only admit childless wives and men with injuries sustained in defence of their city-states. As our ephebe unit had seen no active duty, we had no option but to leave the queue in defeat.

But the temple doctor who treated my tournament injuries had noticed me in the crowd and sent a messenger to summon me. When I was brought to him, he declared he would award me a place because my wounds were suffered in a combat sport, at a festival in praise of Athena. I thanked him for his kindness and he instructed me to come back at dusk when I'd be taken to the sacred spring to bathe.

Every day brings more pilgrims and my hopes of meeting up with a friend I made at the spring festival grow fainter. On the first day, I scoured the Akropolis, starting below the Sacred Gates at the sanctuary of Demeter, but without success. Philemon asked if I was looking for someone but I felt too shy to confess I was. I've been more discreet in my quest since then.

Even though my wish for temple sleep has been granted, I am not wholly at peace. First, because I haven't found my friend, and second, because of the tales I've heard of temple snakes being gathered from their subterranean pit in the tholos and set loose to crawl over the rows of sleeping bodies. The temple keeps records of miraculous healings. I read earlier of a blind woman having her sight restored by a serpent, who healed her eyes with his tongue while she slept. In her dream vision, however, she saw a beautiful youth applying ointment to her eyes.

At last the flicker of lamps indicates the arrival of the attendants. One of them kneels beside me and asks whether I have any questions.

'Will you release the snakes?' I say, trying to sound unconcerned.

'Not tonight. There are too many people. They might be crushed.'

More at ease after hearing this, I repeat the preliminary invocation after him.

I invite a divine presence to come to me in my dreams, and call upon the goddess Mnemosyne to help me remember when I wake up.

Then he hands me the cup and I drink down the draught in one go, eager now to get on with the process. Thank the gods, the bitter taste it leaves in my mouth is less pungent than that on my first visit to the sanctuary. I lie back and close my eyes. At first I am conscious of the coughs and snores of my fellows, but soon I slip out of waking and into dreaming.

— o —

I awake to the sensation of a temple dog licking the scar on my face. My eyes are slow to focus but when they do, I see the familiar form of my temple doctor, kneeling by my side. He shoos the dog away, helps me sit up and holds a cup of honey water to my lips, counselling me to sip it slowly. I expect to see the room as packed with bodies as it was last night, but it is only about one-third full. Four or five other temple doctors are engaged in low conversations with patients.

'How long have I been asleep, sir?'

'You have slept the night through. The sun is up.'

'And where are the incubants who were sleeping next to me?'

'We woke them earlier, a few at a time. It wouldn't do if you all opened your eyes at once, would it?'

I immediately feel foolish.

'Have you anything to relate?' he asks, his tone gentle.

'Yes, sir.'

'Good. Take a little time to collect your thoughts. When you are ready, tell me what you remember.'

I do not need to pause, as I can still see the dream clearly and want to describe it quickly, before my fickle memory releases its hold on it.

'I dreamt I was a child, searching for my mother. I saw a woman walking in a field of wheat and ran after her but when she turned I saw it was the goddess Demeter. I began to cry and she took my hand. We walked together to a beautiful glade by a river where we sat on a carpet of lush grass, shaded by an apple tree. After a while, she picked two fruits from the tree: one gold and one red, and told me to choose. As soon as I took the red apple, she disappeared. After eating the apple, I lay down on the grass and rested until I heard a familiar voice. I opened my eyes to see my mother, weeping with joy. She embraced me and I felt my heart fill with great happiness. I asked her if she could stay with me and she shook her head. She said…'

I try to remember her exact words.

'—She said, *My son, you must take care of your sister*. Then the goddess returned and led her away.'

The doctor waits a few moments and when he is satisfied I am finished, takes some deep breaths.

'This dream refers to your family circumstances. Is that right?'

'Yes. My mother died when my sister, Xanthe, was born. She's fifteen now and has already rejected two suitors.'

'You say Demeter led your mother away. It is unusual for a deity to stand alongside a mortal. What tribe did you mother come from?'

'I believe it was the Hippothontis.'

'And the deme?'

'She was born in Eleusis. She came to Athens when she married my father.'

'Mmm. Her connection to Eleusis probably explains it.' His tone suddenly switches, to one more searching. 'Do you think your mother's death has had a lasting effect on you?'

This question, coming out of the blue, unleashes a torrent of emotion that catches me completely unawares, and I find myself sobbing uncontrollably.

In response, the doctor produces a small pot of herbs which he waves under my nose. I'm glad to say, their scent calms my weeping. He calls an attendant over and instructs him to massage my head, shoulders, the back of my neck and the base of my skull. The man takes his place behind my head, sitting cross-legged on the floor, and begins his work. While his hands knead and glide, the doctor continues his questioning.

'How old were you when your mother died?'

'Five years.'

'Do you remember your distress at that time?'

'I cried only because others in the household were crying. My mother didn't care for me, I had a nurse.'

'You say your mother didn't care for you…what do you mean by that?'

'I mean she didn't wash, dress or feed me.'

'When you were together, did she play with you or tell you stories?'

'If she did, I don't remember.'

The doctor closes his eyes and fills his lungs with air, exhaling noisily. He does this three times, then begins speaking in a low monotone.

'The goddess tells me your mother is a descendant of Eumolpus, first priest of Demeter. With such strong blood, it is no wonder the woman's lot did not satisfy her. She possessed a mind too sharp to be content with household duties. After your birth she suffered melancholia, from which she never fully recovered. With the blessing of the goddess, your mother brings today a message that she loved you but could not express that love because of her sickness of mind. She sees within your sister the seeds of the same condition. Marriage is not the ideal condition for her. Your mother wants you to protect her and says you have it in your power to keep Xanthe from making the same mistake.'

The doctor has stopped speaking, and I allow my thoughts to roam. In truth, his words are borne out by what Xanthe told me on the day of our uncle's party—how she'd overheard the kitchen maids talk of our mother's despondency after my birth. But, as for protecting Xanthe from a life of domesticity, how can I keep her from becoming someone's wife? What else would she do with herself?

My reverie is broken by an increase of pressure at the hands of the masseur. At the same time, the doctor resumes his discourse.

'It could be the same for you, Apollos. Do not drift into a life of restless discontent. Will civic business keep you sufficiently occupied? Contemplate what your true destiny might be. What life are you suited to? That of a statesman? Lawmaker? Poet? Philosopher? Priest? Make your choice and be sure it's a wise one.'

I consider the options he has suggested, noting that 'Pankratiast' had not been among them. I wait to see if the good doctor has any more words of wisdom, but he has closed his eyes and seems to be recovering himself. I watch him shake his body a few times, as if to come back fully into it.

When he opens his eyes, he asks me how I feel about my mother now. This must be a signal to the attendant because he removes his hands, bows to us both, and leaves us.

I sit up and adjust my position so my back is resting against the temple wall, striving to marshal my thoughts to answer him.

'I didn't realise how much I missed a mother's affection until now. At first, I thought my nursemaid, Dorcas, filled the role. But when I grew older and went to school, she spent more time with my sister. And once Xanthe was too old to need her, she went to live with a cousin of our family who required her services.'

I'm about to say I wish my mother had never died, but knowing she'd still be unhappy had she lived, I bite back the words.

'And what of your father? Did he show affection to you and your sister?'

'I have no complaints of him, sir. But he is sadly no longer with us.'

'What have you learned from your dream, Apollos?'

'I'm sorry my mother was unhappy. I wish she could have paid me more attention, but now I've heard the explanation for her reticence, I understand.' I hesitate to go on, because I am unused to expressing such thoughts and feelings, but the words that have sprung to my mind now spring to my lips. 'I don't blame her for neglecting me.'

The doctor nods, as if confirming the appropriateness of my answer.

'And what of her belief that you can help your sister avoid living a life that does not suit her?'

'I have no idea how to do that.'

'That doesn't mean it isn't possible. Be open to opportunities and see what comes.'

I can sense that he considers his work is done but I still have two questions.

'Sir, can I ask the meaning of the two apples the goddess Demeter offered me. What if I had chosen the golden one?'

'The golden apple is a symbol of discord, Apollos. Had you chosen that, I'm afraid your dream would have ended very differently. Luckily, you chose the red. In the context of your dream, it symbolises love.'

Pleasantly relieved, but not much the wiser, I ask the question that has been on my mind ever since I first met the doctor.

'Is there a remedy that will make all my memories return to me?'

Though his expression is sympathetic, the doctor's words are candid.

'Before you bathed in the sacred spring today, I asked whether you could recall the events of your life in the intervening time since sustaining your injuries and you said you could. You also seem cognisant of most of your past, even from the age of five. Ask yourself if the loss of a few minor details is such a tragedy. Perhaps some of them are not worth remembering.'

He gets up slowly and holds out his hand to help me up. I retrieve my cloak and knapsack from an attendant, paying him to sacrifice a cockerel to Asklepios on my behalf, before I walk with the doctor to the door.

'Thank you, sir, I am in your debt.'

'It's my pleasure,' he replies, as we brush hands in farewell. Lowering his voice to a whisper, he adds, 'Remember, you have chosen love. And the heart is the soul's gateway to the divine.'

Chapter 22

Seb woke to the persistent beep of the alarm, not sure which day it was and where he should be. He squinted at the bedside clock he'd had since he was a teenager—like the yew chest, one of the few reminders of his former existence. The clock face showed it was eight-fifteen on Tuesday morning. If he didn't get a move on, he wouldn't have time to record his dream before the biochemistry session in the lab at ten.

When he'd finished writing, he ventured out of his room to make breakfast and noticed Nick still wasn't up. This came as no surprise, since the poker night had gone on until the early hours, and Nick had drunk a good deal of the bottle of whisky he'd taken with him. Seb was glad they'd gone in his car; at least *he* wasn't nursing a hangover.

A bit later, he knocked on Nick's door.

'It's nine-thirty man. You getting up?'

From inside came a grunt, followed by an expletive to the effect that he wanted to be left alone.

On Seb's way back from the lab, he sat in the founder's garden to enjoy the unusually clement weather. Just the day for a bike ride, he thought. That gave him an idea. The afternoon was scheduled for writing up reports of the practicals, but he could do that later. Now would be a good time to pick up his bike from Joe, the man who'd introduced him to natural remedies in the first place.

A nagging voice in his head told him he should be getting in touch with Sybil to arrange a meet-up, but he felt little enthusiasm for another discourse on Greek culture and customs, so he rang Joe, who said he'd be delighted to see him.

He was on the road in next to no time, stopping off to buy a half bottle of rum, which his old friend hugged to his chest when Seb presented it.

'Good to see you, boy. I was wondering when I'd hear from you. Will you join me in a tipple?'

Seb shook his head.

'No thanks, but you go ahead. How are you?'

'Not too bad, not too bad. I keep the arthritis away with one of my *ancient potions*,' he said, winking as he emphasised the last two words. 'Which is the kind of thing you'll be learning how to concoct, no doubt. Except you'll be studying the chemical whys and wherefores.' He opened the bottle and poured himself a tot. 'How do you like the place?'

Seb slipped comfortably back into the easy rapport they'd had on the farm, as he chatted about the Foundation and the scholarship he'd been given. In his turn, Joe passed on what he'd heard about the new farm tenant, along with snippets of news about fellow workers.

As the afternoon wore on and the brandy exerted its influence, Joe began to reminisce.

'I'm glad you're finally getting some proper schooling, lad. I never agreed with Josie taking you away from school. Neither did my Maggie. That's why they fell out.'

This was news to Seb. Joe's wife had been kindness herself to him. Joe used to take him home to see her sometimes, and she'd always spoiled him with cakes and hugs. When she passed away, he'd been devastated.

'I didn't know that.'

'No, well, like a lot of kids you were never one to pick up on, let's say, the *subtleties* of a situation.'

'My mum kept me away from school because I didn't know my own strength and I knocked somebody over in the playground.'

Joe shrugged.

'If that was the case, every other lad in the school would have been kept home.'

'Why, then?'

Joe breathed deeply.

'Do you really want to know?'

Seb felt his heart flutter. Life had been full of revelations lately. He wasn't sure he was equipped for another, but still he nodded his head.

'One of the teachers told your mum and dad you might have, what she called, "developmental problems". She suggested they should get you checked out. That's why your mum took you away.'

'What? You must be joking! I could read and write before I went to school. And tie my shoelaces,' he added, red-faced.

'It wasn't that sort of problem, Seb. According to her, it was your emotional development.'

Seb's heart sank.

'So the school wanted me to see a shrink.' He brooded for a few seconds. 'Why didn't my parents just refuse and leave me in school anyway?'

Joe took another sip of brandy, his eyes becoming misty.

'That's what your dad wanted, and my Maggie agreed. They thought you needed to be with other children, but your mother took offence and nobody could persuade her to change her mind.' He paused. 'My Maggie delivered you, you know. She said you were one of the bonniest babies she'd ever brought into the world.'

Seb couldn't believe his ears.

'You mean, she knew my real mother?'

'She didn't *know* her. She was the midwife who had the job of delivering the baby...you. She tried to persuade the woman to keep you but she was set on giving you up for adoption. It was a coincidence that your new parents turned out to be Pete and Josie. Maggie always said if Josie had been half the parent Pete was, you'd have been all right.'

Seb tried hard to make sense of what he was hearing. Josie might have been a bit remote at times, leaving him to school himself while she went riding, but being outside on the farm with Pete and Joe and the others had made up for that, hadn't it?

'Why did Maggie think that about my mum?'

'Look, I can say this now because the poor woman's passed away. It was always Pete who wanted a family. Josie went along with the adoption for his sake. You see, she always had trouble with her nerves. That's why she gave up teaching. Couldn't stand the stress. Maggie reckoned you didn't get enough mothering and that's why you didn't know how to express yourself properly.'

A memory of Apollos's dream and the temple doctor's questions swam into Seb's mind. Apollos hadn't been able to remember his mother playing with him or telling him stories. Come to think of it, neither could he.

'I've said too much,' said Joe, his voice hoarse. 'I didn't want to upset you, Seb. But you're a man now. You've got a right to know about your past.'

They gazed at each other and Seb gained strength from the kindness in Joe's eyes.

'I spoke to my biological father for the first time yesterday, Joe. His name's Teodor Ophis. Believe it or not, he's the founder of the college. One of the lecturers from Whitwell Hall put me in touch with him.'

Joe put down his glass.

'Well, I'll be…I was just about to tell you his name.'

Seb stared at him in wonder.

'How do you know that?'

'Pete and I were good friends. He confided in me a lot…when things weren't going so well with the business, that sort of thing. He told me he received a very generous monthly payment from your birth father until you turned eighteen. Purely voluntary. Pete never asked for it. Once that stopped, he found it hard to make the books balance. I don't suppose there was much left in the pot for you. Am I right?'

Seb nodded. 'About two thousand, all told.'

'That's tough on you, lad. It should have been a lot more than that. Looks like your inheritance was used to subsidise our wages.'

'My pleasure,' said Seb, feeling suddenly lighter. 'It couldn't have gone to a better cause.'

He stood up to go and Joe staggered to the shed to get his bike.

'Did you keep any furniture, at all?' said Joe, passing Seb the bike.

Seb shook his head. 'I had nowhere to keep it, so I got the auction rooms to do a house clearance.' Then he remembered Joe's birthday gift to him. 'I've still got my chest, though.'

Joe beamed. 'I'm glad to hear it. The wood came from a churchyard yew. They used to plant them next to churches because they believed the yew protected against evil by driving away devils.'

'Why was it cut down?' said Seb, fastening his bike to the roof rack.

'Health and safety. They're poisonous.'

'I promise I won't try to eat it.'

Chuckling, Joe patted him heartily on the back.

'Great to see you, lad. You're always welcome.'

Seb grinned. 'Have you got any more revelations up your sleeve?'

'I think I've already told you this one, but I'll remind you. When you're healing someone, whether four-legged or two, you know you're on the right track if your hands get all warm and tingly.'

Seb laughed and jumped in the car, hooting as he drove off. On the way back, he realised he hadn't had anything to eat for hours so he stopped at a roadside café for an all-day breakfast. While he ate, he mulled over what Joe had told him, revelling in the bit about Teo sending Pete money, and fretting over the allegation that his emotional skills had been undeveloped. He wasn't even sure what that meant.

When the waitress brought the bill, he found he didn't have enough cash, so he used his credit card. As he put the card back in his wallet, he noticed Birdie's address card in the next slot. In the car, he scrutinised the card and saw that he'd be passing her road on his way home. It wouldn't hurt to ring her, surely. Perhaps she could explain the emotional skills thing to him.

Within fifteen minutes he was sitting in her front room, a cup of tea on the table beside him, enjoying the scent of roses and vetiver permeating the room from an aroma diffuser.

'Now then, Seb,' said Birdie. 'What's on your mind?'

He gave her an edited version of his conversation with Joe, leaving out the bit about Teo and keeping in Joe's observations on the wisdom or otherwise of Josie's decision to keep him away from school, including the teacher's reference to his lack of emotional skills.

'I wouldn't worry about it too much, lovey. We've all got different levels of, what they used to call, "emotional intelligence". You don't strike me as being on the *spectrum*, if you catch my drift.'

Seb didn't catch her drift but nonetheless felt reassured by her words.

In the meantime, Birdie had closed her eyes, remaining like that for some minutes.

'The Team are telling me you were very young when you were separated from your birth mother. Is that right?'

'Yes. I think I was two days old,' he answered, wondering who "the team" were and why Birdie's voice sounded different.

'They say the bond was established and your mother didn't leave you lightly. She had to tear herself away and that sadness has never left her. In the same way, your two-day-old self felt the anguish of separation and your present self has not yet recovered. This sense of abandonment is what the teacher detected, but didn't understand.'

Until then, Seb had felt quite calm, but these words triggered an avalanche of racking sobs which had him fighting for breath.

Birdie left the room and returned with a dropper bottle and a blanket, which she tucked around him.

'This is a rescue remedy, Seb. Open your mouth. I'm going to put four drops on your tongue. It'll make you feel better.'

When his grief subsided, she began to speak, this time in her natural tones.

'I sense you've experienced a clearing, not only for the separation from your birth mother, but for the unexpressed sorrow at the sudden passing of your life parents, Peter and Josie.' She paused. 'How do you feel about Josie, after what your old friend told you today?'

'I feel she did her best but I wish she'd let me be the same as everyone else.'

'And your birth mother?'

This scene was feeling very familiar to Seb.

'I don't blame her.'

The similarity between this exchange and the one between Apollos and the temple doctor struck a chord with him, and the doctor's words to Apollos floated into his head: *Remember, you have chosen love*.

'Are you ready to continue, Seb?' said Birdie, breaking into his reflections.

He nodded, wondering what he was letting himself in for.

'The Team are confirming that you've begun a clearing of the emotional trauma you suffered at birth…'

'Sorry, Birdie, but who is this team exactly?'

Birdie's face expressed exasperation at being interrupted, but she nevertheless delivered a civil answer.

'A group of Higher Beings, but they always speak to me as one voice. It's called channelling.'

'You mean you've got a direct line to a supernatural squad?' said Seb, momentarily forgetting that he didn't necessarily believe in the supernatural.

'Yes. It's a gift,' said Birdie, beaming with pride. 'Hold on, your message is coming.'

Birdie began nodding her head rapidly, as if receiving mental dictation.

'They're telling me you also have a burgeoning gift. You receive information out of the blue. Is that right?'

'Er, yeah, I suppose so. Every so often I come out with a word or expression I've never heard before.'

'That's how it starts. It's up to you whether you develop it or not. Think of it as intuition. As you're training to be a healer, I'd say it could prove invaluable.'

Birdie fell quiet, leading Seb to think this would be a good time to make a move, so he pointedly removed the blanket from his legs.

'Just a minute,' she said, 'They haven't finished yet. They're saying there's a female presence of whom you must beware. They're trying to show…'

Seb's phone rang at that point and Birdie shrank back into her normal self, like a deflated balloon.

'My fault, love, I forgot to ask you to turn off your phone. Was it anyone important?'

'Only Nick. I'll ring him back later. What was that about a female presence?'

Birdie looked disconcerted.

'I don't always remember what I've said after I've tuned out. I wouldn't worry about it.'

'Okay. I have to get going, anyway. Thanks a lot, Birdie.'

He stopped short, trying to remember whether he should have called her Bridie instead. He didn't want to offend her.

'I'm Birdie to my friends, and I definitely consider you one,' she said, smiling. 'How's Fliss, by the way? Have you patched up your little tiff yet?'

He felt himself blush.

'Not yet.'

'Well don't leave it too long. She's a good girl and she'd go to the ends of the earth for a friend. I know you think she's been interfering in your private business but she's only doing it because she believes you'd be happier with a family to love you.'

'Are you sure she's not the female I have to beware of?' he said, half-joking, half-serious.

'Don't be ridiculous. That girl thinks the world of you and you'd be mad to let her go.'

When Seb got back to the flat, with the packs of lager Nick had asked him to bring, he found Nick and Jim engaged in a computer game tournament, which they insisted he joined in.

He'd had enough deep talking for one day and was more than happy to indulge in an evening of ersatz blood and guts, courtesy of virtual warfare, sustained by lager and pizza.

That night, he mentally scrolled through the day's events. Bit by bit, his past was revealing itself. And as it did, his mind was getting clearer.

Chapter 23

At last the day has come when we set out on the Grand Procession from Athens to Eleusis. Thousands of pilgrims have been gathered at the Dipylon Gate since sunrise. Vendors have exhausted their supplies of food and drink; our knapsacks have been loaded onto pack donkeys; and the city has issued us with free staffs of bound myrtle to assist us on our way.

Now we are waiting, in white robes and myrtle crowns, for the sacred objects to be brought from the Eleusinion by the purple-cloaked hierarchy of the Demeter priesthood. Only then can we begin the fourteen-mile march along the Sacred Way to escort them to the sanctuary of Demeter in Eleusis.

Even at this time of the morning everyone is excited, and when the procession finally moves off, in the wake of the sacred objects, we all cheer and wildly swing our myrtle branches, like children let out of school.

Once we have passed the cemetery, the priests and priestesses start to sing Homer's Hymn to Demeter, which begins with the abduction of her daughter, Persephone, by the god Hades who carries her off to the Underworld to seduce her. Demeter wanders the earth searching for her, refusing to eat until she finds her daughter.

By the time they get to the part when Demeter destroys the harvest, in retaliation for Zeus failing to rescue her daughter, we have reached the sanctuary of Aphrodite, where the procession comes to a halt.

Philemon and I sit on the sanctuary steps and gaze at the statue of Aphrodite, goddess of love and beauty, the sight of her reminding me of the temple doctor's words: *You have chosen love*. Some pilgrims are plucking branches of myrtle from their staffs to offer the goddess, others are buying votive tablets and terracotta figures from the sanctuary attendant.

'Are you going to invest?' I ask Philemon, paving the way for my own imminent purchase.

'Why not?' he answers, slightly to my surprise. 'And you?'

'Of course,' I say, matching his tone. 'The time is ripe for love, my friend. For both of us, in our own way.'

Philemon's face darkens for a moment, perhaps indicating he suspects I deem his mode of love inferior to mine. But I tousle his hair, as old friends can, and in response he jumps to his feet, sprinting towards the attendant as if we're in a race.

'I'm out of practice,' I gasp, catching up with him as he is choosing a painted tablet of Aphrodite sitting astride a swan.

'You've been eating too much pork,' he laughs.

I inspect the attendant's goods, expecting to see turtle doves and dolphins; instead, I am faced with crude earthenware genitalia, both male and female. In the end, observing my dissatisfaction, he fetches another tray, from which I select the figure of a sea turtle.

Philemon and I each find a niche in the rock to place our offering and stand, arms outstretched, to voice our prayers to the goddess. As I still have not confided in Philemon, I do not name the object of my affections, but simply ask the goddess to bring me love.

Philemon's prayer is in the same vein: he asks for love to come to him, a promising sign he's beginning to recover from the loss of his beloved Diogenes.

The procession soon resumes its advance along the Sacred Way and the priests, priestesses and anyone who knows the words, resume singing the Hymn to Demeter.

We hear that Zeus finally capitulates to Demeter and sends his messenger, Hermes, to order Hades to release Persephone from the Underworld. Her daughter returned, Demeter restores the cycle of seasonal growth and fruitful harvests. But Hades had tricked Persephone into eating some pomegranate seeds before she left, which means she will always have to stay one third of the year underground. And during that time of winter, the earth sleeps with her until her return in the spring.

Just as the last notes of the hymn are sung, we reach the bridge which marks the boundary between Athens and Eleusis. We file across, to be greeted on the other side by the priests of Krokos, who invite us to rest there while they tie saffron-coloured ribbons around the right hand and left leg of every initiate, to protect us against evil spirits.

As we are younger and stronger than many of the crowd, we are eager to get going, but the priests have much to do, there being so many limbs to decorate. When at last their work is done, we move onward to the Bridge of Jests, where masked jesters mock and jeer at some of the illustrious personages in the procession, to the amusement of all.

As dusk falls, the torches are lit and we finally arrive at the Great Forecourt of the sanctuary of Demeter to enjoy an evening of singing, dancing and feasting in honour of the goddess.

— o —

Once we have paid our respects to the god Hades, in his temple set in a cave in the hillside, Philemon and I meet up with our comrades near the Well of Beautiful Dancing, where conjurers and jugglers vie with acrobats and musicians for a few coins to be thrown in their hat. Having satisfied our appetites at the feasting place, we make our way to a hostel, planning to leave our staffs and knapsacks and return to the festivities. Once there, however, being tired after the heat and dust of the day's march, some of our group decide to stay put, Philemon among them.

Those of us who have got our second wind return to the well, in time to see the priestesses perform the dance of the First Fruits of the Harvest while carrying a lighted kernos on their heads, consisting of a circle of pots containing poppy seedpods, wheat, barley, lentils, oil and honey, with the candle in the centre.

Their dance begins slowly but speeds up as the spectators began to clap more quickly, no doubt hoping for one or more of them to lose their headgear. These young women are too nimble, though, to put a foot wrong.

Soon the crowd begins to follow them as they sway and spin in ever-increasing circles around the well, managing to dance with a minimum amount of spillage. Some of them even let go of the kernos as they dance, such is their skill.

In no time, we are swept along with the dance, joining in the laughter and whooping. The priestesses link arms in pairs and the crowd begins to copy them, linking up with whoever's next to them. One of my companions prances off with a matronly woman, another skips away more sedately with a tall, thin man who resembles a scribe. Before I can look to my left or right, I feel a soft hand on my arm and turn to see the friend I have sought since the first day of the festival.

'Pelagia! Where have you been?'

'Keep dancing, Apollos, and I'll tell you when we stop.'

We dance one further circuit of the well and when next we pass close to an ancient olive tree with a vast, twisted trunk, she leads me round it so we can disappear into the shadows.

'Where are we going?' I gasp, my heart pounding from the dancing and from the excitement of finding her at last.

'To my house. There will be no one there. When they finish this dance, the other priestesses are going to the telesterion to keep an all-night vigil over the sacred objects.'

'I don't think I can dance another step.'

She laughs and takes me by the hand. Within minutes we are outside her house. It is within the temple precinct: one of several small dwellings grouped around a large villa.

'What about the slaves?' I say, thinking of her reputation.

'They sleep in the house of the high priestess. We won't be disturbed.'

Pelagia takes me into a reception room and launches into her tale of woe.

'I was supposed to accompany the sacred objects to Athens with the others, but I disagreed with the high priestess on a matter concerning the management of the sanctuary. She seems to forget that my lazy ex-husband always left the running of his estate to me, so I know a sight more about it than she does. Anyway, the night before the procession left, she told me I had to stay here and supervise the cleaning of the telesterion. Can you believe it? I've a good mind to fashion an effigy of her and bind it. That'll clip her wings.'

As she relives the dispute, her colour rises, tinting her alabaster cheeks a delicate pink. To me, it only makes her all the more beautiful. I'm sure she's not serious about making a leaden image of the high priestess. I could never believe my beautiful Pelagia would engage in curse magic.

'So that's why I couldn't find you,' I say, accepting some water and wine. 'I've been looking everywhere.'

'Sorry. I had no way of getting word to you.'

'Five months has felt like five years.'

'For me, too, Apollos.'

She moves closer and touches the scar on my cheek.

'How did you get this?'

'At the games.'

'And did you suffer any other injuries?'

'A blow to the head, broken ribs and some bruising of the body.'

She kisses my scar softly and takes my hand.

'Come. You should bathe after your journey. Then I'll anoint you.'

— o —

I wake some time after dawn in the arms of Pelagia and silently give thanks to Aphrodite for her beneficence at reuniting us. I get up to relieve myself and return to her bed, drinking in the sight of her shapely form and lustrous black hair, so long it almost covers her breasts.

'My love,' I whisper, kneeling beside her. 'I'm sorry to wake you but you must tell me what to do. What happens next?'

Her lids open and she reaches out to me drowsily.

'Stay here and rest with me all day before you go to the telesterion this evening.'

Even in my ignorance of the details of the initiation, I know this can't be right, so I begin to get dressed, which spurs her on to reach for her temple robe and arrange her hair in a style suitable for the morning.

'Do you expect any house slaves yet?' I ask, nervous that, if discovered, my presence in Pelagia's house might lead to her expulsion from the service of Demeter.

'If they come, what does it matter? I'm not required to be celibate. I was married for five years, remember.'

How could I forget? You're as skilled as any of the girls at Nikoleta's place.

But thoughts such as these are inappropriate to voice.

'What about your argument with the high priestess? Are you still out of favour?'

'Bah! Iphigeneia is a bitch. But we're related on my mother's side, so she can't get rid of me. I'll be doling out the happy juice later on, don't worry.'

'The what?'

'The kykeon. We've got to give you initiates something to remember, haven't we?'

'What do you mean? It's made from barley and mint, isn't it?'

'Let's just say it's a special recipe.' She winked. 'Greater than the sum of its parts.'

'I can't wait,' I said, fascinated by her relaxed attitude to the approaching religious rites. Rites which were usually spoken of in hushed tones.

Pelagia leaves the room and comes back with some barley bread soaked in wine.

'Here, have this. You've earned it.'

'I'm supposed to be fasting.'

'Eat it. Who's going to know?'

I devour it and she brings me two more bowls.

'Come into the reception room and you can tell me what's been happening to you. We didn't do much talking last night.' She smiles at me and my heart melts. 'And if anyone asks why you're here, I'll say I instructed you at the Lesser Mysteries and you've come to pay your respects.'

'Which is true,' I answer, giving her a final kiss.

So we withdraw from the bedchamber and sit on opposite sides of the room, for the sake of propriety, which is fortunate because just as I finish telling her about my night in the abaton, a young woman in the garb of a novice priestess enters the room.

'Excuse me, priestess Pelagia. High priestess Iphigeneia requests your presence in the telesterion. She wishes you to guard the sacred objects while the others sleep.'

I sense from the way Pelagia's lips tighten, that this order does not please her, but she nods, tells the girl she will come immediately and signals her to go.

Sighing, she stands up, patting her hair and smoothing her robe.

'Now I have no free time left today, thanks to Iphigeneia.' She takes my hand and looks up at me, her dark eyes misty. 'You asked what happens next. Today you must take your ritual bathe in the sea and change into clean clothes. After that, go to a recording priest who will check your name against his list and exchange your myrtle wreath for a ribboned one. Only the officiating priests wear myrtle in the telesterion. The priest will tell you when and where to assemble. Make sure you take a cup with you for the kykeon.'

'And what of us?' The lump in my throat almost chokes me at

the thought of not being able to see her again.

'I will see you after your initiation.'

'But how? Where? You might not find me.'

'I won't drink any kykeon, so I'll have my wits about me.'

'Do you promise?'

'Yes.'

She walks me to the door and puts her arms around me, pressing her head to my chest.

'Give Philemon and the others my good wishes,' she says, as she opens the door. 'I hope they benefit from tonight's performance. I personally favour the festival of the Lesser Mysteries over the Greater. I enjoy teaching initiates the significance of the myth and the secret chants they need to travel safely through the Underworld. I much prefer it to the conjuring show you'll see later.'

Chapter 24

When I reach the hostel, I'm happy to find Philemon still resting. He greets me gladly, telling me he feared I'd been set upon by thieves. On the way from Pelagia's house, I'd been debating whether to tell him the truth or concoct a tale that I'd fallen asleep by the well, but his heartfelt relief at seeing me prompts me to be straight with him.

'Where are the others?' I ask.

'They've gone to see the lifting up of the bulls.'

'Think I'll steer clear of that,' I say, not one to relish the sight of a gang of ephebes hoisting a sacrificial bull on their shoulders for its throat to be cut.

'Me, too,' he says and we exchange a smile of accord.

As there is no one else in the room, I sit beside him on the floor and begin to explain.

'I was with Pelagia last night, our teacher at Agrai. We became close at that time and vowed to meet again on the second day of the Greater Mysteries, at the feasting place. But the high priestess gave her duties to perform here, so she didn't get to Athens. We finally met last night at the Well of Beautiful Dancing and she took me to her house.'

Philemon's face is a picture of amazement.

'I didn't tell you this before because Pelagia and I agreed to keep quiet about our attachment. I'm sorry, Philemon, if you feel I've been deceitful.'

He shakes his head.

'Love makes deceivers of us all, Apollos. Be sure, I am not offended. I can see in your face when you speak of her that you're lovestruck. But was it not perilous to spend the night with a priestess on temple ground? And is she not married?'

I feel my blood rise.

'I'm no adulterer, Philemon. Her husband divorced her

because she couldn't bear him a child.'

'That doesn't mean *she's* barren. Take care, Apollos.'

The fact that her husband might have been infertile had not occurred to me and I begin to worry about the consequences of our night together.

'I expect she knows what she's doing,' he says quickly.

I am aware that Philemon means to comfort me, but instead it stirs in me doubts about my lover's virtue. My only defence is to pass on her message.

'She sends her good wishes, by the way.'

That seems to please him.

'Do give her mine, when you next see her. Which will be...?'

'Tonight, when the ceremony is over.'

'And afterwards, will you walk to the Rharian Plain for the dancing and feasting?'

Unwilling to commit myself, in case my lover decides against it, I can only say, 'I hope so,' and leave it at that.

— o —

Night has fallen and Philemon and I are waiting in line, having bathed in the sea with the other initiates and changed into fresh tunics, saved for this occasion. We've exchanged our myrtle wreaths for crowns of ribbons and flowers and are each holding a cup, bought from a temple vendor. Once the word is given, we are admitted, amid much pushing and shoving, to the telesterion, the windowless initiation hall, whose west wall is cut deep into the rock of the hillside. At the Lesser Mysteries we learned that our entry into the 'earth' reflects Persephone's journey to the Underworld, although our 'underworld' is bathed in the muted light of wall torches and the heady scent of incense.

The roof of the vast hall is supported by an array of columns. On three sides, there are eight tiers of steps and we are directed to the highest tier by an attendant. The southern wall is bare of steps and has three doors, leading to we know not where. There is an air of excited anticipation and the noise rises as the tiers fill up. Once they are full, people sit or stand at the base of the steps.

At Agrai, Pelagia told us we would see an enactment of the Demeter-Persephone myth, followed by the revealing of the sacred objects which lie within the anaktoron. This stone chamber, whose open-sided roof is raised above that of the main hall, lies in the middle of the telesterion and is only accessible to the hierophant. It is no surprise then, when the door of the anaktoron opens from within and the hierophant, an impressive figure with long curly hair and beard, emerges to announce the start of the play.

But this is not a drama as we know it. For a start, the actors do not have the customary face masks: these masks only cover their eyes. And while there are musicians playing flute and drums, there is no chorus to comment on the dramatic action of the play. More unusual still, the female parts are played by women—something unheard of in any theatre.

As the players enter from one of the doors in the southern wall, behind which must lie a dressing room, the re-enactment of the myth begins, with Persephone kidnapped by Hades, god of the Underworld, as she picks flowers in a meadow.

The actors dance the action without speaking, moving about the hall so all can see them, while the hierophant takes the place of the chorus, singing a commentary in a lyric baritone; frequently and enthusiastically clashing a cymbal for dramatic effect.

Later in the play, the hierophant halts the performance and announces an interval, for the kykeon to be served.

As the players exit, a flock of priestesses appear from another door with jugs of a thick, soupy liquid. The taste is not particularly pleasant but I manage to keep it down. I had hoped to see Pelagia, but there are hundreds upon hundreds of initiates to be served and I do not catch sight of her.

Once the priestesses have gone and we have emptied our cups, the hierophant shouts, 'Good people! Now is the time for you to come to the aid of grieving Demeter, to help her find her daughter, Persephone!'

The attendants exhort us to put down our cups, descend to ground level and follow the goddess and her priestesses, who are bearing torches. When I hear someone whisper that the person playing Demeter is the high priestess, I cannot help but remember Pelagia calling her a she-dog, and find myself laughing out loud. As we move quickly, in columns, following the high priestess around the great hall, weaving and winding like a giant serpent, there is much foolery and merriment. Those who topple over have to be saved by attendants who weave their way through the throng to rescue them, placing them on the steps, out of harm's way.

All at once, a gong begins to rumble and the drums roll; the acrid smell of extinguished torches fills the air and we are plunged into pitch-black darkness. We find ourselves pulled and pushed by unseen hands. The shouts and screams are horrible to hear. I feel myself trembling and sweating with fear, imagining myself imprisoned in the pit of Tartarus, worst hell of all, at the mercy of hostile phantoms, never to see daylight again. I hear a volley of sobs around me and succumb to tears myself. The air is thick with the sound of weeping and wailing.

Once again the gong thunders, this time accompanied by smoke and flashes of lightning. The cries of the crowd reach such a crescendo that I think I will go mad. Until, little by little, a strange and wonderful light illumines the anaktoron from within and an awed silence descends.

I scan the hall, expecting to see broken limbs and bruises but there is no sign of any carnage. All eyes are focused on the outer walls of the anaktoron, now transformed into the fields of Elysium, yellow with corn and bright with poppies, where men and women are eternally at leisure, playing musical instruments and taking part in athletic games.

An invisible choir in perfect harmony begins to sing, heralding the appearance of the beautiful young woman who plays Persephone. She throws off her eye mask and walks slowly around the anaktoron so all the spectators can see her. My heart nearly bursts from my chest with pride when I see it is Pelagia.

Moments later, Demeter appears and enfolds her in a rapturous embrace. Her ecstasy is infectious, giving rise to cries of joy and frantic stamping of feet from the crowd. I can see now that the light within the sacred chamber is coming from a huge fire, whose flames reach upward to the open-sided roof chimney.

The hierophant is next to make an entrance, triumphantly displaying a sheaf of wheat made of gold, which he places in the centre of a display altar. His final commentary, declaimed in exultant tones, celebrates Demeter's restoration of fertility to the earth and her gift of The Mysteries to humankind.

Now is the moment we've all been anticipating—our long-awaited sight of the sacred objects. A hush descends in the telesterion as the hierophant enters the anaktoron and brings out the chest, unpacking the sacred objects and placing them on three trays. He is joined by the chief torch-bearer and the chief herald, who each take a tray and follow him in procession around the hall, while a chorus of voices off-stage lead us in the secret chants Pelagia taught us in the spring.

From where I am standing, unrestricted by a column, I have quite a good view, and I cannot help but find the objects disappointingly mundane: sesame cakes, apples, figs, ears of wheat and barley, pomegranates, lumps of salt, wool, poppy seeds, amber, a conch shell, boughs of ivy. All that is, except one: a carved phallus which he holds aloft, giving rise to much whispering and giggling.

The circuit completed, the three men return the sacred objects to the chest. The hierophant then places one of them into a small basket, which he covers with a veil and hands to the high priestess, still in her role as Demeter. That done, he calls for silence in stentorian tones and instructs us to approach her throne one by one, speak the holy words, and thereafter do her bidding. Only then will we have fulfilled the sacred rite.

I'm beginning to feel lightheaded from the kykeon, and would dearly love to sit down, but in response to his order there is a great jostling for position, and I am carried along with the crowd, nearer and nearer to the throne. Fortunately, the attendants restore order, pushing us back so we can't see what is happening until it comes to our turn.

I have no one to talk to in the queue, having lost sight of Philemon among the hordes during the long darkness, but my mind is still soaring with the gods and time seems to fly. After I don't know how long, I am standing in front of the high priestess and I address her as we rehearsed at the Lesser Mysteries.

'Hail Demeter, lady of much bounty, of many measures of corn. I have fasted, I have drunk the kykeon, I have beheld the sacred objects. I beg to receive a sacred object from the chest, place it in the basket, work it, and take it from the basket into the chest.'

I had thought it would be up to me to choose an object but, to my dismay, she asks me to take the phallus from the chest while she unveils the small basket she is holding, revealing the object therein to be a conch shell. She then instructs me to put the phallus into the basket without letting go of it, demonstrating with her hand a thrusting motion towards the shell. I can feel my face burn as I force myself to perform this louche act. The impassive expression on her face never wavers, however, as she indicates, with a glance towards the chest, that I should put the phallus back.

Bending over the chest to do this, I see something in her lap that makes my blood run cold.

'Hold out your right hand.'

I do as she commands.

'Now touch the snake.'

I fully expect to be frozen with fear, but find myself reaching out and touching the coiled, yellow-bellied serpent.

The high priestess nods in approval, saying, 'Go. You are now a child of Demeter and under my protection, even beyond the gates of Hades.'

I move on, my earlier embarrassment swept away by the feeling that captured me when I touched the snake.

In a daze, I climb the steps and stagger out into the cool night air.

'You took your time,' says a familiar voice.

'Pelagia. I am in rapture. You look beautiful. You are Persephone personified.'

Spouting more foolish compliments, I allow myself to be guided to her home where she makes me drink copious cups of water.

Pelagia is tired so we retire to the bedchamber. Though dog-tired myself, I cannot sleep. Nor can I stop talking, reliving the spectacle in the telesterion without pausing for breath, marvelling at my brush with the divine.

'So your trip to Eleusis was worth it,' she said. 'You had your epiphany.'

'I believe so.'

But then I blot my copybook by demanding that she tell me how the effects were achieved.

'You mean, you don't believe they were the acts of the gods?' she says, mockingly. 'Take heed who you confess that to. You could be accused of impiety.'

'Have you any herbs you can give me?' I plead. 'My mind is racing and I crave sleep.'

She leaves the room, yawning, and comes back with a draught.

'It will take a little time to work. In the meantime, tell me what's worrying you. If you unburden yourself, you'll sleep more soundly.'

So I confide to her my concerns about Xanthe, my memory lapses, my uncertainty about my future profession, and, most of all, how much I love her and how wretched I will be if I can't find a way of seeing her again once I leave Eleusis.

— o —

I am woken by a kiss from Pelagia, who must be freshly bathed and perfumed because she smells wonderful. I respond to her caress and then something Philemon said yesterday makes me turn away from her.

'What's wrong, Apollos? Are you ill?'

I can't think of a tactful way to say what's on my mind, so I blurt it out.

'I'm sorry, Pelagia. I should have thought of this before, but it only occurred to me recently. Was it you or your husband who was unable to…who was…'

'Barren?' she says, with an edge to her voice.

I take her hand and press it over my heart.

'Did he marry again?'

'Yes.'

'And did he have children?'

'There is a child but I have it on good authority that his wife pretended to be pregnant and sent one of her father's slaves to Mount Lycabettos to pick up a newborn boy. If I'd loved him, I might have considered doing the same.'

'How could she get away with that?'

'He often travelled abroad on business and she chose an opportune time. She padded herself out and went to her parents' house for the "birth". They probably sprinkled some pig's blood around, to make it more realistic.'

'What if he finds out?'

'I think he'd turn a blind eye. They were married for two

years before the child "arrived". This way, it makes him look more of a man.'

'If it wasn't his, does that mean you might be fertile?'

Pelagia dropped her cynical pose and giggled.

'I wouldn't be surprised, pledged as I am to a goddess of fertility. If I wasn't before, I probably am now.'

I can't tell whether this is a yes or a no but have now grown tired of the subject and proceed to finish what she'd started, making conversation redundant.

'Do we have to go to the Rharian Plain?' I ask her, some time later, happy to remain in bed now my festival mania has passed.

'I think we should.'

Pelagia reminds me that now I am initiated I can wear a myrtle crown, so I fetch one from the diminishing pile of those handed over yesterday and we walk together to the grain fields. Once there, we join the other celebrants in invoking the rebirth of the crops by shouting, 'Rain! Pour down! Conceive sweet earth! Give birth!'

On the way, Pelagia offered solutions to two of the problems I'd shared with her the night before.

She remembered what I'd told her about the message from the goddess Demeter: that my mother was descended from Eumolpus. This, she said, meant that my sister Xanthe was from the house of Eumolpidai and thus eligible to become a novice priestess of Demeter, just as she herself had been eligible through her bloodline to the other great family of Eleusis, the Kerykes.

'It would solve the problem of Xanthe not being keen on becoming a wife, and give you a reason to come to Eleusis regularly,' she said, clasping my hand tightly and making my blood race with the thought of it.

Chapter 25

Seb rubbed his eyes to help him come into the present moment, his head still full of what he'd witnessed through the eyes of Apollos. He relaxed when he remembered it was Wednesday and the morning was lecture-free.

It took over an hour to write his account of the Greater Mysteries and the accompanying events. After he finished, he turned his attention to a sticky note reminding him to look out for any more similarities to Apollos. The only one that sprang to mind was the parallel between his biological mother giving him away, and Apollos's mother consigning him to a nursemaid. So he wrote that they'd both been brought up from birth by women who were not related to them by blood.

It was only then he linked his dream of the purification ritual to Apollos. Was this the ritual his father, Theas, had performed following the death of his wife, Agathe? Was the newborn baby Xanthe, and Apollos the golden-haired child who'd been the last to cry?

Once he was dressed, Seb messaged Sybil to say he'd had two dreams on consecutive nights. Shortly after, he heard a loud yawn from the other bedroom, so he switched on the automatic coffee machine, considered by Nick a necessity and acquired soon after he moved in.

'That smells good,' said his flatmate, emerging in bare feet and dressing gown, his face the colour of putty. 'Just what I need. Two nights over-imbibing on the trot is neither good for man nor beast.'

'Feeling rough?' said Seb, handing him a mug of pricey Colombian coffee.

'And the rest. Remind me not to touch a drop of alcohol next time I'm within spitting distance of a pack of cards or an Xbox. Decided what you're doing with your poker winnings, yet?'

'Eat.'

'Come on, surely you can think of something more exciting than that.'

'Actually, yeah. My car insurance is due soon. Is that exciting enough for you?'

'Good job you got your bike back then,' said Nick, slumping down on the sofa. 'Seriously, though, we've got to think of some way for you to make money. Have you got any special skills?'

Seb almost spat out the mouthful of coffee he'd just swigged. Something about the question had tickled his funny bone.

Nick started to guffaw as well.

'How about a hod carrier on a building site? Or a strippergram? You've got the abs for it.' He adopted the pose of The Thinker, chin in hand. 'I know! You could ask the lovely Sybil if they need a life model in the art studio. For a fee, of course.'

Seb was trying to think of a clever comeback when he was saved by his ringtone. He grinned at Nick and answered the call, mouthing, 'Sybil', to his friend, who mouthed back, 'Go on, ask her.'

'Hi, Seb,' she was saying. 'Were they good?'

He was still trying not to giggle at the mental images that Nick had planted, so was slow to reply.

'—The dreams, Seb. Did you enjoy them?'

'Sorry, Sybil…yes. They covered a few days,' he said, walking into his room and leaving Nick miming the diverse poses of a life model. 'Apollos was at a festival. It started in Athens and ended up in a place that sounded like "El-assis". And I found out who his secret love is.'

'Great. Don't tell me any more, let me read it. It'll be more exciting.'

'Okay. Do you want me to leave the journal in the admin office?'

'Where are you now?'

'The flat.'

'Tell you what, why don't I drive over and get it? We can discuss it this evening, if you're free.'

Seb was about to ask where she was thinking of holding their discussion when he heard, 'I'll come now,' before the line went dead.

'What was all that about?' said Nick, when Seb drifted back into the living room, journal in hand.

'It was Sybil. I had another dream last night. And the night before.'

Nick burst out laughing and Seb joined in, the juxtaposition of 'Sybil' and 'dream' appealing to their schoolboy humour—most definitely in the ascendant this morning.

'You'll have to go easy on the gorgonzola, boy. No more late-night snacks. So what did Miss Hughes want?'

'She's coming here to pick this up,' said Seb, waving the journal. 'Can you make yourself scarce?'

'Why, what do you want to do?'

'I want to be polite and offer her a coffee, without you leering at her.'

'I do not leer, my friend. Unlike you, I know how to behave in the company of an attractive woman. Anyway, I doubt if the coffee bean would make it past her herbal code of conduct.'

When the door buzzer sounded ten minutes later, Nick raced to answer it. Seb, who'd been absorbed in reading over his dream report, swore under his breath in irritation.

'To what do we owe this pleasure?' said Nick, as if her arrival was a complete surprise.

Sybil hovered awkwardly in the doorway, so Seb strode forward to greet her and give her the journal.

'Can we offer you a drink?' said Nick, a model of courtesy.

Seb wondered if he was aware that his dressing gown had fallen open to reveal a pair of dinosaur-patterned pyjama shorts.

Sybil hesitated for a moment, put the journal in her bag and smiled brightly at Nick.

'That's kind of you, but I'm a bit pushed for time. I'm taking Year Three to a holistic healing college in London. We've been invited to have a look round.'

She directed her next smile at Seb, patting her bag.

'I'll be in touch when I've read the latest episode,' she said, disappearing down the stairs.

'Thanks for frightening her off with your hairy legs, mate,' said Seb. 'Now I still don't know where we're meeting.'

'Calm down, young Sebastian, she said she'd get back to you, didn't she? She seems keen to read it. In fact, I wouldn't mind taking a look at it myself. I want to find out what happens next.'

Seb hesitated. He'd been willing to tell Nick about the first dream, but now he'd got to know Apollos better, he wasn't sure he wanted to share him with anyone else. It was bad enough having to discuss his exploits with Sybil.

Nick's ice-blue gaze held a certain challenge, though, as if this was a test of some kind.

'Okay,' he said, and Nick's expression thawed. 'You can read it if you like.'

— o —

Sybil opened her front door and Seb walked straight into the living room. She'd told him it was smaller than Digby's cottage, but he hadn't expected it to be quite so compact. The stairs were towards the back of the room, on the left, and the kitchen led straight off the living room with no dividing wall. In the space under the stairs stood a small console desk, on it a laptop computer and a table lamp.

'This is…cosy,' Seb said.

'You mean tiny. But I'm single, so a one-bedroom place is all I need. There are compensations. I can walk to work in ten minutes. And the Foundation doesn't charge me any rent. It's a perk of the job.'

Seb took in the cushioned window seat with cupboards beneath and the slim display units either side of the chimney breast.

'Everything seems to be about two-thirds normal size.'

'Except me,' she said, laughing. 'Do you want to sit at the table or here?' She gestured towards two squat easy chairs and he shook his head.

'The table's fine.'

There was just enough room on the table for Sybil to consult his journal and make notes in her own. She asked if he wanted anything to drink and he declined, influenced by the risk of spillage due to a lack of elbow room.

Opposite him, she gave a little shudder of excitement.

'You did well. I'd heard about the Eleusinian Mysteries but only as one of many festivals the Greeks held. It was good to have a ringside seat. I suppose you didn't know anything about the festival before you had the dream?'

'Absolutely not. And I still haven't looked it up.'

'Really?'

'No. I had a lecture this afternoon and I wasn't sure how to spell the name of the place. I knew you'd tell me, anyway.'

He caught a fleeting glint of disapproval before she asked if he had any questions, because she *had* looked it up. The most vivid part had been the last night, so he started with that.

'Did anything supernatural actually happen in the initiation hall?' he ventured.

'You mean, was the whole thing a well-rehearsed magic show? No one can say for sure. There's a theory that a fungal parasite in barley, called ergot, turned the kykeon into a psychedelic drug so what Apollos experienced was probably a mixture of hallucination and special effects. If you remember, Pelagia suggested as much.'

'Fungal parasite? Are we talking magic mushrooms here?'

'Er, yes, I suppose so. Ergot does look like a tiny mushroom.

It can cause vertigo, cold sweats, trembling, visions.'

'Ah. That explains why the ceremony wasn't as clear as the rest of the dream. I remember fragments of the play, some of what the hierophant was doing but not the whole thing.'

'Apollos had a good view of the sacred objects, though, didn't he?'

'Yes. The hierophant and the two other priests made sure everyone could see them. But Apollos couldn't understand what was so special about them. And there weren't any oohs and aahs from the congregation either.'

'Perhaps the custom was to observe them in silence. The Mysteries were celebrated for well over a thousand years, so the sacred chest probably contained some other, more ancient, symbols of the harvest, for example, pestles and mortars for grinding grain. In fact, if you think about it, the fertility ritual Apollos had to enact, with the phallus and the shell, could also have been enacted with a pestle and mortar.'

Seb frowned and looked away, embarrassed.

'A bit graphic, wasn't it?'

'To us, yes, but their lives were completely dependent upon the land, much of which was substandard. In a year of drought the people went hungry. The allegory of the sex act symbolising seeds being planted in the earth was one they understood. That's why they shouted for the earth to conceive. Some writers even hinted that the high priestess and the hierophant actually copulated during the play and some of the initiates followed their example!'

Seb shifted uncomfortably on the hard wooden chair.

'Well, if any of that *did* happen, Apollos didn't notice.'

'He was probably too stoned,' said Sybil, and Seb's face broke into a surprised smirk.

'I suppose it could have been expressed symbolically in dance,' said Seb. 'Don't they call it *hieros gamos*?'

Sybil stared at him.

'You've done it again.'

'What?'

'Surprised me with a nugget of wisdom.'

'No more than I surprised myself,' he muttered, offended nonetheless at effectively being called an ignoramus, even though *he* didn't know where the nugget had come from. Unless he chose to believe Birdie's theory that he'd channelled it.

'I forgot to ask,' said Sybil suddenly. 'Did you see everything through Apollos's eyes, as you did in the second dream?'

He nodded.

'That's a shame. An objective view would have been perfect this time. You could have solved the mystery of The Mysteries.'

'What do you mean?'

'Well, what went on in the telesterion is documented up to a point. The dramatisation of the myth and the showing of the objects is common knowledge. But the top-secret thing about the Greater Mysteries was said to be the vision. The question is, what did the initiates witness en masse and why did it make such a powerful and lasting impression on them?'

Seb tried to picture the most memorable part of the ceremony, conscious now that his recall was filtered through a mind which had been well and truly addled by an hallucinogenic drug.

'I suppose it could have been when the outer walls of the central chamber turned into a pastoral scene.'

Sybil didn't look convinced.

'Was that really so spectacular? The vision is supposed to activate a great revelation, leading to a spiritual rebirth. A mural doesn't quite cut it.'

'How was it done, though?'

She shrugged.

'They probably used painted scenic panels, like the ones that decorated the *skene* structure in the Greek theatre. There was plenty of time to put them in place during the blackout.'

'I find it hard to believe there are no records. Surely someone must have squawked.'

'Apparently not.' Sybil shuffled through her notes. 'The punishment for revealing the secrets was a curse from the Eleusinian priesthood, followed by death. So you can't blame them for not "squawking", can you?'

'You mean I could be in trouble?'

She looked puzzled for a moment, then laughed.

'I think you'd be covered by a statute of limitations, considering what you saw took place almost two and a half thousand years ago.' Sybil consulted his journal. 'Can you recall how Apollos felt when he touched the snake?'

Seb turned the journal to face him and read the part Sybil indicated.

'Uh, yeah. You remember he'd been afraid of snakes when he was in the abaton? Well, when he touched the snake in the initiation hall, it was more than a feeling of conquering his fear. It was as if he was at one with the snake. It's hard to explain... he felt...'

'At one with the cosmos?'

'Something like that.'

'That fits in with historic descriptions of initiates experiencing feelings of ecstasy and oneness, which would correspond with the sort of reaction people had to LSD in the sixties and seventies,' she said, with an air of satisfaction.

'So the mystery of Mysteries boils down to ancient Greek psychonauts blissing out on acid,' he said, hoping she'd leave it there.

Sybil gave him a searching look.

'Unless you can tell me otherwise.'

Seb recalled the intense feelings of peace and joy which had engulfed Apollos as he left the telesterion after his 'brush with the divine', which had stayed with him even after the drug had worn off. But being in no mood for a Sybil-sermon implying that an acceptance of the divine would solve all *his* problems, he kept his thoughts to himself.

'No. Only the snake episode.'

'Fair enough. Do you have any memory of the hierophant giving specific instructions on how to behave after death?'

'Um, possibly. There was some engraving on the altar that he kept referring to when he was drawing symbols in the air. He asked the initiates to copy him, and to remember the symbols. But most of them were half-asleep, or on cloud nine, by that time.'

'That doesn't surprise me,' said Sybil. 'They weren't all strict devotees by any means. For many, the festivals were an excuse to feast, make merry and,' she added, smirking, 'get laid.'

'Makes sense,' he said, continuing to replay the scene in his mind. 'And there was something about drinking from the river of memory but not from the river of forgetfulness when they got to the Underworld. Did they really believe if they learned all that hocus-pocus, they'd go straight to heaven?' said Seb, scornfully.

'More or less. The Lethe river of forgetfulness was said to flow through the Underworld. Dead souls drank from it so they wouldn't remember their past lives when reincarnated. The initiates were taught instead to drink from Mnemosyne, the river of memory, which would stop the cycle of reincarnation. It allowed them to go straight to Elysium, where they'd spend eternity in comfort and peace. That's why Elysium was depicted on the walls of the anaktoron.'

'Did the Greeks believe in reincarnation?' said Seb, shocked.

'Some of them. The Eleusinian and the Orphic cults certainly did. Other cults subscribed to a ghostly afterlife with a deep pit of suffering and torment for the very wicked, called Tartarus.'

Seb looked pained.

'I find it hard to believe that a civilisation which introduced democracy to the world would be despotic enough to require their citizens to believe in heaven and hell.'

Sybil made no response, having begun to scribble in her

notebook. Seb watched her, noticing how her lips pursed slightly whilst she was concentrating. When she looked up, there was a new softness in her eyes.

'Shall we talk about Apollos's dream in the abaton, starring Demeter and his mother? What do you make of it?'

Seb brought to mind the emotion Apollos had felt when reporting his dream to the temple doctor—mirroring his own catharsis yesterday, at Birdie's—and his breath caught in his throat.

He waited a few moments before replying.

'I think it was incredibly sad when he cried. But the temple doctor talked him through it and he seemed to come to terms with what happened.'

'Yes. His dream had a good outcome. He forgave his mother.'

'He said *he didn't blame her*. Is that as strong as forgiving? I'm not sure.'

Sybil looked as if she was about to say something about splitting hairs, but instead asked another question.

'Did you make a note of any more similarities between you and Apollos?'

'Yes, at the end of the journal.'

She read it and nodded in approval.

'That's a good observation. Actually, motherhood is the theme of the Persephone myth. Demeter literally went through hell to rescue her daughter. She was the exception, though. Greek mothers in general had a bad press. Look at Medea, one of Euripides' characters. She killed her own children in revenge for her husband taking another wife, whereas Demeter shone as an example of unconditional maternal love.'

'I wouldn't know about that,' said Seb, roughly, 'never having experienced it.'

Sybil blushed.

'Sorry, that was insensitive of me.'

Seb shrugged, while inwardly admitting how disturbing this

dream analysis could be.

He tried to stretch his legs, his shins making painful contact with the spindle of Sybil's chair. Stuck behind the small table, he was starting to feel claustrophobic, wishing he'd taken the other option she'd offered him. But he'd been too impatient to wait another two days for the consultation suite to be available.

Sybil must have sensed he was feeling confined, because she suggested a break. Seb followed her into the kitchen area and remained standing, while she occupied the solitary bar stool beside the narrow worktop.

'So, what do you think of his girlfriend?' said Seb, eager to cut to the chase. Much as he enjoyed writing up the dreams, he found the follow-up sessions frustrating because Sybil never got closer to a conclusion.

'She's certainly a character to be reckoned with. In those times, religion was the only area of activity where women could hold authority and have a certain amount of freedom and independence. I hope she manages to rescue Xanthe from the claustrophobic life of a Greek housewife, even if her only motive is to keep seeing Apollos.'

'Could there be a future for Pelagia and Apollos?' said Seb, surprising himself at how much he wanted it to be so.

'Doubt it. Pelagia's not wife material,' she said, laughing. 'But then, he's too young to marry, so she's probably perfect for him at this point in his life.'

'That's if he ever existed,' said Seb, a strange feeling of loss sweeping over him. 'Isn't he just a figment of my imagination?'

Sybil's reply held a hint of impatience.

'But how can he be, Seb? You're no historian. You couldn't make up the sort of things you've described. You've never heard of most of the activities and customs of Apollos's era.' She paused. 'With the exception of incubation therapy, of course.'

'I don't have an explanation,' he said, feeling confused. 'I thought that was your job.'

'Do you believe in reincarnation?' she said, her voice shaking slightly.

'The rebirth of the soul? To believe that, I'd have to believe in an immortal soul. I told you, I'm an agnostic.'

'Well, I do. And I think your dreams possibly took you to a past life.' She made a note in her notebook. 'I'll have a word with someone who knows about regression and get back to you...'

Seb brought his cup down on its saucer with some force, bringing her speech to a halt.

'Thanks for the tea, Sybil.' He picked up his journal and grabbed his coat from the newel post. 'I'm sorry, but I've had enough of being your lab rat. You promised some sort of diagnosis and treatment of a phantom "condition" but you haven't delivered. This mad theory of reincarnation has just about put the tin lid on it.'

He opened the front door and glared at her startled face.

'See you around. Good luck finding another mug to experiment on.'

Chapter 26

Seb stopped off at the common room for a drink and found Nick playing pool with a girl. The bar itself was still shuttered. Nick hailed Seb when he saw him, so he sauntered over in time to see the girl sink the black.

'Good shot, Suzy,' said Nick, winking at Seb. 'If the bar was open, I'd buy you a drink.'

Seb looked at his watch. It was nine o'clock.

'It'd be open by now if it was going to be.'

'Fancy going into town?'

Nick's invitation was directed at both of them, but Seb guessed his friend was in the mood for a twosome.

'You go ahead. I might track Fliss down.'

Suzy excused herself for a bathroom break and Nick gave Seb a searching look.

'How did your session go with Sybil?'

'Not too good. I ended up telling her to find another mug to practise on.'

'You what? *Mein Gott*, Sebastian, you do have a way with the ladies, don't you? What happened?'

'She said I could be a reincarnation of the ancient Greek... talked about consulting someone who knows about regression. It's bad enough being put under *her* microscope, now she wants to involve someone else. There's no end to it.'

'But the other day you said you wished she'd hurry up and make a diagnosis. Isn't that what she's trying to do?'

Seb scowled.

'I just feel like I'm an exhibit in a freak show.'

'Don't be daft,' said Nick, patting him on the back. 'Have you got your journal with you?'

Seb tapped his coat pocket.

'Let me take it off your hands,' said Nick, with a winning

smile. 'I'll even throw in my professional opinion on the character arc.'

'The what?' said Seb, distractedly.

'The transformation of a character over the course of the story. Has ' h Wotsisname, Apollos, changed since you first encountered him?'

Seb thought about Apollos after his night in the abaton, and nodded.

'Good. That means you're dreaming along the right lines...'

Seb knew Nick was joking but what he'd said sounded suspiciously like something Sybil would say.

Suddenly the air was shattered by a raised female voice.

'Are you coming, Nick?'

Suzy was standing at the door, tapping her feet.

Nick held out his hand and Seb reluctantly handed over his journal. What else could he do? He'd already promised he would.

'Thanks. I'll guard it with my life.'

'You'd better.'

— o —

Fliss reread the email she'd received from the tracing agent, providing the telephone numbers and addresses of two entries in the name of Anna Norland, taken from the Oslo phonebook.

He said that women of that generation had followed the tradition of not taking their husband's name, so even if Anna had got married, there was a good chance one of them could be her. Provided she was still living in Oslo.

She should have been feeling elated that her efforts on Seb's behalf had come up with two possibilities, but as he'd made it crystal clear he didn't want to contact his mother, instead, she felt thwarted.

On top of that, he hadn't called her since the fashion shoot when he'd been so touchy about Lynette. She certainly wasn't going to call him. Her brother always dropped girls he described as 'too much hard work' and she'd more or less come to that conclusion about Seb.

At that moment, her bedroom door opened and her mother's head appeared.

'Didn't you hear me calling, Felicity? There's someone at the door for you. He says he doesn't want to come in.'

'Sorry, I was listening to music. I'm coming.'

Downstairs, she found Seb standing in the porch.

'Thought you might want to go for a drink,' he said, his eyes shifting from hers to the road.

'Where?' she said, making him suffer by adopting a false air of indifference, even though the sight of him was making her heart trip the light fantastic.

'Bull's Head?'

'It's my day off tomorrow—I feel like going to a club tonight. How about Underworld?'

'I've heard the drinks are expensive,' he said, shuffling his feet. 'Anyway, I'm not a member.'

'I am. Sit in your car while I get changed. Won't be long.'

She changed into a short, black lace dress and new red stilettos and ran downstairs, almost immediately dashing back up to grab a pair of men's trousers from the fitting room. On her way out, she paused at the open sitting-room door.

'We're going dancing,' she said to her parents, who were seated side by side on the sofa, their backs to her.

'Okay,' said her mother, without looking round. 'Don't wake us up when you come in.'

'I won't,' she said, kissing the tops of their heads.

When she was out of earshot, her father observed, 'She's in a good mood, she must like him,' and her mother replied, 'I wonder if he's the one Birdie was telling me about. She said he was very good-looking but a bit troubled...'

'Aren't we all?' said her husband, patting her hand.

— o —

Underworld was a few miles out of town and Fliss had to give Seb directions. Once there, she explained that sometimes the doorman didn't admit people wearing jeans, so to be on the safe side, he'd better change into this pair of trousers she'd brought with her, before they went in.

She'd half expected him to refuse, but he meekly obliged and within minutes they were descending the steps to the nightclub and heading for the bar, where Fliss approached a female bartender who greeted her by name.

'Long time, no see. Last time you were with your posse, weren't you?' said the girl, eyeing Seb up and down approvingly. 'Who's this?'

Noting Seb's embarrassment, Fliss kept the introductions brief.

'Heidi, this is Seb. He and his friends were on the latest shoot. Have you seen it on the website?'

'No, but I'll have a look. I must pay you a visit, my wardrobe needs a bit of a makeover.'

Their chat was cut short by a bunch of customers stacking up behind them, so Fliss ordered the drinks.

Heidi placed them on the counter and Seb pulled out a £20 note, courtesy of his poker winnings. When she returned, she gave him £15 change. He looked on the point of querying it, but Fliss took his arm and said, 'Let's find a table.'

When they were seated, she explained.

'Heidi gives me mates' rates and I do the same when she comes to the shop.'

'Bit risky for her, isn't it?'

Fliss shook her head.

'Her uncle runs this place. It's all above board.'

When they finished their drinks, they got up to dance and stayed there for a few tracks. On their return to the table, they found a reserved sign beside two fresh drinks.

'Looks like we've lost our table,' said Seb.

Fliss took a seat and picked up the margarita, motioning Seb to do the same with the beer.

'Don't worry, it's something Heidi does when I come here with my friends. I'll settle up with her later.'

'Cheers,' said Seb. 'This is the life.'

Happy to see he was enjoying himself, Fliss wondered if it was a good time to broach the subject of Anna Norland. She was still trying to decide, when Seb moved his chair closer to hers.

'Let me tell you about some dreams I've been having.'

The music was loud, even though they were sitting a good way from the dance floor and Seb bent closer to her ear, the proximity of his lips causing her spine to tingle.

'It all started the first weekend at college. There was no one around, I was at a loose end, and the director of the Foundation invited me to experience one of the treatments, so I spent that night in the sanctuary in the founder's garden…'

Fliss listened, wide-eyed, to Seb's graphic account of his dreams. He also described Sybil's role in the process, confessing that he'd walked out on their latest follow-up session earlier that evening. After talking uninterrupted for some time, he sat back in his chair.

'Hope I haven't bored you with all that,' he said, puffing air out of his cheeks as if he'd just finished a marathon.

'Of course not,' she said. 'It's amazing how clearly you remember it all.'

'So what do you think?'

A clique nearby was being quite rowdy, giving Fliss an excuse to mirror Seb and lean in close to his ear.

'Didn't you once tell me that it was the picture of the tholos on the Foundation website that attracted you to the course?'

'Yes. That and the snake logo which matches my mother's brooch.'

'And do you remember the first time I saw you? You pushed a van uphill, single-handed. If you'd lived in those times, you'd have been strong enough to take part in combat sports, like Apollos, wouldn't you?'

He shook his head.

'Not if I'd been an agricultural worker. It was only the moneyed classes who could afford to work out in gymnasiums and compete at games festivals. That's where Apollos and I differ.' He paused, a hint of remorse in his eyes. 'I only know that from Sybil.'

'So her feedback does have its uses?'

'If I was studying Classical Culture, but I'm not.' Seb sighed heavily. 'I know I shouldn't have lost my temper but it was the reincarnation thing that got me. I'm not into that kind of mumbo jumbo. I want to qualify as a traditional healer, not a psychoanalyst.'

'I'd have thought that people interested in natural medicine would tend to be open to ancient beliefs like reincarnation.'

She wanted to say more: that his vivid dreams suggested he'd inhabited that time and place before, and maybe something in Apollos's life would help him understand his own. But she was afraid he'd walk out on her the way he had on Sybil.

He slumped in his chair.

'I'm wondering if I'm cut out for this course. I'm not saying I'm closed to different aspects of the healing process. It goes without saying that the mind affects the body and vice versa. It's the other bit I'm not sure about.'

'You mean the spirit? Don't you believe we have a soul?'

'I don't know—some sort of animating force, maybe, but not something that lives on after we die. Anyway, even world religions can't seem to agree on what exactly constitutes a soul. I read somewhere that Plato thought everyone had three!'

Fliss giggled, almost bursting with happiness that Seb was at last confiding in her. Part of her didn't care what he believed in, as long as this newfound intimacy between them would never end.

'It could be just the brain fooling us,' he went on. 'Look at the Greeks. They got high on psychedelic drugs and thought they'd had a spiritual epiphany.'

Fliss could happily have sat there all night listening to him, but he looked as if he expected a reply, so she revved up her brain and added something to the debate.

'You could look at it the other way round. Taking the drug meant the initiates' mystical experience was guaranteed. It doesn't mean the experience was any less valid.'

'You've got a point,' he said, standing up and nodding in the direction of the men's room.

'See you in a minute.'

As Fliss watched his retreating figure, she panicked that she'd said the wrong thing and he was about to do a runner, but halfway there he turned and smiled, putting her racing heart at rest. Seconds later, she felt a sharp pain in her right foot, followed by the dull thud of a body landing on the floor beside her.

Tears of pain sprang to her eyes as she watched a slack-jawed hulk being pulled to his feet by his bull-necked companion. Rather than apologising for the blow to her foot, however, he began to bombard her with an expletive-charged tirade.

Apparently, he felt that her shoe had been protruding too far into his path and it was entirely her fault that he'd tripped over it, with the result that his head had made painful contact with the metal base of the table.

Fliss recoiled in repulsion as the man loomed over her, blood dripping from a cut over his eye, spraying her with beery saliva as he cursed her. She searched wildly for Seb in the crowd, without success, so she sank back in her chair and hid her face in her hands until all at once the man's diatribe became fainter. She opened her eyes to see Heidi standing in front of her, asking if she was all right.

Fliss winced as she gingerly removed her right shoe.

'That idiot's just ruined my favourite shoes. Has he gone?'

'Yes, don't worry. He's been escorted off the premises.'

Heidi knelt beside her to examine the damage done to her foot, at which Fliss burst into tears.

'Doesn't feel as if anything's broken. Stand up. See if you can put your weight on it.'

Supported by her friend, Fliss managed to hobble to the staff room, where she rested her leg on a stool while Heidi bandaged her bruised and swollen foot.

'I'm not much good at this,' said Heidi, frowning. 'Tony, the floor man, used to do the first aid. But at least you'll be able to walk to the car without getting your foot dirty.'

Fliss laughed weakly.

'You've got some work to do on your bedside manner, Heidi.'

There was a knock on the door and Seb entered.

'Your uncle said you'd be in here. How's the patient doing?'

'Not too bad,' said Heidi. 'Did the yobbo give you any trouble?'

When she heard Seb had been involved, Fliss blanched, but said nothing.

'Nah. I just handed him over to the doorman. He's barred him and his mate.'

'Good. That was some arm lock you put on him, by the way. He's one hefty brute.'

'Do you get many punters like that?' said Seb.

'Not as a rule. We're a bit low on security at the moment. There's usually a floor man patrolling the club but he left last week.'

Seb sat down opposite Fliss and began gently massaging her bandaged foot.

When Heidi saw what he was doing, she sniggered.

'You're not a foot fetishist, are you?'

Seb grunted and Fliss suppressed a smile.

'No, he's a student at Whitwell Hall.'

Heidi rolled her eyes but Fliss didn't return the signal.

'What did you do before?'

Seb answered without looking up.

'Worked at the Dog and Duck, Fairley.'

'Did you have to deal with any dodgy customers?'

'Occasionally. The girls were the worst.'

Both girls looked startled for a moment until he raised his eyes, which were crinkled in a smile.

Seb lowered Fliss's foot on to the floor.

'Best thing for that is bed,' he said, helping her up.

'I bet that's what you say to all the girls with foot injuries,' said Heidi, gurgling with glee at her own joke.

'Whatever,' said Seb, linking arms with Fliss. 'Come on, let's get your coat.'

'Wait a minute,' said Heidi, urgently. 'Would you be interested in a bit of casual work here, till we get a replacement floor man?'

Seb stopped in his tracks.

'I could be.' He took a flyer from a pile on a table and wrote his name and number on the back. 'Ring the manager of the Dog and Duck if you want a reference.'

Fliss was quiet in the car, engulfed in equal part by the pain in her foot and guilt at involving Seb in the whole sorry business.

Seb must have sensed she didn't want to talk because he put on some music, glancing her way occasionally to check on her. When they got to her house, he helped her up the path and kissed her at the door.

'Thanks,' she whispered. 'We should have gone to the Bull's Head, shouldn't we? I'm sorry for dragging you to Underworld.'

'Don't be,' he said. 'I might get some work out of it.'

Fliss wasn't sure she wanted him working in such a place but he was already walking away from her, towards his car.

Chapter 27

Roger Digby surveyed his visitor across his desk. He hadn't expected to be having a one-to-one with Sebastian Young this early in the term. But the boy had requested a meeting today and, being the scholarship student—albeit a somewhat unwilling one—if he needed support, it should be forthcoming.

'So, Sebastian, how's everything with you?'

'Okay, thanks.'

'Course to your liking?'

'Yes.'

'Happy with your accommodation?'

'Very.'

Roger leaned back in his chair, relieved that the lad hadn't so far presented him with a list of complaints. He could see though, by the way he was biting his lip, that something was eating him.

'So what's brought you here today?'

Seb hunched his shoulders, as if struggling with a crucial decision. Finally, he found his tongue.

'It's concerning Syb…Miss Hughes.'

Roger felt the blood drain from his face in anticipation at what might be coming next.

'I've been, er, rather rude to her, and I want to apologise. I've tried to ring her…left messages, but she hasn't answered. I planned to talk to her at the end of yesterday's lecture but she introduced a guest speaker after break and left the room. So I wondered if *you* could pass my apologies on to her.'

Roger's imagination went into overdrive. Had the two of them become romantically involved? How so? Wait, he remembered now. He'd sent her to finish off the incubation therapy. This was potentially extremely serious. If anything unprofessional had ensued, he needed to know about it.

He gave Seb a piercing look.

'You'll have to be more specific than that, Sebastian, if you want me to step in. Has this, by any chance, got something to do with the night you spent in the sanctuary?'

Seb looked surprised.

'Yes. It's about me being her case study.'

Roger listened with increasing interest while Seb explained what had happened. When the narration got to the scene in the cottage, he had to fight hard to keep a straight face as the lad stated his aversion to the concept of reincarnation and owned up to telling Sybil he no longer wanted to be her 'lab rat'.

'I'm afraid I told her to find another mug to experiment on.'

At this, Roger gave a shout of laughter, seasoned with a large pinch of relief.

'Perfectly reasonable. At your age, I might well have said the same thing.' When Seb looked doubtful, he added, 'Or the equivalent, for the times.'

'Glad you feel that way,' said Seb, 'I wish Miss Hughes felt the same.'

Roger looked thoughtful.

'Have you got to rush off?'

'No. I'm okay till two.'

Roger picked up the phone and rang Brenda, instructing her to take a note to wherever Sybil was teaching, asking her to ring him as soon as possible after her class finished.

'She'll be free at one, so it shouldn't be too long a wait,' said Roger, and proceeded to make small talk about the herb garden, which Seb gladly absorbed.

A few minutes later, the phone rang.

'Ah, Sybil. Thanks for responding. I have our scholarship student here, who'd like to have a word with you. He's explained the situation to me and asked me to intercede on his behalf. Now if you have the time—I'm off to lunch shortly—I'll gladly let you have the use of my office so you can both clear the air, so to speak.'

Seb held his breath while she replied, trying to make out whether her response was positive or negative. She must have been talking and walking at the same time because a few moments later the door opened and in she came, flushed and flustered.

Roger rose and gave her his seat.

'I hope this little misunderstanding can be resolved,' he said looking hard at Sybil. And to Seb, 'The official introduction to the abaton experience comes in the second term. I hope your premature induction won't leave you with a bad impression of it. For some people it's a very effective therapy.'

As soon as he left the room Sybil burst into tears.

Seb was so stunned he could only sit with his eyes averted as her shoulders heaved.

When her sobs gradually lessened, she stuttered an apology which added all the more to Seb's embarrassment.

'But it was I who behaved badly,' he said. 'Why should you be sorry?'

'Because I put too much pressure on you.' Tears began to course down her cheeks again. 'You're feeling your feet, trying to get used to a new regime, a whole new way of life. Roger's right, I've probably set you against sanctuary sleep for good because I wouldn't let you terminate the process when you wanted to.'

Seb thought of how he'd been attracted to the Foundation by the images of the tholos and the snake-entwined staff on the website. And of the group visit to the sanctuary, when certain Greek words had come to him—words he'd never consciously heard or seen before—as they also had in his sessions with Sybil. Not least, he took into account Birdie's theory that he might have channelled them.

'I think I overreacted to your theory of reincarnation,' he said, diplomatically. 'I realise now there are certain incidents which, from your point of view, might have pointed to it. But personally,' he added quickly, 'I'm still on the fence.'

Her face broke into a watery smile.

Seb wondered if he should tell her the rest of the revelation he'd had, sitting in the founder's garden early yesterday evening: when he'd worked out why he'd had the dreams.

A shaft of autumn sun broke through the window behind Sybil. Her eyes followed its beam, which alighted on the founder's photograph. And that's what decided him to tell her the truth.

'If I tell you something about my birth, Sybil, will you keep it secret? At least, for the time being?'

'Of course, Seb,' she said, curiosity transforming her dejected slump into a ramrod back.

Seb walked over to the photograph and handed it to her.

'Do you notice any resemblance?'

She looked from the photograph back to him.

'You've got the same colour hair and a similar physique. What are you getting at, Seb?'

'Teodor Ophis is my father.'

Saying the words out loud felt good. Better still, he found he could say them without feeling disloyal to Pete.

'What makes you think that?' she said, looking at him as if he were mad.

'Do you remember the brooch I had with me, on my interview day?'

He watched her features recast themselves from concern for his sanity to a dawning recollection.

'Yes, I do. It was the staff of Asklepios. I wanted to ask you how you got it but you seemed to be in an awful hurry.'

'It was pinned to a note my biological mother left, which I didn't get till recently. I had no idea the brooch came from Teodor, just that it was a present to her from my father. I only found out he was my father three weeks ago, when I uncovered my original birth certificate.'

Transfixed by this news, Sybil remained quiet for a full

minute, after which she showered him with questions. He answered every one of them, including his dealings with Dr Sharma.

'Sunny's a dark horse,' she said, but seeing Seb's expression cloud, she added, 'Of course, I'll never discuss this with him.'

When her questioning tailed off, Seb expounded his theory, formed the day before in the founder's garden.

'At first, I didn't have any interest in finding my biological father, even after I discovered who he was. As far as I was concerned, the only parents I ever had, Peter and Josie, were dead. It was only when I had the second dream that I suddenly had this great urge to find out more about Teodor.'

'That's right,' said Sybil, 'You asked *me* and I told you that Sunny was the only member of staff who'd been here when the professor was around.'

Seb tried to mentally place himself back on the sanctuary bench so he could revisit the sense of epiphany he'd experienced, and explain it to her.

'The way I see it now is that, on some level, I knew that the dreams were telling me I was linked, through blood, to Greece… and to the Asklepion sanctuaries.'

'Hmm,' said Sybil. 'I see. You think the dreams were prompting you to link up with Teodor, the living bearer of the same blood as you, who built the Asklepion sanctuary here.' She paused for thought. 'So whereas I thought your connection was with Apollos, something in you felt it was with Teodor. And that's why our sessions weren't working for you.'

Seb nodded, thankful that she'd understood.

'That doesn't mean you can't still have a connection to both of them, though. Maybe your bloodline stretches back to Apollos?' she said tentatively.

'If it does, it's too diluted to mean much,' he said. 'Anyway, we don't know if Apollos went on to have any children.'

'Unless you keep dreaming,' she said.

'I don't need to now, do I?' he said, picking up his rucksack and getting to his feet. 'I've found my father.'

Sybil stood up, too, but walked around the desk to position herself between him and the door.

'There's just one thing I'm curious about. Do you feel a similar urge to find your biological mother? You haven't mentioned her but you must know who she is.'

'She's Norwegian.'

'Does that make a difference? There was quite a lot about mothers in the dreams.'

'Teodor told me about her.'

Sybil nodded expectantly. At first Seb was loath to elaborate, feeling he'd revealed enough already. More to her, in fact, than Fliss, who knew nothing of Teo.

'Are your birth parents in touch?' Sybil persisted.

'No.'

He weighed up whether to enlarge on the subject and came down on the side of expediency. If he stayed the course, he'd be within her orbit for three years, so it wouldn't hurt to keep Sybil onside.

'She was a mature student, with a husband in Norway. Teodor thought she was going to leave her husband but she went back to him. I was a mistake, obviously. Their method of birth control let them down. So I don't think either of us will be getting in touch any time soon.'

'I see.'

Sybil looked as if she wanted to continue the discussion, but Seb had had enough.

'So shall we say case closed?' he said, holding out his hand.

'I respect your decision, Seb,' she answered, reluctantly taking his hand.

Seb grinned from ear to ear, elated that their peace treaty was signed and sealed.

'Although,' Sybil added, 'the mind-detective in me would

love to follow up your feelings about your mother.'

'You sound like my girlfriend,' he said, feeling a buzz just saying the word.

Seb exited the room leaving Sybil looking surprised. Walking down the corridor with a spring in his step, he felt glad to be alive.

— o —

At the sound of her business phone, Fliss switched off the gas under the soup she was heating and limped out of the staff room and into her office. It was Nick.

'Hi Fliss, how are you?'

'Not too bad. How did you get this number?'

'It's actually on your website.'

'Of course it is. You're quite the detective. What can I do for you?'

'I was thinking it's about time I spent my Belinda voucher. Are you around today? About five?'

'Yes. I've put the sweater and trousers by for you, as you asked.'

'Great. I hear you've hurt your foot. Seb said some bozo tripped over you.'

She sighed. 'My dad had to drive me to work today.'

'I'll give you a lift home tonight, if you like. What time do you close? Six?'

'Yes. That's really kind of you. See you later.'

Fliss took her personal phone from her bag in the staff room and scrolled to Seb's number. When he answered, she wished him good luck for tonight, his first night as relief floor man at Underworld.

He told her he'd just apologised to Sybil, sounding relieved and happy; she told him Nick was coming in later and would be giving her a lift home, and he made a joke about telling the staff to stay clear of the changing room. After saying goodbye, she added, for the very first time, 'Love you.'

For a few seconds there was silence at the other end, but he managed a soft, 'Likewise,' which made her heart sing.

She was downstairs, sitting behind the cash desk, when Nick came in.

'I have strict instructions from Seb not to lay a finger on you,' he said, kissing her cheek. 'But he didn't say anything about lips.'

Beside her, Amy giggled.

Fliss smiled and handed Nick the clothes.

'You'd better try them on to make sure.'

'I hope you're not suggesting I'm getting a beer belly, young lady. Stay there and I'll prove you wrong.'

When he came out of the changing room in a cream zip-neck sweater and slim grey trousers, he strode to the front of the shop, his body in complete alignment like a catwalk model.

'Perfect,' said Amy.

'Great bum,' remarked a customer who'd just walked in, as he paced back to the changing room, and the three of them giggled.

'I suppose you want paying for these now,' he said, appearing at the till a few minutes later with his credit card and the vouchers.

'Why have you got Seb's as well?' she exclaimed.

'It's okay, it's legit. Seb needed some cash and I bought his voucher off him.'

When Fliss took Nick to the staff room to wait for her, she returned to the subject of Seb's finances.

'How short of money is he?'

Nick stroked his chin, looking uncomfortable.

'He told me but I'm not sure if it was in confidence.'

'Please, Nick. You know what he's like. If I ask him, he'll be too proud to admit he's hard up. I won't drop you in it. Honestly.'

'Okay. He said he had two thousand to last him for the next

three years.'

'But he's got a scholarship. Doesn't that include living expenses?'

'Apparently not. He said the grant covers his fees and accommodation.'

'So on top of that he has to buy food, clothing...'

'Car insurance, gas. Everything else, in fact.'

'No wonder he jumped at the chance of some casual work at Underworld,' said Fliss, glumly.

'Yeah, he mentioned that. It's not a long-term solution though, is it?'

'No. I'm worried that he'll have to leave college when he runs out of money.'

'Me too,' said Nick. 'I wasn't too sure about him to begin with, but he's cool once you get to know him. He's the kind of guy who'll always have your back, you know?'

Fliss nodded, her heart in her boots at the thought of Seb having to watch every penny.

'When he said his parents had a farm, I assumed they'd left him more than a couple of thousand.'

'Apparently not. They were his adoptive parents, right?' said Nick. 'He told me they died in an accident.'

'Did he tell you he found his original birth certificate recently, with his birth mother's name on it?'

Nick shook his head.

'Why would he?'

'Some people would want to trace their birth parents but he's not interested.'

'I can understand that.'

'If you were adopted and someone else found out certain information, like a phone number which might connect you with your birth mother, wouldn't you be pleased?'

'Probably not. I'd say it was my place to trace them if I wanted to, not theirs. Life's complicated enough without other people interfering.'

Fliss sighed.

'By the way,' said Nick. 'What about those dreams he's been having? I've been reading his journal. It'd be great material for a screenplay.'

'You'd better get someone to write it. You could star in it,' she said, glad he'd changed the subject before it occurred to him that the 'someone else' finding out 'certain information' was sitting next to him.

'No need. I'm a trained screenwriter. I've just been waiting for inspiration...'

Once Nick had dropped Fliss home, he thought about paying a visit to Underworld later in the evening to see how Seb was doing. But after fixing himself something to eat, then getting engrossed in a DVD, he found the moment had passed and stayed home instead.

— o —

Seb stepped into the staff room, as requested by the manager, who liked to see all the staff before they left. It was almost three in the morning and all he wanted to do was get home to bed, so he hoped this wouldn't take long.

'Any problems tonight, Seb?' Heidi's uncle had the face of a pugilist and the manner of a softly-spoken assassin.

'Nothing major. A bit of ragging from a couple of cretins. Calling me "Tarzan", that kind of thing.'

'Asking you where Jane was, were they?'

'Yeah.'

'Might be related to that incident on Wednesday. Those two who were barred run with a gang from the Bridgewater estate. I say gang, but they're not criminals, just a bunch of Jack the lads. All mouth and trousers, most of 'em.'

'That's good to know.'

'Right, well, are you up for joining us again tomorrow night?'

'Sure.'

'Okay. Good night. See you tomorrow.'

Seb left by the back entrance and walked to the small staff car park. His was the only car there. The manager had told him that he always used a taxi firm, so he could have a drink and not worry about driving home.

He took his key fob out of his pocket and pressed unlock. As he bent down to open the car door, he felt something heavy smash into the back of his skull. Then everything went black.

Chapter 28

Fliss finished getting ready for work and turned on her phone to find a voicemail from Penbury General Hospital. It was in connection with a patient who'd been admitted to the Accident and Emergency unit. Her number was on his mobile phone contacts list and if she could supply them with information about his next of kin, would she please ring this number.

She wondered who it could be. Her own contacts list was extensive. Then her thoughts flew to Seb. He was the one most likely not to have an entry under Mum, Dad or Home.

With shaking hands, she called the number. It rang for a long time before a female voice answered. She explained she was replying to a message and the speaker took her name and asked her to hold on while she got someone who could give her more details.

While she was waiting, her father called out to her from the bottom of the stairs.

'If you want a lift, Felicity, you'd better get a move on. I'm playing golf at ten.'

'I'll be five minutes, Dad. I'm in the middle of a call,' she said, irked that her foot was still too painful for her to drive herself.

Finally, a different voice came on the line.

'Hello, Miss Logan. I'm Dr Perera. I understand you know Mr Sebastian Young?'

'Yes, I do.'

'Are you a relative? If not, do you know of any?'

'Seb's an orphan. He doesn't have any living relatives.' She was pretty sure this wasn't true, but now wasn't the time to raise the subject of absent parents. 'I'm his girlfriend.'

'Well, I'm sorry to have to tell you that he was admitted by ambulance early this morning, having sustained a blow to the head, and hasn't regained consciousness yet.'

Fliss felt sick.

'Was there anyone with him when he came in?' she said, her voice unsteady.

She heard the rustle of notes.

'It says here he was unaccompanied. Police and ambulance were called by the manager of the nightclub, who told the driver he was a casual employee and all he knew was his name.'

'So what happened? Did someone attack him in the club?'

'I have no idea. You'll have to ask the police that.'

Fliss groaned. Seb wouldn't have been anywhere near that club if she hadn't forced him to take her in the first place. She heard her father coming up the stairs and asked the doctor to hold.

'Dad, change of plan. Can you take me to the hospital instead, please? A friend of mine's been taken in as an emergency.'

Her father pointed to his watch and mouthed, *Only if we go now.*

She nodded and returned to her conversation with the doctor, who sounded as irritated as her father had looked.

'Miss Logan, I don't have much time. Can you tell me if Mr Young has any current medical conditions? Is he on any medication? Does he have any allergies?'

'Not as far as I know.'

The doctor asked a few more questions, most of which she couldn't answer. When he'd completed the check list, she asked if she could see Seb.

'Yes. Though he'll have to be moved within the next couple of days.'

'Where to?'

'Marylebone Neurological Hospital. We don't deal with cases like his here.'

On the way to the hospital, Fliss rang Milena to ask her to open the shop, and left a message for Heidi to get in touch if she had any information about what had gone on last night.

Her last call was to Nick. Before she broke the news, she asked if Penbury General had left him a message about Seb.

'No. Why? What's happened?'

After she told him she was on her way there and why, she burst into tears. Nick gulped and said he'd leave immediately.

When her father, who'd listened in silence, pulled up outside the hospital, he said, 'Is this the boy who called for you in the week?'

She nodded, still tearful.

'Let's hope it's nothing serious, eh? Call me if you need a lift to work.'

She kissed his cheek and began to hobble, as quickly as she could, towards the Intensive Care Unit. Nick arrived soon after, looking pale and anxious. Instinctively, they hugged each other, Nick saying that they must be strong for Seb's sake. When she'd gained control of her tears, they entered the ward and Fliss gave her details to a nurse, who recognised her name.

'So you got my message. He's been unconscious since he came in, so I only had his mobile phone contacts to go on. You're his...?'

'Girlfriend.'

With Nick standing beside her, she felt shy declaring it, particularly as they'd known each other such a short time. But as far as she was concerned, she was.

'And you?' asked the nurse, smiling at Nick.

'His friend. We share a flat.'

'Dr Perera said Sebastian didn't have any relatives?'

'That's right,' said Nick. 'His parents died in an accident.'

'His adoptive parents,' said Fliss quickly, the germ of an idea forming in her mind.

'I see. I was looking for an entry under Mum or Dad. That explains it.'

'Did you contact anyone else?' said Fliss.

The nurse gave her a sideways look.

'He didn't have many contacts listed, so I went for the two female names. They're more likely to respond quickly.'

'I bet the other one was Sybil,' said Nick.

'That's right,' said the nurse, twinkling an eye at him. 'But, as far as I know, she hasn't been in touch yet.'

Fliss's heart swung between unease at having her newly acquired status weakened by Sybil appearing on the scene, and a sense of relief that Seb's contact list held no nasty surprises.

'He's a student. She's one of his tutors,' she said quickly. 'Can we see him now?'

The nurse led them to a side room where Seb lay on a bed with a raised back rest, his eyes closed. There were various tubes attached to him, the most recognisable being an intravenous feeding tube and a catheter to drain his bladder. Fliss's heart ached when she saw the livid, sutured wound on the back of his partly shaved head.

'He's in a coma,' the nurse said, in a low voice. 'You can still talk to him. It's possible he'll hear you.' She indicated the chair beside the bed and Fliss sat down. 'You can hold his hand if you want.'

The nurse disappeared and came back with another chair for Nick. At first, they simply observed him quietly. Then they started talking to him about familiar things but his eyes remained closed. Fliss thought she saw his left eyelid flutter when she took his hand but there was no more response than that.

At eleven o'clock, Nick said he'd find a coffee machine. She told him to take his time, maybe have one in the café, and bring her one back.

As soon as he'd gone, she gently kissed Seb on the cheek, which felt worryingly cool to her lips, saying she'd be back soon. Then she headed for the day room where she switched on her phone, accessing her emails and making a note of the two phone numbers the tracing agent had sent her. Her mind was racing as she dialled the first one, thinking of the consequences if it all went wrong and Seb never forgave her. But she couldn't stop herself: something had been prompting her to do this all the time she'd been holding Seb's hand.

The voice that answered was a man's. She'd already rehearsed what she was going to say.

'Good morning. Do you speak English? I want to speak to Anna Norland, please.'

'*Engelsk? Nei. Vent.*'

He hadn't ended the call, so she assumed he'd gone to fetch somebody.

'Hello.' Seb's mother would presumably be the same generation as her own mother, but the voice that answered sounded elderly. 'I am Fru Anna Norland, can I help you?'

'Hello. I live in Whitwell, near Fairley. I'm trying to trace the owner of a gold brooch.'

'A brooch? What is that?'

Fliss's heart sank. Seb's mother would have known the word, considering that was the only thing she'd ever given him, apart from his life.

'A brooch is something you pin on a dress or coat.'

'*Ah, brosje*. But I haven't been to England. I learned English at school.'

'I see. Do you have a daughter of the same name?'

'A daughter? No, two sons.'

Fliss apologised for disturbing her and rang off.

She dialled the second number and this time a woman answered. Fliss followed the same formula and when she mentioned the brooch the woman asked her to describe it.

'It's in the shape of a snake, entwined around a staff.'

'Yes, I know it. Who are you?'

Fliss's moment of elation turned to panic as she searched for the right words to keep Anna on the line. Then she had a flash of inspiration.

'I'm speaking from Penbury General Hospital. We admitted

a young man called Sebastian Young in the early hours of this morning with a severe head injury. He's in a coma and we're trying to trace any close relatives, to let them know.'

Fliss heard Anna gasp. When she replied, her voice was shaking.

'I'm very sorry about that but I don't understand why you're calling me. He has adoptive parents. Haven't you told them?'

'It appears his adoptive parents are no longer alive. Can I put you down as his next of kin?'

Fliss held her breath while Anna remained silent, willing her to agree.

'It's difficult. We don't know each other.' Her voice broke as she whispered, 'He was adopted at birth.'

Fliss couldn't resist the opportunity to voice her thoughts.

'Perhaps it's time you got to know him, then.'

At that moment, Nick walked into the day room.

'Your wish is my command,' he said loudly, holding up a cardboard cup.

She placed a finger to her lips.

'Hello, Ms Norland. I'm sorry, I'm being called to an emergency. Can we contact you if there's any change in Mr Young's condition?'

She waited until she'd heard Anna's faltering 'yes' before she rang off. Leaping to her feet, she punched the air, leaving Nick gaping at her in astonishment.

'I'll explain in a minute,' she said, 'I need to see the nurse. Stay here.'

The nurses' station was deserted so Fliss walked along the corridor, looking into side wards and rooms. She found her in Seb's room, checking the monitors. Fliss waited until she'd finished, making a mental note of the name badge she was wearing.

'There's been a breakthrough, Angela.'

The nurse gave a little start.

'A breakthrough?'

'Yes. We've traced his birth mother. But she's in Norway. I've got her phone number and she wants to be kept informed of his progress.'

'Well done,' said Angela, warmly. 'You'd better come with me and I'll put her details on his notes.'

When they reached the reception desk, Angela looked questioningly at Fliss.

'She'll go down as his next of kin.'

Fliss nodded.

'That's what she is.'

'Of course, if...*when* he regains consciousness it's up to him who he nominates.'

'Sure,' said Fliss, focusing on the when, not the if.

'I'll ring her in a couple of hours,' said Angela, as she completed the paperwork. 'She'll have to call Marylebone Neurological Hospital for updates after he's moved.'

'When will that be?'

'Probably tomorrow. Don't worry, he'll be in the best place.'

Fliss returned to the day room where she found Nick leafing through a women's magazine.

'The only thing I could find,' he said, with a grin. 'It's a bit of an eye-opener, I have to say. Now drink this lukewarm coffee and tell me what you've been up to.'

Relieved to be able to confide in someone at last, Fliss embarked on the saga of Anna Norland. When she got to the part about the tracing agent, Nick shook his head in disapproval, but had a change of heart when she reached the finale.

'Nice one, Detective Logan,' he said, getting up. 'Thanks to you, our work here is done for today. Need a lift to Belinda's?'

'Yes, please. Let's just say goodbye to Seb,' she said, already halfway out the door.

The sight of Seb, all alone and still dead to the world, brought Fliss down to earth with a bump.

'See you soon, big fella,' said Nick, patting Seb's arm. 'Hang in there.'

He turned abruptly and left the room. Fliss could see Nick was upset so she stayed back to give him time to collect himself.

'I'm going now. I'll see you tomorrow, my love,' she whispered, her mouth close to his ear—as it had been in the club, just before the ill-fated event that had sparked this tragedy. 'Please, please get better. You've got so much to live for.'

'That's a big old head wound, isn't it?' said Nick, as they walked to the car park. 'I'd like to get my hands on the bastard that did it.'

As they drew away from the hospital, Fliss got a call from Heidi, which she put on speaker for Nick's benefit. She said her uncle's taxi driver had found Seb unconscious beside his car. Her uncle called the police and told them about the trouble earlier in the week. He was able to give them the suspect's name. The taxi driver found Seb's keys on the ground and they were being kept in the office for whoever picked up Seb's car.

'Tell her me and Jim'll take care of that,' said Nick.

After that, Heidi said how sorry she was and how guilty she felt for putting Seb forward for the job, but Fliss told her not to blame herself. How could anyone have known what would happen?

'I'll keep tomorrow free,' said Nick when he dropped her off. 'Give me a bell if he's still here and I'll pick you up.'

— o —

Sybil got a taxi from the station and was back from her weekend in North Wales by suppertime on Sunday. Lovely as it was to see her parents, the train journey could be a bit of a nightmare: crowded and noisy with weekenders. At least this time of year wasn't too bad: well past summer and not too close to Christmas.

She turned on her phone for the first time since switching it off on Friday evening. The mobile reception where her parents lived was rubbish, so there'd been no point in keeping it on. It was no hardship. She rather enjoyed being unobtainable: it gave her a feeling of freedom.

She'd told her close friends she'd be away, so there were no missed calls, just a voicemail from Penbury General which she listened to in stunned dismay. After speaking to a member of staff, she dialled Sunny's number.

Only two days ago she'd promised to keep Seb's secret. Given the gravity of his present situation, she was now about to break that promise.

Chapter 29

Teodor Ophis disembarked from the Eurostar and took the underground train to Baker Street, depositing his small suitcase in the luggage storage facility beside the station. From there it was a short walk to Marylebone Neurological Hospital where his son lay in a coma.

When he gave his name to the ward receptionist, she fetched a doctor. Once he'd heard everything the doctor had to report—which boiled down to Seb's condition being stable, with little progress since he arrived—he asked to see his son. The ward rounds were about to start, however, so they asked him to come back in an hour.

He took this opportunity to head for the restaurant, where he carried his tray of food to an empty table in a quiet part of the room. A few minutes into his meal, he became conscious of an approaching figure. Without looking up, he positioned his laptop case opposite his own plate.

The diner was undeterred, however. A female voice asked, 'Is this seat taken?' and he looked up to see an attractive middle-aged woman holding a tray laden with a pot of tea, a sandwich and a slice of chocolate cake.

'No. It's free,' he said, removing the case. 'I see you haven't lost your sweet tooth, Anna.'

'Nor you your penchant for meatballs, Teo.'

'Actually, they're my second favourite. They'd run out of lamb intestines.'

She allowed herself a smile and sat down.

They regarded each other in silence for a few moments. It was over twenty years since their son's birth; all that time they hadn't seen or spoken to each other. Yet here they were, reunited in a hospital cafeteria to find out how close he was to death or permanent brain injury.

Anna poured her tea and Teo returned to his meatball pasta.

'Would you mind if I asked you a question?' she said, finally.

'No. Go ahead. Ask as many as you like. As long as I can ask *you* one for every one you ask me.'

'Deal,' she said, extending her hand as if to shake on it and swiftly withdrawing it when he made no reciprocal move.

'I didn't expect to see you here, Teo. How long have you been in touch with Sebastian?'

'One week to the day. I video called him last Monday afternoon.'

'How did all that come about?' she said, her fingers tightening on her cup.

'That's two questions. It's my turn now. Why are you here?'

'The hospital in Penbury was looking for his next of kin. They said they traced me from the gold brooch you gave me. I can't think how.' She paused. 'You know his adoptive parents are dead?'

Teo nodded. 'Like you, I was unaware of that until recently. But you haven't completely answered my question. You could have refused to come. So why are you here?'

Anna's face crumpled and she rummaged in her bag for a handkerchief.

'When I heard he was alone in the world, what else could I do? I flew in yesterday. Now I can't wait to see him. How did you get the news?'

'Somebody called Sybil rang me last night. She's a lecturer at the Foundation. Sebastian had told her we were related.'

'Looks like the universe was in a benevolent mood,' said Anna. 'We were clearly meant to reconnect with him.'

Teo closed his eyes briefly and nodded.

'How is your father?'

Anna's mouth twisted and Teo knew the answer to his question before she even gave it.

'He died a couple of years ago. I miss him so much. But I'm

glad his name lives on in Sebastian.'

'Did you ever tell him he had a secret grandson?'

She shot him an indignant glare. 'Of course not. Did you ever tell anyone you had a secret son?'

He shook his head, looking around at the tables filling up.

'Where are you staying, Anna?'

'In Highbury, with a herbalist friend. And you?'

'I haven't booked anywhere yet. I've just got off the Eurostar.'

Her eyes widened in surprise.

'Where are you living now?'

'Paris.'

'Ah. I looked you up on the Internet yesterday, but I couldn't find you.'

'I like to keep a low profile,' he said. 'There's not enough hours in the day to provide references for all the students who want one...'

He trailed off, aware of the lameness of his explanation.

'Are you sure you weren't hiding from me?' she said, with a forced brightness.

Discomfited by her words, he frowned and looked away.

'I'm sorry,' she said, hastily. 'I don't know why I said that.'

'I'm at the University Paris Descartes,' he said, choosing to ignore her apology. 'But I've wound down a bit in the last year. I supervise the occasional PhD student. How about you?'

'I have a small practice. I get by.'

Teo chewed his food thoughtfully. After a few moments he said, 'Your turn.'

'Do you have any other children?'

'No. You?'

'No.'

Anna was the first to ask the unspoken question which hung in the air.

'Do you have a wife or...?'

'No wife or partner. These days my life is almost monastic.

Are you still with Erik?'

She shook her head.

'We're divorced. Ironically enough, he left me for a woman he got pregnant. I suppose you could call it karma.'

Teo stared at the table. Then he remembered Anna's question: what had led to his video call to Seb a week ago.

'Do you remember Sunny Sharma?'

'Of course I do. He was one of my tutors.'

'Well, he's still teaching at the Foundation and, you probably don't know this, Sebastian is a student there. In fact, he's the one and only scholarship student. He didn't have the usual qualifications...got in on an entrance exam, Sunny said. Did very well.'

There was pride in his voice when he spoke of their son and Anna's drawn face relaxed into a soft smile.

'He recently found his original birth certificate,' he continued, 'so he approached Sunny, who gave me his number. I was happy to talk to him. He's a nice kid.'

Anna's smile had faded.

'You mean, Sunny knew about what happened between us?'

'No, no. I never told a soul. But Sebastian showed him the brooch. There was some flim-flam about writing an article about me, so I went along with it, but as soon as Sunny mentioned the brooch I knew why he wanted to "interview" me.'

'Didn't you recognise his name when he got the scholarship? I would have.'

'Anna, I had no idea there even *was* a scholarship student until a week ago. I have no contact with the Foundation now. I handed that over to a trust after you...'

'Abandoned our baby?'

'If you want to put it like that.'

Anna produced her hankie and started dabbing her eyes again.

'What I can't understand is why he was doing security work

in a nightclub. That sort of environment always attracts trouble.'

'We can only assume he needed the money. He never mentioned it when we talked.' Teo clasped his forehead. 'If only I'd known he'd been orphaned, I could have given him an allowance. Then none of this would have happened.'

'He's effectively been orphaned twice,' she said, her voice trembling. 'First by us and then by the Youngs.'

They finished their food in silence, lost in their own thoughts.

He consulted his watch.

'Time to get going.'

Walking to the lift, they made a striking couple. He, tall, tanned with greying temples. She, tall, slim, with silky dark hair and green eyes. When they entered the ward, the receptionist greeted them with a warm smile.

'Sebastian's parents? I'll get a nurse. She can show you where he is.'

The nurse took them to his room, suggesting they talk about memorable times during his childhood: a beloved pet, perhaps, or a special holiday, in the hope of stimulating a vivid memory which would bring him back to consciousness.

They nodded as she talked, waiting till she'd left before regarding each other helplessly.

'What use are two strangers like us going to be to him?' said Anna.

'We can only try,' said Teo. 'What do you think of him?'

'He's beautiful. He looks like you.'

Teo looked pleased.

'He's got your eyes, though.'

Anna sat at her son's bedside.

'I don't know what to say,' she whispered. 'I'm a stranger to him and vice versa. He has every reason to hate me for giving him up. I'm probably the last person he wants to see.'

Teo sat on the other side, taking Seb's hand and massaging his fingers, one by one.

'He asked me about you, you know. Wanted to know why you didn't keep him.'

'What did you tell him?'

'The truth.'

'How did he take it?'

'Let's just say, he didn't think much of our method of contraception. He asked if I had a picture of you. But I didn't.'

Anna took hold of Seb's left hand and began massaging his fingers in the same way as Teo.

'Are your hands getting warm?' said Teo, and she nodded. 'Let's do his feet.'

They moved to the end of the bed and did the same with his toes.

'Stay there,' said Teo, slowly making his way behind the bedhead, carefully avoiding the lines and tubes. He inspected Seb's head wound, then placed his hands beneath the back of Seb's head, cradling the occipital bone.

After five minutes or so, Seb's eyes opened and he began rambling incoherently. Teo bent over him but his eyes were blank and staring. His body began to thrash about, the lines and tubes straining to remain embedded.

Anna ran to one side of the bed to restrain him and Teo hastened to the other.

By this time, Seb had pulled himself up, so Anna found herself cradling his torso as one would a child, which seemed to calm him down.

'Sing to me, Dorcas, sing to me…' intoned Seb, repeating these words over and over, like a mantra, tears running down his cheeks.

Anna's heart heaved with grief at the sight of her son in such distress.

'Sing to him,' said Teo.

'Sing what?'

'Something you'd sing to a child. He seems to have regressed.'

'I can sing *Gjendines Badnlat*, but it's Norwegian.'

'Hurry,' said Teo, glancing at the glass-panelled door. 'If a member of staff sees us, they'll want to know why the emergency buzzer hasn't been pressed.'

So Anna began to sing the folk lullaby her mother and grandmother had sung to her. She started at normal volume, her voice gradually becoming quieter and the tempo slower. As she did so, Seb relaxed, leaning into her like a baby, his body growing limp.

Soon they were able to settle him down so there was no visible sign of his earlier anguish. They returned to their places beside his bed, where they spent the afternoon talking about their lives in the intervening years since they parted, interrupted only by a nurse taking readings from the monitors.

At five o'clock, Seb opened his eyes, blinked and looked around.

'Where am I?' he whispered.

'In hospital,' said Teo, gently. 'You hurt your head but you're going to be all right.'

'Who are you?' said Seb, looking at Anna.

'I'm your mother.'

'Which one?' he said, his head a confusion of Dorcas, Agathe, Demeter, and Josie.

'The one who gave birth to you, named you, sang to you and wishes she'd never let you go,' she sobbed.

'When can we go home?' said Seb.

His parents' eyes met.

'Good question, my boy,' said Teo. 'Now you're awake, your mother and I will have to leave you for a little while to let the medics check you out. You'll probably have to stay here for one or two more nights. After that, we'll take you home.'

Chapter 30

Fliss sighed heavily as yet again Seb's phone went to voicemail. It was ten days since she and Nick had visited him in the Marylebone hospital, and they hadn't seen or heard from him since.

Nick had picked her up from work at six on the Monday evening, but the traffic had been bad and they'd got to the hospital late. The staff must have been on a break, or changing shifts—whatever the reason, there was no one to approach. They eventually found Seb in a side room, propped up on pillows, staring into space. He managed a weak greeting although he didn't say their names: they'd been so delighted he'd come out of the coma, that it didn't seem to matter.

On Tuesday, Fliss rang the hospital and found he was doing well, so she and Nick decided to leave their next visit till the following day, so that Nick and Jim could pick up Seb's car from Underworld. When they got to the hospital on Wednesday evening, he'd gone.

The male nurse they saw told them his parents had discharged him. Fliss said did he mean his mother, but the nurse checked the records and said it had definitely been a man and a woman. They asked for Anna's mobile phone number but he said it was against the rules to give out personal information. Since then, they'd heard nothing and Fliss had been torturing herself with the knowledge that if it hadn't been for her, Anna Norland wouldn't have come and taken him away.

Her mobile rang. It was Nick.

'Any news on the missing person?'

'Nothing. I've been ringing Anna's home number in Oslo every day but there's no answer there, either.'

'Maybe the guy who came with her, whoever he was, lives at a different address. He might even live in London.'

'But why hasn't Seb himself been in touch?'

'He's probably still groggy,' said Nick. 'Anyway, I've got a bit of news. I was looking for some batteries for the door buzzer and I remembered Seb had some. So I looked in his desk drawer and there was his birth certificate. He must have got a hell of a surprise when he found out who his old man was.'

'What do you mean?'

'His father's down as Teodor Ophis, the actual founder of the college.'

Fliss was momentarily paralysed by the shock of betrayal. Why had Seb excluded her from such a significant discovery?

'You still there, Fliss?'

'Yes. He told me his father wasn't named on the birth certificate.'

'Well, it's there in black and white. Maybe he just wanted to keep it to himself. Don't take it personally, you know what he's like.'

'Would the college know where the founder's living?'

'Is that relevant? I assumed the "parents" who took him were his mother and some guy she was married to or living with.'

'Relevant or not, he has a right to know.'

'Okay, I'll ask in the office. But I'm not gonna say he's Seb's father. Got to go, Ayurveda's calling.'

Nick rang off, leaving Fliss to pore over the shop accounts, number crunching being the only way she could stop her galloping mind from agonising over whether she'd ever see Seb again.

— o —

Anna and Teo were talking in the large drawing room they called the 'salon' when Seb joined them. The scar was still visible but a fine down of hair had already begun to grow over it. His physique still conveyed strength and power, even though he hadn't yet regained the weight he'd lost. His shoulders, however, had rounded, as if he were protecting himself against an unseen foe.

'Good morning, darling. How are you?' said Anna, getting up and kissing his cheek.

'Fine,' he said, automatically. 'What's happening today?'

Anna and Teo exchanged glances.

'Anna's flying back to Oslo, Seb. We told you yesterday, remember?'

'Yeah, that's right,' he said, looking away. 'Are you going, too?' he asked Teo, in the tone of a fearful child.

'No. I'm staying here with you, while you get better.'

Seb's expression cleared.

'Can we all go out together first?'

Anna looked at Teo.

'I don't see why not. I've finished packing.'

'We can go for a walk in the Jardin du Luxembourg if you like, before we leave,' said Teo. 'Put your jacket on in case you get cold.'

As they strolled in the gardens, Seb lagged behind, gazing at the children's boats bobbing on the octagonal pond. This gave them the opportunity to speak privately.

'Are you sure you want me to put my apartment up for sale, Teo? Shouldn't I keep it just in case...'

'In case living with me doesn't work out?' He took her hand. 'You know me well enough to trust me, Anna. Whatever happens, I'll take care of you. You have my word.'

'At least I'll have a warmer winter in Paris than Oslo,' she said, smiling up at him. 'I'm looking forward to throwing out my thermals.'

'That might be going a bit far,' he said, grinning. 'It can get pretty cold here, too.'

They walked to the Medici Fountain and paused by the statue of a giant observing two lovers.

'Polyphemus,' said Seb.

'What, darling?' said Anna.

'He's naming the statue,' said Teo. 'The scene depicts the giant Polyphemus catching his lady love with another man. It's a Greek myth.'

'How would he know that?' said Anna.

'Ask him.'

But in reply to her question, Seb simply shrugged.

'We'd better go,' said Teo. 'Otherwise your mother will miss her flight.'

On their way back from the airport, Teo played Bach's Goldberg Variations on the stereo; he'd noticed Seb liked it. He waited a few minutes before asking if any memories from before his coma had come back to him.

'It's hard to say. Nothing here seems familiar. It's like the dreams I used to have. It feels as if I'm in another country.'

'But you are, Seb, you're in France. We brought you here to recover. You haven't got anyone to look after you in England.'

'Haven't I?'

Teo sighed. Maybe bringing Seb to his apartment hadn't been such a good idea. It had cost a small fortune to hire a private ambulance to get him to Paris. But what had been the alternative? A student flat with no one to give him the care he needed.

'I'll show you some pictures of your college later, Seb. They might jog your memory.'

'All right.'

His father wished he'd sounded a little more enthusiastic.

'What was that thing you were telling me about Asklepios last night?' said Seb, sounding much more interested in that.

'Why don't you tell me how much *you* remember first, Seb?'

'Zeus killed Asklepios with a thunderbolt because he'd made a potion out of snake's venom which could bring people back from the dead and Hades objected...'

'That's how the myth goes, yes. Hades didn't want to be put

out of a job. What happened next?'

'Zeus relented, made him a god, and placed him in the cosmos as a constellation...called...'

'Ophiuchus, which is Greek for Serpent Bearer,' said Teo.

'Yes. You were showing me where it was in the sky on our walk last night...you told me there's something important about it.'

'Yes. Astronomers have recently identified a key building block for life in a cloud of stardust in that very constellation. This organic compound is actually helping to form new stars. What's happening is a mirror image of how our own solar system was formed.'

'*Everything comes from everything,*' said Seb, dreamily.

'*...And everything is made out of everything and everything turns into everything*. Leonardo knew what he was talking about, didn't he, Seb?'

For the rest of the journey their thoughts, accompanied by the strains of a baroque harpsichord, claimed them.

When they got back, Teo went to the plan chest in his study and extracted the folder containing his designs for the Foundation sanctuary. The salon was spacious enough to accommodate a sizeable dining table, on which Teo spread the plans. He called Seb, who wandered into the room, an apple in his hand.

'I'm hungry.'

Teo sighed. His son seemed to have reverted to a period in his childhood when he was capable of washing and dressing himself but still needed someone to feed him at regular intervals.

'Look at this first and we'll eat afterwards.'

Seb finished the apple and took a seat at the table. He gazed at the plans for a few minutes, then pointed to a drawing of the tholos.

'I've seen a building like that.'

Teo left him browsing and went to find the photographs of the finished project. He placed one of the tholos on the table.

'Is that it?'

'Yes. I've been inside.'

Teo spread out all the photos and Seb pointed to some pictures of the interior of the abaton.

'I slept there. That's when the dreams started.'

This was the second time today Seb had mentioned having dreams.

'What sort of dreams?'

'About Apollos. I had to write them down and tell Sybil about them.'

Teo gave a start at the name. 'Tell me about Sybil.'

'One of my lecturers. But we disagreed.'

Teo felt a surge of relief. It was a woman called Sybil, describing herself as a lecturer at the Foundation, who'd phoned to tell him about Seb's injury. If Seb remembered her, he should be able to remember other familiar faces and places.

'What did you disagree about?'

'I'm not convinced there's a God. Or an immortal soul.'

Teo looked perplexed.

'But Asklepian therapy is all about awakening the soul so a person can become completely whole. The spiritual phase of human development means growing beyond the personality and into the soul. One of the most important aims in life should be to keep one's soul fully embodied. Without it, we lose our link to the divine.'

Seb had become very still. He'd fallen into one of his reveries, so Teo left him to it and prepared lunch, ready for whenever he snapped out of it.

In the evening, Anna phoned and he told her that Seb had spoken about Sybil.

'Do you have her number?' she said. 'Someone who's had regular contact with him might jog his memory. You and I are no use to him because we have no shared memories.'

'You're right. I'd been hoping to keep a low profile, for Seb's sake. It could be embarrassing if it got out that his scholarship was endowed by his father. But his health's the most important thing. He needs to see people he knows. I'll have to get on to Sunny.'

— o —

Jim and Nick were in the campus bar when Jim asked him if he'd heard from Seb yet.

'Not since his birth mother turned up out of the blue and spirited him away to God knows where, mate,' he replied.

'Seems weird, that,' said Jim. 'Have you asked in the office if she's been in touch?'

'Yeah. I asked Brenda today but she said they haven't heard from anyone, so they have no idea where he is.'

Nick kept quiet about his second question to Brenda, which was the one about Teodor Ophis.

'That's a coincidence,' she'd said, 'someone else was asking me about him recently. In fact, come to think of it, it was Seb. He said he wanted to write an article about him for the magazine.'

'That's right,' he'd said, thinking on his feet. 'I'm going to finish it for him, but there's a couple of things I want to check up on first.'

'All I know, dear, is that one of the staff told him Dr Sharma might be able to help.'

Nick had left it at that. He could pull the wool over Brenda's eyes, but Sharma—Sunny by name and frosty by nature—wouldn't have given him the time of day.

Anna Norland had to return home some time. They'd just have to wait until she did.

Chapter 31

Fliss and Nick took a taxi from the Gard du Nord to Teodor's apartment in the Latin Quarter, close by the Place du Panthéon. On the train, they'd been discussing how Teo had learned of Seb's injury, coming to the conclusion that Anna must have contacted him. Which meant that Nick's theory about the other 'parent' being her husband or lover had been blown out of the water.

A female French voice responded to the buzzer. Fliss gave their names and the door opened to the sight of a lady of mature years surveying them from the top of the stairs.

'Professeur Ophis is at the université,' she said, in heavily accented English. 'I am Ruth, housekeeper.'

She told them to leave their coats and cases in the hall and showed them into the salon, which resembled an elaborately furnished drawing room in a stately home with its high windows, panelled walls, and baby grand piano in one corner.

A large oil painting of a woman dressed in the fashion of the early nineteenth century hung above the antique fireplace in front of which sat Seb, his grey twill trousers, white shirt and V-neck navy jumper giving him the air of an overgrown schoolboy.

Fliss called his name when she saw him and he looked up from his book, a trace of apprehension in his eyes.

'What are you doing here?' he said, looking from her to Nick and back again.

She'd been warned by Anna that Seb wasn't back to his normal self, so she answered, as brightly as she could, 'We've come to see you.'

Nick took a seat beside Fliss on a blue velvet sofa with a gilded frame.

'How are you, mate? We had a bit of trouble tracking you down. Did your dad tell you?'

Seb brightened at the mention of his father.

'Have you spoken to Teo?'

'Yes. He rang Dr Sharma to ask if you had any college friends who'd be willing to come and talk to you about stuff…to help you get your memory back. I said I'd be glad to, and your dad invited me over. Can you remember my name?'

'It's Nick. I'm not a vegetable, just a bit forgetful.'

Nick laughed but Fliss didn't join in. Seb looked tired. His face was pale and drawn and he looked out of place in this plush apartment.

'What date is it today?' said Seb, looking around as if searching for a calendar.

'Monday, November the fifth,' said Nick. 'Guy Fawkes Day. Remember, remember, the fifth of November…'

'. . .Gunpowder, treason and plot,' said Seb, mechanically. After a pause, he added, 'You'll be missing all the fireworks.'

Fliss felt like applauding but she didn't want to make him feel like a performing poodle, so she restrained herself. She was waiting for him to ask who she was, as he clearly couldn't place her, but he was still focusing on Nick.

'So Sharma let you off college?'

'He didn't have to. This is Reading Week. Worked out quite well, hasn't it?' Nick grinned. 'You can show me round gay Paree without feeling guilty that you're keeping me from my studies.'

Seb's face clouded.

'I don't know how to get anywhere in Paris.' He shifted his gaze to Fliss. 'I remember being in a house with a small white dog. Were you there, too?'

'Yes.'

His eyes cleared for a moment, then reverted to the impassive expression which seemed to be default mode for him at present.

'Give me a clue,' he said softly and her heart wept.

'My name's Fliss and…' She baulked at using the word 'girlfriend' with him in his present state, so simply said, 'we're friends but I'm not on your course.'

'Right,' he said, with no trace of emotion and no apparent curiosity to find out more.

An embarrassing silence followed, broken by Ruth bringing a tray of coffee and biscuits.

After helping himself, Nick was the first to pick up the conversational ball.

'Fliss spoke to your mum on the phone. She asked her to come and see you here, for the same reason I was invited.'

'How do you know Anna?' said Seb, fixing Fliss with a baffled gaze.

'I…found her number in the Oslo phone directory.'

'I haven't seen her lately,' said Seb, sounding sad.

Fliss felt sad, too. She hoped Anna hadn't deserted him for a second time.

She exchanged a look with Nick, unsure how to continue, and sensed that Nick was feeling the same.

'Where are you staying?' said Seb, like someone making small talk at a party.

'Your dad said there was enough room here, as long as you didn't mind sharing with me,' said Nick, getting up. 'Come on, why don't you show me our room?'

Seeing the two boys making for Seb's bedroom, Ruth beckoned Fliss to follow her to a small, plainly furnished bedroom, where she pointed out a card with the Wi-Fi code.

Once she'd unpacked, Fliss picked up her laptop and followed the sound of voices to Seb's much larger room. She hovered in the doorway, taking in the porcelain ornaments and bibelots covering every side table; the fitted bookcases; the two double beds. Over by the window, a pool table struck a discordant, post-millennial note.

'Do you want to see some photos of you and Nick doing a fashion shoot?' she said, uncertain whether to walk into the room.

'We were going to have a game,' said Seb.

'We can play pool later,' said Nick, joining Fliss and walking down the hall to the salon, with Seb at the rear.

They sat either side of Fliss at the dining table while she navigated to the pictures of the photo shoot on the Belinda website.

'See,' she said, pushing the laptop nearer to Seb. 'There you are. Do you remember that day? It wasn't very long ago.'

'Vaguely,' he said. But Fliss wondered how much he was bluffing.

'Do you recognise him?' said Nick, pointing to a picture of Jim looking into Amy's eyes with convincing intensity.

'Not sure. Where are *you*?' he said to Fliss.

'I was taking a video,' she said, feeling a glimmer of hope that he'd finally shown some interest in her, as she clicked on to her vlog.

But he watched it impassively, with no apparent interest, so she closed her laptop in defeat. They progressed to reminiscing about other shared experiences; Seb nodded every so often, but had little to add to their accounts.

Later in the afternoon Teo arrived home, welcoming them effusively and suggesting they eat at Seb's favourite bistro, just five minutes away.

They went for a walk afterwards. Fliss suspected it was aimed at tiring Seb out so they could discuss him. It had the desired effect because he went to bed as soon as they got back.

Teo settled down in an easy chair with a brandy and asked them how they thought Seb was doing.

Nick answered first.

'It's what, almost two and a half weeks since he was attacked? I'd have thought his memories would have started coming back by now. So far he hasn't recognised much of what we've shown him or told him, has he, Fliss?'

Her chin quivered.

'No. And even when he said he did, I think he was just pretending to remember. He doesn't seem to know me at all. Has he seen a doctor since he's been here?'

'He's seen a neurologist,' said Teo, reaching for the brandy to top up their glasses. 'Recovery times from post-traumatic amnesia are variable, depending on the duration of the coma, for example. But even with Seb being comatose for only three nights and three days, the neurologist can't guarantee a perfect cognitive outcome. It's a case of wait and see.'

'When do you think he'll be able to return to the Foundation?' said Nick.

'When I'm satisfied he can manage the course and fend for himself. Obviously, outside of term time, he can come here.' He cleared his throat. 'His mother will be moving in before long, once she's completed her business in Norway.'

Fliss rejoiced when she heard this, delighted that Anna had come through for Seb at last.

'I was hoping we'd be able to take him back with us on Friday,' said Nick. 'Fliss and I can keep an eye on him between us.'

Fliss found herself adding silently, *That's if he wants me to.*

'Why don't we take him out tomorrow to see the sights?' she said. 'He said he didn't know his way round. He even sounded a bit frightened of going out.'

Teo looked serious.

'Do you think it was selfish of me to bring him here? The neurologist advised me that a recovering amnesiac should be surrounded by familiar sights and sounds.'

Fliss felt a surge of sympathy for Teo.

'We all do things on the spur of the moment, without thinking through the consequences,' she said, recalling how she'd impersonated a hospital ward clerk to give Anna the news about Seb, never dreaming that by doing so, she was paving the way for them to practically kidnap him.

'I've been meaning to ask you, Teodor. What happened to

Seb's phone?' said Nick. 'If you'd called the contacts when you were still in London, we could have worked something out then.'

'He could have stayed at my house. I'd have arranged for a nurse to visit. Or even nursed him myself! I'd have kept him safe and sound, instead of being at my wits' end wondering where he was for a week,' said Fliss, her face flushed with brandy and anger.

Teo shrank back in his chair, clearly shaken by her outburst.

'My dear, there was no phone in his hospital locker and none in the bag that arrived with him. Just clothes, a watch, and a wallet.'

'What about the brooch?'

'No. No brooch either. Do you think he had it on him?'

'He took it everywhere,' said Fliss, and Teo looked even more perturbed.

'I wonder where they are,' said Nick. 'Don't know what I'd do without my phone.'

'I have no idea. Possibly still in one of the hospitals. I wasn't there when the ambulance collected him from the Marylebone. Anna and I travelled ahead so we could get things ready here. We did think it odd there wasn't a phone, but he hasn't asked for it at all.'

'Penbury General definitely had it because that's how they got in touch with me,' said Fliss, still sounding aggrieved.

'Well, perhaps when you get back, you could make some enquiries,' Teo said gently. 'I'm sure Seb would be grateful. By the way,' he said, visibly relieved to change the subject. 'Someone *you* probably know, Nick, is making a flying visit to see Seb on Thursday. She's the person who informed me of Seb's injury, so I'll be forever indebted to her. He mentioned her when I showed him my plans of the sanctuary. Said he'd spent a night there and told her his dreams. I'm hoping the sight of her will unlock a few more memories.'

'You mean Sybil?' said Nick. 'So it wasn't Anna who told you about Seb?'

'No, we both turned up at the hospital at the same time.'

Nick gave Fliss a meaningful glance as if to say, *Another of our theories shot down in flames.*

'Apparently the hospital had also left a message on Sybil's phone,' Teo continued. 'Seb had confided in her that I was his father and when they asked if she knew of any next of kin, she felt a responsibility to contact me.'

'How did she get your number?' said Fliss, sharply. She was seething. It was bad enough that Seb had withheld the identity of his father from her, but a hundred times worse to hear that he'd revealed it to another woman.

Teo hesitated.

'From Dr Sharma. We're old friends.' He looked at Nick. 'I'd rather my relationship to Seb doesn't become common knowledge around the college. I prefer to leave that decision up to him.'

'Understood,' said Nick. 'By the way, I've brought something with me that might help to prepare him for Sybil's visit. I haven't had a chance to show it to him yet.'

He left the room and returned with Sebastian's dream journal. Teo opened the journal and scanned the first page.

'Do you think Seb would mind if I read this?'

'Not at all. He gave it to me, so why not you?'

'Tell me more about Seb,' said Teo expansively. 'What impressions you have of him, how he spends his spare time...'

Fliss stayed with them for long enough to be polite, then excused herself and went to bed in what she guessed was once a maid's bedroom. Sleep didn't come swiftly, though, kept at bay by one persistent thought: what was the point of her being there? She'd expected Seb at least to recognise her, even if he was hazy about events. Nothing she'd said or done so far had seemed to make much impression on him at all. Worst of all, he'd deceived her with what Birdie would call 'a sin of omission'—omitting to tell her about Teo.

And now, to add insult to injury, Sybil's arrival was about to condemn her to an even bigger role of spare part.

Chapter 32

Nick showered, dressed and went in search of Seb, whose bed had been empty when he woke up. He found him lounging on a daybed in Teo's bedroom, which was even vaster than Seb's.

'Hey, *mon ami*, why are you hiding away in here? I am your guest. Your job is to amuse me.'

Seb looked up from his dream journal.

'I didn't want to disturb you.' He paused, to consider his next remark. 'You need your beauty sleep.'

'Touché. Glad to see your sense of humour's inching back, but your timing needs some work. That book looks familiar. How far have you got?'

'I read it through yesterday. I'm reading it again before Sybil gets here.'

'What time's that?'

'About noon, according to Teo. Apparently, she happens to be visiting friends in Paris this week.'

'That's handy,' said Nick, wondering which had come first: arranging the visit, or accepting the founder's invitation to his inner sanctum. He gestured towards the journal. 'Does it ring any bells?'

'Yeah. In fact, it feels more real than where I am now.'

Nick looked round at the elaborate lampshades, crystal chandelier and enormous gilt wall mirror.

'I hear you, man. This place feels like a set for *Liaisons Dangereuses*. The sooner we get you back to reality the better. Teo must be loaded to own this place.'

'It's rented,' said Seb, distractedly. 'None of the furniture is his.'

'That'll be tough on your mum,' said Nick, with a smirk. 'She won't be able to replace it with Ikea when she moves in.'

Seb let slip a furtive smile.

'I think you just insulted my mother.'

'I'm trying to gee you up, you dope. My mission is to get you in good enough working order so we can take you back to Blighty. If you're still floating around like a dying swan, your dad'll never sign your demob papers.'

'Ever the diplomat, Nick,' said Seb.

'That's more like it,' said Nick, grinning. 'You're beginning to sound less like a zombie.'

Seb shook his head in mock disbelief and got to his feet.

'I'm getting some breakfast. Coming?'

When Nick had finished gorging on croissants, he took out his phone and began checking it.

'Don't you miss your mobile?' he said to Seb.

'No. Who would I ring?'

'You'll need one when you get back, to keep in touch with your folks. And your friends.'

'Then I'll get one. I miss my brooch more.'

Distracted by the sound of the shower, indicating that Fliss was up and about, Nick let Seb's comment pass.

'Do you mind if I ask you a personal question, Seb?'

'You're going to ask it anyway, so go ahead.'

'What feelings have you got for Fliss? I mean, do you remember what kind of relationship you had with her?'

'She said we were friends.'

'It was more than that.'

'Did we sleep together?'

'I would say definitely.'

Seb continued calmly buttering his baguette, prompting Nick to be blunt.

'Do you still fancy her?'

In reply, Seb hunched his shoulders and held out his palms in a gesture that was almost Gallic.

'To be honest, I don't have any strong feelings for her.'

'Really?' said Nick, feeling gutted for Fliss. 'She thinks the world of you. And you were just as keen on her before you went into the coma.'

Seb added some apricot jam to his bread and looked thoughtful.

'Sometimes I get a hint of how it was with us but almost immediately someone else comes into my mind.'

Nick was all attention.

'Who? Not Sybil, surely?'

'No. Pelagia.'

'You mean the priestess that Apollos was having it off with? How can you be in love with a dream?'

'Yes, Seb,' said a voice behind them. 'That's what I'd like to know.'

Fliss stood in the doorway in a towelling robe, her hair still damp from the shower, her cheeks a fiery red.

'I'm sorry,' said Seb, having the grace to blush. 'I know that sounds ridiculous, but the snatches of Apollos's life in the journal feel more vivid to me than anything you've told me about my life in England.'

'Really?' said Fliss, bitterly. 'You used to complain about Sybil suggesting your problems might be psychological but after what you've just admitted to, I agree with her. I wish I hadn't bothered to come!'

'I do appreciate you being here. Both of you,' said Seb, sheepishly. 'I'm confident about using the metro now…'

But Fliss had already begun the march back to her bedroom.

'I think you can wave goodbye to the relationship you had with a living, breathing woman, mate,' said Nick, 'which is going to make it quite awkward if we all travel back together.'

— o —

Fliss hauled her suitcase onto the bed and started to pack. Her hope of getting back with Seb was a complete illusion—what the

Greek-obsessed Sybil would probably call a *chimera*. Why should she stay one more minute here with someone who couldn't care less about her? She opened the Eurostar App on her phone. Now she'd made the decision to go, she'd try to get away as soon as she could, preferably before Sybil arrived.

She was reading the instructions for changing her ticket, when her phone started ringing. She gave a little scream of frustration at this interruption, but when she saw the caller was Birdie, known for her thrift, she assumed the conversation would be short. Birdie, however, would not be deterred.

'If it's expensive from my end, why don't you call me back? I'm dying to hear all about Seb.'

Reluctantly Fliss obliged, trying to restrict the conversation to the details of Seb's reunion with his parents, how he'd ended up in Paris and how far he was on the road to recovery. When all the i's had been dotted and the t's crossed to Birdie's satisfaction, she started asking more personal questions.

'And are you back to normal now, the two of you?'

'Not really,' said Fliss, guardedly.

'When someone loses their memory, even when they start to recover it, there's bound to be gaps. And those gaps could include happy times and...you know...intimate moments. Bearing in mind you haven't known him that long, don't worry if he's not on the same page as you yet.'

'We're not even reading the same book,' said Fliss, dissolving into tears.

'Oh, my dear little girl, don't cry. What's happened to make you say that?'

Fliss opened her heart to Birdie about Seb's coldness, her words tumbling over each other, finishing with what she'd overheard him say that morning.

'So he thinks he's in love with someone he's dreamed about?' said Birdie. 'Tell me about the dreams.'

Fliss told Birdie as much as she knew about Apollos and his

love for the priestess and of Seb's journal and how Sybil was on her way this very day. She even confessed she was planning to return home early because she couldn't bear being frozen out for another second. When she finally drew breath, she expected Birdie to commiserate with her, but she was met by silence.

'Birdie. Hello, are you still there?'

'Yes, I'm still here. You'll have to bear with me, lovey, I've got someone else on the line.'

For a few moments, Fliss thought Birdie was answering a Call Waiting, until the identity of the other caller became clear.

'The Team are telling me that Seb's head injury affected a part of his subtle body they call "the well of dreams". This was his means of travelling safely between this world and ancient Athens. At present, he seems to be stuck in Apollos's persona and for that reason he thinks he's in love with Pelagia.'

Fliss knew when Birdie started referring to 'The Team' she was receiving guidance from what she termed 'Upstairs'. Although not entirely committed to their omniscience, Fliss nonetheless decided to take their message seriously, on the grounds it was the only glimmer of hope on the horizon.

'Could you ask The Team if there's a way of getting him back to being his old self, Birdie?'

'Hold on, they're conferring.'

Fliss imagined an oval boardroom table around which several superhumans in long robes discussed the rip in the fabric of space and time through which Seb had been catapulted by a vengeful hooligan, and how he could be returned to safety.

'—This Pelagia's presenting a bit of a problem,' announced Birdie, dramatically. 'Once that young lady gets her claws into a man, it's a hell of a job to prise them out! Looks like she put a love spell on Apollos and it's transferred to Seb. They're showing me a small wax voodoo doll representing Apollos and one of herself, bound together with a silver chain.'

Fliss was trying to get her head round this, when Birdie

revved up again.

'It seems he had a dream when he was unconscious: the only one he hasn't recorded in his journal. If he discusses it with his mentor, they say there's a chance this anomaly can be resolved.'

Fliss waited to see if Birdie had any more channelled words of wisdom, but The Team must have ended the call because when she next spoke, it was in her normal voice.

'This puts a different complexion on the imminent arrival of Sybil, doesn't it, love?' she said, shrewd as always.

'You mean that she's the mentor he has to discuss his latest dream with, who could be the catalyst for his recovery,' said Fliss, feeling peeved that it had to be Sybil and not herself.

'It doesn't do to question the message,' Birdie said reprovingly. 'The Team have a bird's-eye view of unfolding events that we don't.'

'But it leaves me on the sidelines again.'

'Don't make this all about you, Flissy. It would be selfish to leave him in the lurch now. Your role is just as important as Sybil's. You've got to encourage him to remember his last dream, so he's ready to tell it to her. When he called round, I could see he had the gift of intuition and the potential to use it to become a gifted healer. You've got to help him get back on track.'

'When did he come to see you?'

'A few days before he got his head bashed in. He didn't tell you, then?'

'No. Why did he visit *you*?'

'He happened to be passing and popped in for a chat. He'd been to see an old friend who told him his adoptive mother had taken him out of school because a teacher had questioned his emotional development, so we did a bit of clearing.'

Fliss's heart sank at this fresh instance of Seb confiding in anyone but her.

'He never mentioned that to me.'

'Well, you weren't talking at the time, were you? I take it you *did* make up, otherwise you wouldn't have gone to the nightclub together, would you?'

'And none of this would have happened,' said Fliss, in floods of tears again.

'Come on now, girl, pull yourself together. Go and put on some war paint and stand by your man!'

Thirty minutes later, Fliss walked into the salon, looking for Seb. Hearing a wolf whistle, she turned to find the perpetrator was Nick, who'd raided Teo's bookshelves and appeared to be reading a textbook on the therapeutic use of medicinal plants and their extracts.

'I see you've made an effort to impress Sybil,' he said, cheekily. 'Have you two met before?'

'No, we haven't. Talking about effort,' she said, 'are you trying to fool her into believing that you're actually doing some reading in Reading Week?'

'It's no effort at all. And if I become teacher's pet in the process, where's the harm?'

She laughed. Now that she'd been given something to do by The Team, she felt a whole lot better.

'Where's Seb?'

'Hiding from you, I should think. When I asked him how he felt about you, I never dreamed he'd drop that bombshell.'

'You're telling me. But I talked to Birdie and she said I was making it too much about me and how I feel. I can't blame him for being honest.'

She detected something approaching admiration in Nick's eyes.

'He's in Teo's room. It gets the sun in the morning. He goes there to rest sometimes.'

Fliss found Seb staring out of the window at the street below.

'Seb, I've come to say sorry.'

He turned away from the window and looked her up and down. Today she'd swapped her jumper and jeans for a short, black leather dress with a V-shaped back. She'd packed it because the last time she'd worn it he'd kissed the back of her neck and told her how hot she looked.

'Sorry for what?'

'The way I reacted earlier. It was rude.'

'That's okay.'

He seemed to have nothing further to say, so she sat down on a spindle-legged chair and started to talk about his dreams. When she felt she'd sufficiently gained his attention, she asked if he knew what happened after Apollos returned to Athens from Eleusis.

'…So did Pelagia's plan work out? That Xanthe would become a trainee priestess, giving them an excuse to meet regularly?'

'How do you know about my dreams?' he said, frowning. 'I thought I only showed my journal to Sybil and Nick.'

'You told me all about them the night we went to Underworld.'

Teo had told her Seb had no memory of the attack and she wondered if he'd blocked out all memories of the club, but he responded with a nod.

'Were you in the telesterion with me?'

'I don't know what that is.'

His eyes flickered and he shook his head, as if trying to shake out the cobwebs.

'I'm getting confused. What were you saying before? About Pelagia?'

Fliss gestured towards Seb's journal, lying on the daybed.

'Do you mind if I read the last page?'

'No, go ahead,' he said, his voice saying one thing and his scowl another.

Fliss proceeded to read it out loud, while Seb resumed staring out of the window.

On the way, Pelagia offered solutions to two of the problems I'd shared with her the night before.

She remembered what I'd told her about the message from the goddess Demeter: that my mother was descended from Eumolpus. This, she said, meant that my sister Xanthe was from the house of Eumolpidai and thus eligible to become a novice priestess of Demeter, just as she herself had been eligible through her bloodline to the other great family of Eleusis, the Kerykes.

'It would solve the problem of Xanthe not being keen on becoming a wife, and give you a reason to come to Eleusis regularly,' she said, clasping my hand tightly and making my blood race with the thought of it.

At the last sentence, she noticed Seb clasping his own hands together, miming the action of the lovers, Pelagia and Apollos.

'You had another dream after that, didn't you, Seb?'

'Yes,' he said, turning to face her. 'How do you know?'

There was a desk next to the fireplace and Fliss placed the open journal there.

'A little bird told me.' She pointed to the journal. 'Why don't you write it down now, before Sybil comes? She'll want to see it, won't she?'

'I don't enjoy discussing my dreams with Sybil.'

'Do it for yourself, then. It's a good memory exercise.'

Seb surveyed her with more interest than he had done all week.

'Why are you cajoling me, as if I'm a child?'

'Because you've been acting like one!' she snapped, beginning to fear he'd refuse. 'If you really want to know, my old friend Birdie said you should do it. You probably have no idea who Birdie is, any more than you know who I am, but whether you care or not, there are people who love you and want you to get better. If you won't do it for me, do it for her.'

Fliss's heightened state of emotion seemed to galvanise him and he covered the ground between them in moments, startling her by circling his arms round her waist and kissing her on the lips. At first she responded, then pulled away when she realised it was like kissing a stranger.

'What are you doing?'

'Nick said we'd slept together. I was checking to see if I felt anything.'

'And did you?'

Seb declined to answer, choosing instead to take a seat at the desk, where he picked up a pen and began to write.

Chapter 33

When I enter the house of Aristokles, after nine days away from home, I expect a welcome befitting a graduate of the Eleusinian Mystery School but instead, my uncle greets me with a serious face, leads me into the men's hall, and talks of his morning spent at the Assembly.

He tells me the debate was dominated by the subject of Corinth's denunciation of Athens in the Spartan Assembly, leading to a vote on whether we had violated the Thirty Years' Peace Agreement. The vote was carried and Sparta had summoned delegates from the rest of the Spartan Alliance for a federal congress.

'The Corinthians could never forgive our alliance with Corcyra,' I say, thinking sadly of the battle at sea where Philemon's mentor, Diogenes, lost his life.

'Nor our treatment of Potidaea,' says my uncle. 'Laying siege to a Corinthian colony is turning out to be a costly mistake, financially and politically.'

'Does this mean I need to polish my shield?' I ask, my blood rising at the anticipation of combat and falling swiftly at the prospect of being separated from Pelagia.

'Nothing's certain yet. The delegates have yet to vote on whether to go to war with us.'

'When are they voting?'

'Tomorrow.'

As my uncle is looking tired, I excuse myself, saying I will see him at supper.

I go in search of my aunt and Xanthe. They're nowhere to be found on the ground floor, so I knock on the door of the women's room. Xanthe opens it and throws her arms around my neck.

'Apollos! I thought you'd never come home. Are you all full of secrets now?'

I kiss her and take a pair of gold tunic pins in the shape of wheat sheaves from my knapsack.

'These come from Eleusis. A lady sent them to you.'

Xanthe's eyes open wide as she inspects them.

'They're lovely. Who is she? Does she know me?'

Before I can answer, Aunt Eupheme rises from her weaving stool and comes to kiss me.

'Welcome home, Apollos. I'm glad to see you're looking so well.'

'I brought you some honey from the sanctuary bees, Aunt. I hope it's to your taste.'

'You're a good boy, Apollos. And even better now you're a son of Demeter.'

Xanthe is tapping her foot, impatient for answers to her questions, but I have to confer with my aunt first.

'May Xanthe be excused for a moment, Aunt?'

'Yes, of course. Go and find Echo, Xanthe. See if she's hungry.'

'I'll find you in the courtyard, Xana,' I say, as she drags herself away.

As soon as I hear my sister's steps descending the stairs, I draw up every vestige of charm and diplomacy I can muster.

'Dear aunt, I have an idea I'd like to discuss with you. If, in your wisdom, you see fit to grant the scheme your approval, it might answer the question of what to do about Xanthe...'

— o —

I awoke this morning rejoicing at how the expedition to Eleusis has reinvigorated me: getting up is no longer the laborious and painful task it was. My zest for life has returned and with it a zest for love. In consequence, my first thought was of Pelagia. How long will it be before I see her again?

She asked me to send a message when my uncle made his decision. I insisted that I was my sister's official guardian and it could be *my* decision but she advised against it, warning that my uncle's disapproval would be to the social disadvantage of both herself and Xanthe.

Yesterday my aunt promised she would pass my suggestion on to Uncle Aristokles. I stressed to her that the priestess who would train Xanthe was of noble birth, but Aunt Eupheme is nobody's fool and enquired if I'd had any previous dealings with this priestess. I answered that she'd been our group tutor at the Lesser Mysteries and she gave me a look which made the blood rush to my face.

I'm taking breakfast with my sister in the family room. I've said nothing to her about my scheme in case it comes to naught so I try to answer her questions without giving too much away.

'Tell me why the lady sent me the tunic pins, Apollos.'

'Probably because I told her I had a sister who sang at the Panathenaea.'

'Is she very beautiful?'

'Yes, very.'

'Did you meet her at the festival?'

'We'd already met in the spring. She's one of Demeter's priestesses.'

In the background I can hear my aunt giving orders to the kitchen maid. She passes through the family room on her way upstairs but gives me no sign of any progress on the matter.

When Xanthe goes upstairs to join my aunt, I depart for the gymnasium to meet Philemon and my trainer, Brygos. After putting me through my paces, Brygos declares me fit enough to resume light training, eliciting from me a promise to come prepared the following day.

After visiting the baths for a massage, Philemon and I meet up with some friends who bring us up to date on city affairs. Inevitably, the conversation turns to the current conflict.

'Perikles didn't help matters by imposing a trade embargo on Megara,' says one of our comrades.

'Why did he do that?' asks another, raising a laugh at his ignorance.

'There's a piece of sacred land consecrated to Demeter between Eleusis and Megara which the Megarians illegally occupied and cultivated.'

'Not only that, they killed the herald sent to warn them off,' adds another.

'They deserve to be punished! They're allies of Sparta. Don't forget, they're notorious for giving shelter to our runaway slaves, as well,' bays a staunch supporter of Perikles.

'It still doesn't make sense to punish Megarian merchants for what a few hungry Megarian farmers did,' says Philemon, mildly, and I find myself nodding in agreement.

The discussion continues until someone suggests a series of races around the track, a welcome diversion from such a thorny topic.

On our way back, Philemon asks whether I've broached the subject of Xanthe as a novice priestess with my uncle yet. I'd taken the opportunity, during our return journey to Athens, to further unburden myself to him and he'd listened with a sympathetic ear.

'Not directly. I've disclosed the plan to my aunt. She's acting as my diplomatic envoy. But like the Spartan situation, we know nothing yet.'

'Good luck, Apollos,' he says, as we part. 'I hope the gods bring you good news on all fronts.'

'And you, old friend.'

Aristokles is standing in the courtyard as I enter, deep in thought.

'Good afternoon, Uncle. How are you?'

'Good afternoon, Apollos. I've been waiting for you. What's all this your aunt's been telling me about Xanthe becoming a novice? Is this some nonsense your sister's cooked up to indulge her love of warbling and prancing about?'

My heart sinks. Although a good head shorter than me, his manner frequently makes me feel like a small boy.

'She knows nothing of it, sir.'

'Pah! Well you can forget all about it. It's a mad idea. She's of marriageable age and that's all there is to it.'

Being determined in this matter I move closer, straightening to my full height and looking down at him.

'I believe for a person of her sensibilities...so like our mother...it would be for the best.'

At the mention of my mother, his face pales.

'Agathe. My poor sister.' he whispers, his eyes filling with tears.

It is then I press home my advantage.

'When I spent a night in the sanctuary of Asklepios I had a vision.'

I pause for effect and Aristokles is all attention.

'First I beheld the goddess Demeter, and then my mother, who embraced me and asked me to look after my sister. The goddess Demeter herself led my mother away. The temple doctor affirmed that Mother had suffered from melancholia after giving birth to me, and that Xanthe might suffer in the same way unless she lives a life more suited to her.'

'Is this true, Apollos?' said my uncle, his mouth agape.

'I swear it. Xanthe is eligible to serve the goddess through her mother's bloodline—the blood you share. It is because of this lineage that our mother has the goddess Demeter's support. Before I left Eleusis, I obtained permission from the high priestess Iphigeneia for Xanthe to live within the sanctuary.'

Aristokles utters a deep sigh of defeat.

'Very well. Who am I to dispute a sacred edict? But you'd better tell the girl before you arrange it. She's headstrong and we don't want her running back and forth because she can't make up her mind.'

As soon as my uncle goes indoors, Xanthe leaps from a hiding place behind the courtyard vines.

'Apollos!' she cries, 'does this mean I don't have to get married?'

'Yes. No. I don't know.' I wasn't sure. Some priestesses were married, some not. 'You'll have to ask Pelagia, the lady who sent you the present. She's going to be your teacher. I'll take you to meet her soon. Are you sure it's what you want?'

Her smile is as bright as the sun.

'Of course it is. As long as Echo can come with me.'

There were always dogs around temples. Must be the smell of the sacrifices.

'Why not? Providing you see she behaves herself.'

After Xanthe has hugged me half to death, I go to the storeroom, cut a piece of papyrus from the roll, and hastily scribble a short letter to Pelagia saying Xanthe has been given permission to accept the position and asking when I can bring her to Eleusis. I keep the letter formal, in case Pelagia leaves it lying around.

Having fastened the roll with thread, I walk to the Dipylon Gate, where there's usually a messenger hanging around. Failing that, I'll look out for a traveller who's willing to carry a letter for an obol or two.

Luckily, I find a messenger who's on the point of leaving for Eleusis and beyond. I tell him where I live so he can deliver a reply, pay him, and make my way home.

— o —

My slumber is broken the next morning by several hard raps on my chamber door. I jump up and open it to the sight of my uncle, wild-eyed, his hair dishevelled.

'Apollos, I've just had word from our neighbour. The carrier pigeons have returned from Sparta bringing grave news of the vote. The delegates at the federal congress have declared war on Athens!'

Chapter 34

As Fliss walked down the hall, the bathroom door opened, and she came face-to-face with a flame-haired young woman, in cargo pants and a baggy blouse, who held out her hand.

'Hello, I'm Sybil. You must be Seb's girlfriend. He mentioned you the last time I saw him.'

Sybil wasn't quite what Fliss expected. She'd heard Nick referring to her as 'the luscious Miss Hughes' and, with Nick being such a fashionista, she'd expected Sybil to be stylish as well as shapely. The person before her, however, looked as if she'd flung on whatever clothes were handy when she'd got out of bed.

The same went for her magnificent auburn hair. It was long, wavy and in desperate need of a good cut. As for makeup, her eyelids wore a quick smudge of green shadow, her lips a gloss of insipid pink.

It was for these reasons that Fliss found her rather endearing. In fact, now they'd actually met, she felt the resentment she'd harboured towards Seb's dream mentor promptly vanish in a metaphorical puff of smoke.

'I'm afraid my French is rusty,' said Sybil. 'The housekeeper was trying to tell me something about Professor Ophis but I couldn't understand.'

'He has a meeting and won't be back till later in the afternoon. That's probably what she was trying to tell you,' said Fliss, steering Sybil into the salon, where Ruth was laying out the customary coffee and biscuit welcome on the large coffee table.

When he saw them, Nick broke off his laboured conversation in pidgin French with Ruth to greet the newcomer.

'Hello, Miss Hughes. A very timely arrival. I keep saying "oui" but I'm not sure what I'm agreeing to.'

Sybil smiled.

'This is surreal, isn't it? Who'd have thought we'd be meeting in the founder's swanky apartment halfway through the first term! Good to see you, Nick.'

'And you,' said Nick. 'We're hoping to get Seb back where he belongs pretty soon, if we can. Where is he, by the way?' he said, addressing Fliss.

'Still in Teo's room. He's writing up his journal.'

Nick and Sybil looked puzzled.

'He had another dream while he was in hospital but hadn't got round to logging it till today. I'll check on him in a few minutes.'

'I hope he remembers it,' said Sybil, looking anxious. 'There were a few loose ends to be tied up.'

Fliss poured the coffee while Nick brought Sybil up to speed on Seb's progress. When he told her about Seb's avowal of love for Pelagia, she looked shocked.

'You mean he's saying he loves two women?'

'No,' said Fliss. 'Just her. He hardly seems to remember me.'

'How upsetting for you,' said Sybil. 'I hope it's only temporary.'

'I suppose it's one of the dangers of reliving a previous incarnation,' said Fliss, trying to sound objective, but loathing the priestess Pelagia with every atom of her being.

Sybil's eyes widened with interest.

'That's my theory, too, but Seb wouldn't hear of it. He dismissed the idea completely and stormed out of our last session.'

'But he apologised afterwards, didn't he?' said Fliss.

'Yes. And that was when he told me Teodor was his father, because he wanted to prove that his dreams were meant to connect him to Teodor rather than Apollos. And as he had, at last, contacted his father he considered his case closed.'

A lightbulb went on in Fliss's head. The reason Seb had told Sybil about Teo was to get her off his back—understandable considering how much he'd hated being her guinea pig.

The other two were staring at her and she realised she was smiling broadly.

'Um, I spoke to a psychic friend of mine this morning who knows Seb,' she said, bringing herself back to the moment. Fliss consulted the note she'd made of Birdie's words.

'Seb's head injury affected a part of his subtle body called "the well of dreams". This was his means of travelling safely between this world and ancient Athens. He seems stuck in Apollos's persona and for that reason he thinks he's in love with Pelagia.'

Sybil gasped.

'So I was right. His session in the labyrinth *did* unlock the energy centre at the base of his skull.' Seeing the others exchange enquiring looks, she added, 'It's known as *the zeal point*. Alternatively, *the well of dreams*. It's the reason he was able to dream so vividly and, as it's also linked to memory, why he was able to remember the dreams in such detail.'

'Being stuck in someone else's head sounds serious to me,' said Nick, looking worried. 'Teo will have to get a psychiatrist involved, surely?'

'I haven't finished yet,' said Fliss, quietly. 'Birdie received a message that there was a missing dream. She said, "If he discusses it with his mentor there's a chance this anomaly can be resolved." That's good news, isn't it?'

'Who's the psychic?' said Nick.

'Birdie.'

'I didn't know she moved in such exalted circles,' he said, his eyes twinkling.

'And you are the mentor,' said Fliss, smiling at Sybil. 'How lucky that you're here.'

'Serendipity strikes again,' said Sybil, looking less anxious. 'I have to say, I'm feeling more confident now we've got a bit of divine guidance backing us up.'

'Would you mind if Nick and I sat in on your discussion?' said Fliss, voicing a thought that had been buzzing in her head ever since she'd spoken to Birdie.

Sybil hesitated, and Fliss added, 'As observers, of course. We wouldn't join in.'

'In that case, yes. But you'll have to check with Seb first.'

'Of course. I'll go and see if he's ready.'

Fliss knocked softly on the bedroom door. There was no reply but she went in anyway. He was still sitting at the desk but his pen was not in his hand.

'Have you finished, Seb?' she said, doing her best not to sound like a mother addressing a toddler.

'Yes.'

'Sybil's here. Shall I bring her in?'

He turned to face her and she saw his eyes were red.

'Might as well, I suppose.'

Her heart lurched at his tone. He sounded defeated.

Seb held out the journal.

'I usually give it to her beforehand. It won't take long to read.'

'Do you mind if Nick and I come in with Sybil?' she said, taking the book. 'We'll be very quiet.'

'Whatever you want,' he sighed, rearranging the cushions on the daybed and stretching out on it.

Nick and Sybil were deep in conversation when she got back to the salon. They hadn't heard her coming so she stayed behind the door and listened in.

'I used to love *Time Guards*,' Sybil was saying. 'I can't believe you were in it.'

'Yeah, I was Gideon.'

'Gideon the time traveller. I can see the resemblance now. In one episode, I remember, you travelled to the future to find a cure for all ills.'

'That's right. My girlfriend, Chyna, had an incurable disease and I was sent to find a panacea.'

'But you didn't get back in time to save her.'

'Sadly, no. The actress who played Chyna had been demanding more money so the only option was to kill her off.'

'Harsh,' said Sybil, giggling.

'That's show biz,' said Nick. 'They ended up killing off the whole series. That's why I got fed up with acting. You're too much at the mercy of other people.'

'So you decided to come to the Foundation and learn how to make your own panacea?'

'I certainly intend to give it my best shot.'

Intrigued as she was with their conversation, Fliss needed to interrupt, in case Seb fell asleep and refused to be disturbed.

'Here's the journal,' she said, striding into the room and handing it to Sybil. 'Seb thought you'd want to read it first.'

Sybil looked pleased and decided to read the dream out loud so they'd all, literally in this case, be on the same page.

When she finished reading, she consulted her smartphone to check some facts.

'Let's go,' she said, looking solemn.

Seb was in the same position as Fliss had left him: reclining on the daybed, facing the window, his eyes closed. Fliss and Nick took a seat by the fireplace, behind Seb. Sybil placed a small chair towards the end of the bed and sat down.

'Hello, Seb,' she said softly. 'Are you awake?'

'Hi, Sybil. Fancy seeing you here.'

'My sentiments exactly,' she said, laughing. She reached into her bag. 'I've got something for you.'

He sat up and opened the recorded delivery package, addressed to his flat.

'Brenda signed for it, as there was no one home. It's been sitting in her tray. Luckily I found it before I left for Paris.'

Seb shook the contents of the package on to the bed.

'The elusive phone,' he said, immediately replacing it in the padded envelope. He picked up the other object and kissed it.

'I've been wondering where you were.'

Fliss strained to see what it was and glimpsed a glint of gold.

It's his mother's brooch, she mouthed to Nick.

'There's a note here from a ward clerk at Penbury General,' said Seb. 'I'll have to write to thank her.'

'Or phone,' said Sybil, crisply. 'How are you feeling by the way? Bad luck, that moron attacking you.'

'Which one, Tellias or the geezer from the nightclub?'

Sybil looked bemused until she realised Tellias was the man who'd beaten Apollos in the pankration contest.

Seb uttered a hollow laugh.

'Don't worry, I haven't completely lost it. I'm joking. I suppose the others told you I can't stop thinking about Pelagia. Does that make me crazy?'

'You tell me,' said Sybil.

'There's nothing to tell. Have you ever fallen deeply in love with anyone?'

'A long time ago,' she said, looking pensive.

'Well, that's how I feel. I can't explain it.'

'Let's talk about the latest dream,' said Sybil, slipping into teacher mode. 'At first it felt as if everything was going to plan, didn't it?'

'Yeah. I felt really happy, until...' He gulped, and Sybil gave him time to recover himself. '. . .Sparta declaring war on Athens meant I'd be cut off from seeing Pelagia.'

'You mean "he" would be cut off from seeing her.'

Seb pulled himself up. 'Yes, I'm talking about Apollos. I feel sorry for him so I'm empathising.'

Sybil looked unconvinced but went ahead with her potted history lesson anyway.

'Ultimately, yes, they would be separated. But the conflict didn't start immediately so they would have had a few months together. There was an attempt at diplomatic negotiations, until the Thebans—hated by Athenians for their past support of the

Persians—forced Sparta's hand by mounting a surprise attack on one of Athens' allies. The Athenian empire ended up at war for twenty-seven years, which would certainly have kept Apollos and his comrades busy.'

'Or dead,' said Seb, flinching.

'And even if he'd survived the first year of the war, he could have died from the plague that devastated Athens,' said Sybil, gently, as if breaking the news of the death of a loved one.

'A plague?' said Seb, sounding shocked. 'How did it start?'

'It came in through the port of Piraeus, a few miles away. The Spartans were burning Attican farms so the farming population poured into the city. They built makeshift shacks and some of them even occupied the temples and wrestling schools. The overcrowding meant the plague spread like wildfire.'

'How long did it last?' said Seb, wearily.

'About four years, on and off. A quarter of the population of Athens died of it, including Perikles himself.'

'But Xanthe and Pelagia didn't live in Athens, did they?' he said, a note of entreaty in his voice. 'They would have been based in Eleusis so they would have escaped.'

'Possibly. But their daily lives would have been restricted. They couldn't have travelled to the Eleusinion at the Akropolis, or Aristokles' house, or to meet Apollos.'

Sybil stopped speaking, allowing the silence to continue while Seb lay back on the cushions, his hands covering his eyes.

Nick and Fliss regarded each other with perplexed expressions. Seb seemed more dejected than ever.

Finally, Sybil spoke.

'Do you have any questions, Seb, or are we done?'

'No more questions, Sybil, just a favour.'

'What would that be?'

'Could you tell my father you think I'm okay to go back home tomorrow.'

— o —

Nick had managed to arrange three seats together for the journey back. At first, Seb took the window seat and Nick sat beside him but a bit later Seb came back from the men's room and asked Nick to shift up. Seb was now sitting between Nick and Fliss, his right hand reaching for hers.

'You all right?' he said.

'Yes, thanks. You?'

Nick had been looking out of the window but was now observing them from the corner of his eye.

'Is the anomaly all resolved now?' she said.

'I would say so,' he said, squeezing her hand. 'Like Apollos, I was following doctor's orders to "choose love". Except I got *my* love confused with his.'

'It's no wonder, considering you had a bottle bounced off your bonce,' said Nick, grinning from ear to ear.

'You haven't told us why you had a change of heart,' said Fliss. 'Was it something Sybil said?'

'In a way. When she spoke about the war, an image flashed into my head of Apollos lying on a battleground, a Spartan in a red cloak pulling a sword out of his side. As I watched the blood pour from the wound, for a moment I felt as if I was dying, too.'

Fliss moved closer to him.

'What a horrible experience.'

Seb seemed to be lost in the memory, because his eyes never flickered.

'While the blood was draining out of him, I felt all of *his* emotions drain out of me.'

'Sounds like a sort of exorcism,' said Nick.

'Was that when you fell out of love with Pelagia?' said Fliss, eagerly.

Her question dragged Seb back to the present.

'I guess it must have been,' he said, with a wry grin. 'Though

I do quite miss her.'

Affronted, Fliss promptly withdrew her hand from his and decided to pull the plug on the priestess.

'It's not the great love story you think it is. Birdie's convinced that Pelagia put a love spell on Apollos, which transferred to you.'

'I was certainly mad with love,' he said pensively, and Fliss hoped he wasn't comparing the intensity of his feelings for the priestess with his feelings for her.

'And what about Apollos, do you miss him?' she said gently.

'No,' he said firmly. 'He's part of the past and I want to concentrate on the future.' But the sadness in his eyes told a different story.

Then Nick piped up.

'You know, if I was turning this stuff into a screenplay, I'd go along with Sybil's theory and make the contemporary character a reincarnation of the ancient Greek. Any feelings on that, big man?'

'Only that we don't have to die to be reborn. Six months ago, I became an orphan and today I've got two parents. My life's going to be different from now on. That's more real than imagining Apollos and I share the same soul. If that was so, what about all the other bodies the soul's migrated to in between? Am I supposed to remember all of them, as well?'

'You said, "share the same soul". Does that mean you believe you have one?' said Fliss, holding her breath.

'I haven't got much choice,' he said, with a wry smile. 'From what my dad said, it's compulsory for the scholarship student.'

'But do you really mean it?'

'Well, I went along with the beliefs of my first parents, I might as well do the same with my current lot.'

'Is that a yes, Seb?' she said, in a tone any headmistress would be proud of.

'I suppose so.' He accepted her effusive hug with a smile.

'That still excludes reincarnation, though. I had to draw the line somewhere.'

The train deposited them at St Pancras. Further down the line, they were picked up from Penbury station by Fliss's parents, who took them straight to a restaurant.

Mr Logan ordered champagne to celebrate Seb's homecoming and Nick proposed a toast.

'I'd like to wish Seb, my fellow time traveller, a speedy recovery to perfect health. I need him to get his head straight so he can help me with my coursework.'

Everyone laughed and took a sip of champagne but Nick hadn't finished.

'May you remember all the good times and forget all the bad.'

Fliss and her parents clapped enthusiastically but Nick still didn't sit down. Instead, he glanced at his smartphone, for a reminder of a quote.

'Here's hoping that the saddest day of your future be no worse than the happiest day of your past. Whatever that means,' he said, assuming a mystified expression. 'Anyway, buddy, we're glad to have you back.'

— o —

Tired out from the day, Seb opted for an early night. As he entered his room, the blue lapis lazuli stone by his bed glinted a welcome. Seb regarded it for a long time, then wearily undressed.

Before he got into bed, he placed the stone in its organza bag, pulled the drawstring tight, and consigned both it and his dream journal to the yew chest that Joe had made for him.

From now on, he would face whatever life had to throw at him as himself, not as a spellbound observer of ghosts from the past.

Also by this author

Transforming Pandora

Pandora Series – Book One

978-1-78099-745-2

Showcased by The People's Book Prize 2014

Newly widowed Pandora is looking for meaning in her life when she gets an unexpected visit from a supernatural guru. But when romance intervenes, she finds she has choices to make, not just between two suitors, but whether to take the path to enlightenment. Will she choose love or light—or can she have both? You don't have to be a New Age flower child to enjoy this novel: an intriguing mixture of coming-of-age and old enough to know better!

This charming novel blends romance with spirituality. Carolyn Mathews is a talented writer, adroitly balancing the emotional and spiritual themes that drive this multilayered metaphysical romance. A rich cast of characters supplement the basic love story and keep the plot moving. Whether you're looking for romance or spiritual guidance, this well-written novel of love and rebirth satisfies both.
~P. J. Swanwick, Fiction for a New Age

Well-written and engaging, *Transforming Pandora* is an enjoyable read. I highly recommend it.
~Alice Berger, Berger Book Reviews

Inventive and accomplished use of language and assured handling of the different elements of the story, make for a great read.
~Lois Keith, author of *A Different Life* and *Out of Place*

Squaring Circles

Pandora Series – Book Two

978-1-78279-705-0

Free spirit Pandora is shaken by the sudden death of her mother and the presence at the funeral of a mysterious stranger from across the Atlantic. When her mother's grave is disturbed, she turns detective and finds herself drawn into a world of intrigue, centring round a devious couple's plot to exploit a healing circle for their own ends. Her partner Jay's collaboration with an attractive singer and her own encounter with an old flame add to the confusion. Will she succeed in her quest to bring equilibrium to the lives of those she loves, or will the decisions she and Jay make set them up for more heartache?

Squaring Circles is a rich and delicious slice of modern British life, topped off with an intriguing dollop of paranormal whipped cream. This brilliant novel captivated me from the black-humor-filled opening scene until the last sizzling paragraph. The writing is masterful throughout, each sentence thumping with energy and flowing with great momentum, with sparkles of humor sprinkled generously throughout. This is a sequel to *Transforming Pandora,* and like the first instalment, this is a novel of many characters and almost non-stop conversation, delightfully narrated by the protagonist, Pandora. Carolyn Mathews' rare literary artistry will leave readers blessed and uplifted, not to mention highly entertained. This is a delightful book!
~Ram Das Batchelder, author of *Rising in Love: My Wild and Crazy Ride to Here and Now, with Amma, the Hugging Saint*

This story has it all: family secrets, family crises, intrigue, duplicity, legend, magic, mystery… I love the way the author has cleverly blended the many and varied forms of spirituality into the everyday lives of the characters, skilfully demonstrating

how thin are the veils between this world and the dimensions beyond. Carolyn Mathews' writing is fast-paced and beautifully readable, with a great sense of place and a cast of truly believable characters. I was hooked from the first page and genuinely sorry when I reached the end. By that time, I felt as though the characters had become firm friends, and they will stay with me for a long time. Highly recommended.
~Sue Barnard, author of *Nice Girls Don't* and *The Ghostly Father*

Pandora's Gift

Pandora Series – Book Three

978-1-78535-175-4

When Jay loses their home and business in the financial crash and Pandora's job as a TV panellist comes under threat, the appearance of an archangel seems to be just the good omen they need. The message he brings, however, forces Pandora to disappear on a secret mission to fulfil a prophecy, endangering both her relationship and a precious gift she's been given. Events bring Pandora to her knees, but the light at the end of the tunnel may yet lead her to a miracle.

Carolyn Mathews is a master of the breezy conversation that carries a cargo of concealed inner conflict, mixed intentions and all-too human illusion. In her latest Pandora novel, she sets sailing a whole flotilla of these packed messages in bottles, to jostle down the troubled streams of Pandora's life.
~Jessica Moss

Pandora's Gift is a beautiful completion to a series that has captured the heart, the imagination and very essence of life, living, and ultimately the spiritual entity we each have deep inside.
~Ian Banks, Blue Wolf Reviews

I really enjoyed this series. I love Pandora and how she faces everything that is thrown her way. Of course, an angel in a hot body does help. But how she navigates the paranormal world that she travels really adds to the story. I mean, could you step away from your life like she did to fulfil your destiny? The Pandora series has a little bit of everything and a wonderful finish. I recommend checking it out. It was not what I expected it to be but it was a great read. I can't wait for more books from Carolyn Mathews.
~J Bronder Book Reviews

FICTION

Put simply, we publish great stories. Whether it's literary or popular, a gentle tale or a pulsating thriller, the connecting theme in all Roundfire fiction titles is that once you pick them up you won't want to put them down.

If you have enjoyed this book, why not tell other readers by posting a review on your preferred book site.

Recent bestsellers from Roundfire are:

The Bookseller's Sonnets

Andi Rosenthal

The Bookseller's Sonnets intertwines three love stories with a tale of religious identity and mystery spanning five hundred years and three countries.

Paperback: 978-1-84694-342-3 ebook: 978-184694-626-4

Birds of the Nile

An Egyptian Adventure

N.E. David

Ex-diplomat Michael Blake wanted a quiet birding trip up the Nile – he wasn't expecting a revolution.

Paperback: 978-1-78279-158-4 ebook: 978-1-78279-157-7

Blood Profit$

The Lithium Conspiracy

J. Victor Tomaszek, James N. Patrick, Sr.

The blood of the many for the profits of the few… *Blood Profit$* will take you into the cigar-smoke-filled room where American policy and laws are really made.

Paperback: 978-1-78279-483-7 ebook: 978-1-78279-277-2

The Burden

A Family Saga

N.E. David

Frank will do anything to keep his mother and father apart. But he's carrying baggage – and it might just weigh him down ...

Paperback: 978-1-78279-936-8 ebook: 978-1-78279-937-5

The Cause

Roderick Vincent

The second American Revolution will be a fire lit from an internal spark.

Paperback: 978-1-78279-763-0 ebook: 978-1-78279-762-3

Don't Drink and Fly

The Story of Bernice O'Hanlon: Part One

Cathie Devitt

Bernice is a witch living in Glasgow. She loses her way in her life and wanders off the beaten track looking for the garden of enlightenment.

Paperback: 978-1-78279-016-7 ebook: 978-1-78279-015-0

Gag

Melissa Unger

One rainy afternoon in a Brooklyn diner, Peter Howland punctures an egg with his fork. Repulsed, Peter pushes the plate away and never eats again.

Paperback: 978-1-78279-564-3 ebook: 978-1-78279-563-6

The Master Yeshua

The Undiscovered Gospel of Joseph

Joyce Luck

Jesus is not who you think he is. The year is 75 CE. Joseph ben Jude is frail and ailing, but he has a prophecy to fulfil ...

Paperback: 978-1-78279-974-0 ebook: 978-1-78279-975-7

On the Far Side, There's a Boy

Paula Coston

Martine Haslett, a thirty-something 1980s woman, plays hard on the fringes of the London drag club scene until one night which prompts her to sign up to a charity. She writes to a young Sri Lankan boy, with consequences far and long.

Paperback: 978-1-78279-574-2 ebook: 978-1-78279-573-5

Tuareg

Alberto Vazquez-Figueroa

With over 5 million copies sold worldwide, *Tuareg* is a classic adventure story from best-selling author Alberto Vazquez-Figueroa, about honour, revenge and a clash of cultures.

Paperback: 978-1-84694-192-4

Readers of ebooks can buy or view any of these bestsellers by clicking on the live link in the title. Most titles are published in paperback and as an ebook. Paperbacks are available in traditional bookshops. Both print and ebook formats are available online.

Find more titles and sign up to our readers' newsletter at http://www.johnhuntpublishing.com/fiction

Follow us on Facebook at https://www.facebook.com/JHPfiction
and Twitter at https://twitter.com/JHPFiction